Currents of Blue

Currents of Blue

A TALE OF SEA GLASS, TIDES, AND TIME.

SEA GLASS

BOOK TWO

SHARON BRUBAKER

This is a work of fiction. Names, characters, places, events and incidents are either the products of the author's imagination or used in a fictitious manner. Any resemblance to actual persons, living or deceased, or actual events is purely coincidental.

Copyright © 2023 by Sharon Brubaker

Ebook ISBN: 979-8-9889689-2-4
Paperback ISBN: 979-8-9889689-3-1
Printed in the United States of America

Cover design by Dark Queen Designs

Acknowledgments

It takes a village to create a book, particularly a historical novel. My heart and my thanks are with the following:

Many thanks to my very patient and loving family. You are amazing!

Thanks to Alice Lundgren for her friendship, fun field trips, research assistance, support, beta reading, and edits.

Thank you to Nancy Landis, Fox Hollow Farm (www.foxhollowsheep.com), for tutelage in wool farming.

Special thanks to my brother-in-law Butch Grassmyer for his memories of Vietnam. Thank you for your service!

Thank you to Linda Roller (thelibertybookshop.com) for saving my soul with friendship and respite at her Airbnb, always having the right book for my research, and excellent editorial suggestions.

Thank you to Walt Steinbacher for your outstanding memoir, *Point Man Up*. Thank you for sharing your story. I am very honored to have met and talked with you. Thank you for your service.

Many thanks to Meredith and Brandon Boas of Grunge Muffin Designs.

Many thanks to Laura Minker for the information on antique carousels.

Thanks to Cathy Bramble, Carolyn, and Wayne Fletcher for the information on Tolchester.

Thank you to Wiesy Lauffer, www.virginseaglass.com, who

patiently listened to the kernel of the story and educated me on cobalt blue sea glass at NASGA. Finally, the gorgeous, very, very old shard of cobalt blue I purchased from you made it into the book!

Many thanks to Lynne Robertson, https://backfromthebeach seaglassjewellery.co.uk/, for creating the heart-shaped, cobalt blue ring, a great inspiration in writing this book.

And thanks to Lynne Robinson, of www.Dragonfly-swings.com for tutelage and information on alcohol ink art.

Many thanks to the International Sea Glass Association (ISGA), of which I am proud to be a professional member.

Thank you to Kent County Historical Society, Chestertown, Maryland, for your excellent research facilities. Thank you to Nelder Smothers, Librarian at Aberdeen Proving Ground, Susan L. Thompson, Command Historian, Public Affairs Office, G9/Strategic Communications, U. S. Army Communications-Electronics Command (CECOM), Aberdeen Proving Ground, Maryland, and Amburr Reese, Aberdeen Proving Ground, Public Information. And a special thanks to my daughter, Robin, for being my guide at APG.

Thank you, Nicole Maggi, editor extraordinaire!

Thanks to Luke Hartmann for the cobalt blue sea glass ring that started the story.

Prologue

The true essence of everything is energy. In "essence," things cannot ever "be." They are always there in some form, as energy cannot be created or destroyed. The energy changes form. Time exists through our thoughts created by our soul's energy. And so, love, time, and energy will always exist in each shard of sea glass.

The small, cobalt blue bottle was tossed high and landed with a plunk in the Sassafras River on Maryland's eastern shore in 1860. Its journey of medicine, poison, and murder took it to the bottom of the river, where it slowly made its way over many years to the Chesapeake Bay. It hit a rock, and fissures formed, eventually breaking the small bottle into myriad shards that traveled with time and tides to other shores on the Chesapeake Bay.

Whispers from our souls live on everything we touch. The sea glass we find holds echoes from the past. This story lies within these echoes and beyond.

One

LOUISA – 1918

Technically, sea glass is formed in the ocean's salty waters, and beach glass is from freshwater.

The fog rose in the morning sunshine, seeping insidiously into the sky like the grief that enveloped Louisa. Other times, it was like a heavy blanket, smothering her. And sometimes, it dissipated so that she could see the light of day and breathe freely. She perched on a creaky, wooden chair staring over her Baltimore neighborhood's rooftops and chimneys in the small crow's nest of a room perched above the attic of Grandmama's townhouse. Grandmama. Louisa's heart wrenched. It had been just over a month since she had died. The house was hollow without her fierce spirit. The shock of her death left Louisa numb and empty like the scoured shell she kept on her bookshelf.

Grandmama was one of the many felled by the Spanish Flu. Memories of the creak of wagons carrying the coffins of those stricken still sent shivers up Louisa's spine. Louisa never felt so alone when they were isolated from the outside world when Grandmama was sick. The white cloth adorning their door warned of the flu within.

She tugged at her braid, askew from sleep, and curled her bare toes under her nightgown to keep them warm. Pearly smoke drifted from the chimneys, dissipating in the cool November air. The sky, still pale blue in its early arousal, was cloudless.

Her tea sent steamy wisps of clouds, a miniature model of the smoke pulsing from the chimneys that adorned the rooftops like urns. Tearing her eyes from the window, she looked around the tiny room. This small, drafty room had cracked paint and an unpolished wooden floor. Louisa loved this garret room. This room was her refuge. She could see Baltimore's harbor from the windows and a slim, blue line of bright water as the sun broke through the fog. The little room was barren except for the small wooden chair and table where Louisa rested her elbows. It was a safe little nook, a snug hug of a room that gave her the freedom of the vista yet a boundary to keep her safe.

So much loss. Louisa's heart ached with the burden of grief. Several years prior, her parents had died, and she had come to live with Grandmama in Baltimore. Despite Grandmama's uncompromising views on life and the strict rules on Louisa's upbringing, it had been a good life. It had been tough sometimes, but now that she was alone, Louisa missed Grandmama's gruff but loving countenance. She was an orphan now with her parents and grandmother dead. She knew of no other family.

On the little table next to her was a letter from Willie, her first and true love. She hadn't heard from him in weeks and weeks, and oh, how she missed him! He was fighting in France in what people called 'the war to end all wars.'

Dearest Louisa,

I am writing from a trench covered in stinking mud and surrounded by stinking men. Oh, how I long to be on the beach in Tolchester, sitting next to you and watching the sunset in the sky. To feel sand between my fingers and toes would be a joy.

*Sitting next to you is a dream I want to come true again some-
day. I love you. I miss you.
     Your Willie.*

The letter was threadbare from reading so often. Last summer, in Tolchester, they had fallen in love and corresponded since he'd left for the front. She hadn't received a letter in more than a month. She was worried and heartbroken. In her heart, Louisa knew letters could be delayed, but doubt crept into her mind this morning. Their few weeks together last summer had been magical. Now, with Willie not responding to her letters, Louisa wondered if the summer romance had all been a foolish, romantic dream of a child.

A year ago, she was a child. The war and Grandmama's demise changed all that. She felt like one of the soldiers, picking herself up by her bootstraps and carrying on. Today was a day she needed to carry on.

It was considered de rigeuer for young women to volunteer for the war effort. Months ago, Grandmama grudgingly permitted Louisa to work as a volunteer nurse at Fort McHenry. Injured troops came in from the war with horrific injuries and terrible stories of the front. Over one hundred buildings were overflowing with injured men. Her volunteering had fulfilled a part of her that had been restless. And the soldiers, nurses, and doctors depended on her.

The recent bout of Spanish flu had been lethal to Baltimore. Medical schools, churches, theaters, and schools were closed due to the flu epidemic. Over seven hundred people had died, including Grandmama. She was a strong woman, but this flu had conquered her indomitable spirit like had so many others. The streets were like a ghost town, and coping with the pandemic's changes had been difficult for all. Fort McHenry was where Louisa felt she could be useful as she worked through her grief.

She tugged on her braid again, holding back tears as she sipped her now-cold tea.

A wavery but demanding voice came up the attic stairs, calling her name, "Louisa!

Miss Louisa! Come down from that old attic!"

It was Emma, the oldest and dearest servant in the household. Since Grandmama's death, Emma had lovingly hovered over her as if she felt the need to replace Grandmama.

"I am coming, Emma," Louisa called down the stairs.

Louisa stood, folding Willie's letter carefully. She picked up her cold tea in one hand and held the letter in the other. Looking at the sea of rooftops, she remembered sitting on the beach with Willie for a brief moment, gazing at the vista of water and sky over the Chesapeake instead of the rooftops over the city before descending the stairs to see what this day would bring.

Two

WILLIE – 1918

Sea glass is sometimes referred to as Mermaid's Tears.

Willie's nightmares were vivid, color-slides of ravaged, bloody faces and bodies of his comrades in arms and enemy soldiers. They were larger than life as each frame of his dream flashed face after bloody face behind his eyelids. It was orchestrated by a concert of whizzing bullets, exploding rockets, and the cries of men as they thwumped to the earth, either injured or dead.

Willie felt the cold bite of fear. When he and the troops went to the front to the 'war to end all wars,' the bravado was sucked out, just like the drying mud sucked the life out of his skin and clothes. The wet, heavy, stinking mud squished inside his boot. Flashes, bangs, and booms were all around. He remembered his sergeant shouting, "Over the top! Over the top!" and hearing volleys of fire from the enemy. His buddies were falling like heavy trees around him. Willie tried to fire his gun, but his fingers didn't want to work this time. He saw a Hun coming toward him, grimacing and growling, ready to skewer him on his bayonet. Willie didn't give the man a chance. He rose and, in fight or flight instinct, growled back at the Hun and skewered him through. Bang! Flash! Willie screamed over and over. He lived this nightmare again and again.

But today was different. Willie's heavily bandaged head covered his useless eyes. His ears made up for lost vision as he concentrated on the claxon of sounds in the hospital ward. There was the sound of feet, mostly walking, but sometimes running, as the shoes thwapped on the floor. Cries of men, shouts, and moans of pain were a constant background noise, like the concert of crickets on an autumn night. The rattle of instruments on rolling metal carts added percussion to the din. He thought he heard American voices. Perhaps he was in an American hospital in France? He didn't know. He didn't hear the trace of an accent or the melodic sound of swiftly spoken French that he had gotten used to over the last year. Over the cries and moans of the men, someone was giving orders in precise, correct English.

Footsteps approached his bed and began talking to him in soothing tones. Hands held his head, talking to him, guiding a spoon to his mouth, and changing his clothing and dressings. He couldn't see, and he couldn't speak. His vision and words were still on the field with the ravaged men.

He was drowsy from the food and the white noise of the hospital. He fought sleep. When he slept, the nightmares returned. He could only use his voice when he screamed during the nightmares. And when he screamed over and over, the blessed prick of a needle went into his arm, and the nightmares stopped for a short while.

The dreamless naps held Willie's nightmares in limbo. When he awoke again, he heard the snores and groans of other men in the ward. He wondered what time of day it was. He couldn't tell with his sightless eyes and heavy gauze bandages. He heard a noise and tensed. When he realized it was the footsteps of someone approaching the bed, he relaxed. The footsteps came closer and closer and seemed to stop a few feet from the bed. Then he heard an odd sound, like a maniacal chuckle, before the crash of metal and medical implements plummeted to the floor with a loud bang.

Willie couldn't help it. His body jerked and became rigid before his limbs started to tremble. They shook involuntarily and hard as he tried. He couldn't stop them. The maniacal chuckle became a laugh as someone picked up the metal tray and implements that had fallen to the floor. The maniacal chuckle turned to a sinister laugh. The footsteps walked away. Willie was left to tremble involuntarily. He moaned in frustration. He called for help. No one came.

Three

ELLIE – 1969

Pale lavender sea glass is rare and usually over 100 years old.

Ellie woke to the slightly off-key rendition of the Beatles' "Ob la di, ob la da" belted out by her Aunt Penny. The song wafted in through the screened window of the vintage camper Aunt Penny housed permanently at a small campground perched on the Chesapeake Bay. Like many at the campground, Aunt Penny's camper had been modified in unusual ways to make it more livable year-round. The vintage 1949 Prairie Schooner had a wooden carport over the main part of the camper. It extended to a multi-room mini-cabin cum storage area and studio. It was so different from the spacious suburban home she had grown up in on the outskirts of Baltimore. But Ellie liked the compact and well-thought-out design of the trailer.

Ellie pulled on a pair of shorts and a t-shirt and cringed at the door's high-pitched squeak as she exited. When she rounded the end of the camper, she found Aunt Penny bouncing from foot to foot in an awkward dance as the music blared. Aunt Penny sang and busily folded, tied, and rubber-banded t-shirts. She placed them in neat, little rows like little mummies on a clean board set up on sawhorses. Pots of colored dye and squirt bottles filled with more colorful liquid lined one end. Ellie smiled fondly at her aunt, a textile artist who sold her tie-dye creations at local farmer's markets and fairs. She worked outside on this fine May morning.

"Good morning, Aunt Penny," Ellie interrupted her song.

Penny stopped singing, dancing, and binding the t-shirts to give Ellie a sunshine-filled smile.

"Morning, Luv," she greeted Ellie.

She grinned at her aunt, whom her mother would call a 'spectacle' in a short, tie-dyed dress of her creation. Barefoot and deeply tanned, she was covered by a heavy canvas apron spotted with various dyes in an op-art design of splashes and daubs. It would be obvious to anyone that she was supremely happy in her element.

Ellie had been sent to live with her as a 'punishment' after Ellie told her ultra-traditional parents that she wanted to quit school to become an artist. Her father insisted that a few weeks with Aunt Penny, a working artist, would give Ellie a 'reality check.' They thought she would come scurrying home to their traditional suburban life.

Their plan backfired splendidly. Ellie adored her Aunt Penny. Aunt Penny and Ellie were kindred spirits. When Ellie first arrived, Aunt Penny had grasped her chin firmly. She looked Ellie squarely in the eye for several minutes before declaring that Ellie was indeed an artist. Aunt Penny demanded that she get the hell out of that, finishing school with their strings of pearls and tweed skirts. Tradition would finish her! Ellie quite agreed.

"I'm glad you're up and about," Penny announced. "Now, I can take a break and go in and have some breakfast."

"Glad I could oblige," Ellie stated drily, grinning back at her aunt.

"You have," Penny answered primly. "I've been working hard this morning. I washed the shirts in that special soap a few minutes ago. Now I'm getting a bunch tied up so we can dye them. But first, let's have some breakfast."

They returned to the camper. Ellie prepared bowls of yogurt, homemade granola, and dried fruit while Penny made coffee. They took their bowls outside to sit in Adirondack chairs near a small firepit.

The campground was beginning to wake up as well. As Penny and Ellie ate breakfast, the quiet campground began the slow rise of human activity. Ellie heard pots and pans clanking through camper windows and smelled coffee brewing and bacon cooking. A few people meandered through the campground on morning walks on their own or with their dogs. Others maneuvered with a morning ride in their golf carts. Penny raised her hand and greeted everyone. It was a happy community for the most part, and Ellie had discovered in the few weeks she had lived there that the year-rounders were a pretty tight group of friends. The summer season didn't officially begin until this weekend, so most people milling about were people Aunt Penny knew.

When she finished her bowl, Penny sat musing with her coffee and staring toward the sliver of silvery-blue water at the head of the Chesapeake Bay, obviously pondering something. After a few minutes, she broke their silence. "Are you ready to work on some dyeing yourself?"

Ellie was surprised at Penny's question and looked at her aunt's face, askance. "What?"

Penny repeated the question, adding, "We're getting into the festival and fair season. I can work on a few higher-end Shibori pieces if you can handle doing the tie-dye t-shirts and socks. We have the Farmers' Market each weekend, but we also have a few art festivals coming up. And, if you're interested, you can learn Shibori too."

Ellie was surprised but pleased that her aunt trusted her to complete the tie-dye. They cleaned up their breakfast, and Ellie went out to the shed. Aunt Penny worked outside on the picnic table with the intricate fabric tying for the Shibori pieces.

Ellie snapped a pair of plastic gloves and put on an apron over her shorts and t-shirt as she surveyed the rolled and tied shirts on the bench. She proceeded to dip and squirt the t-shirts with dye. She loved the color saturating the fabric and how the colors melded into one another, creating new shades. As she worked, she recognized some patterns Aunt Penny used to tie the t-shirts. Others were new and would be a surprise when she unbound them. She smiled involuntarily at the sound of pop music from the transistor radio where Aunt Penny was working. Occasionally, Penny would break out and sing a phrase of the song playing. Still, Ellie knew that, for the most part, Aunt Penny was hunched over the fabric, concentrating on the knots with her tongue between her teeth.

The next step was placing the t-shirts in plastic bags and putting them in the sun for twenty-four hours. Aunt Penny recently found a new product called Ziploc bags. It was perfect for this process. Soon, colorful puddles of color were inside plastic bags laid out in the sun to set the dye.

When she completed everything, Ellie stopped to stretch and survey her work. She was done until the t-shirts were cured and didn't feel like tie-dyeing the socks today. She didn't think Aunt Penny would mind. It was a beautiful day. The sun was high in the sky. She wanted to go for a swim.

She removed her gloves and apron and checked to see if she could roust Aunt Penny from her work. Penny was fully into her project, concentrating on tying small lentils into the fabric, which created patterns when dyed. She shooed Ellie off and told her to go swimming on her own.

Ellie didn't hesitate. She changed into her bathing suit and topped it with a colorful gauze sundress Aunt Penny had picked up in India on one of her travels. She headed out the door with a towel and book, her oversized sunglasses perched on her head.

Her flip-flops slapped against the dusty road to the beach, kicking up small puffs of sandy dirt as she walked. Ellie noticed the campground filling up, remembering this weekend was Memorial Day and the official start of summer. Guiltily, she remembered the Farmers' Market and Art Fest this weekend and almost turned around to work on tie-dying socks. Ellie justified her actions, telling herself she would tie dye socks after a quick swim and an hour or so on the beach. Maybe she would treat herself to something from the snack bar, too.

Some families had already staked their claim to a portion of the beach next to the marina, the boat house, and the snack bar. Children dug in the coarse sand and played cheerfully in the water, splashing about. It was mostly the moms keeping a close eye on the kids and unpacking picnic baskets for lunch. Ellie found a spot to put down her towel and book before she strode into the water.

The water was still chilly as the weather had not turned blistering hot yet, heating the shallow edges of the bay. She remembered what Aunt Penny said: when school ended in June, the bay would be like bathwater and just perfect. Ellie paddled around. She didn't like the feel of the bay grasses that tickled her legs. She thought she felt a fish bump into her as well. Were there crabs and eels? Spooked, she kicked her legs, freeing herself from the bay grasses, and floated on her back. Floating on the bay felt like floating in the sky, like the cottony clouds that skittered overhead. She watched a bald eagle soar through the sky and the noisy osprey chittering overhead, drawing attention away from their nests. Further away, a tern dove into the water, barely making a splash. She floated dreamily, thinking of nothing, enjoying the connection between the water and the sky. A splash of water on her face woke her from her reverie. Two children dove and kicked, sending plumes of water into the air. So much for her quiet reverie. Ellie left the water to lie on her towel and open her book.

She tried to read. She did. The noise of persistent pounding distracted her from the words on the page. She looked around, trying to locate the distraction. There it was, over by the marina at the boathouse. She raised her sunglasses and squinted to see more closely. A shirtless young man was whaling away at the boards with a hammer and nails. She saw that Carl, the campground director, was there as well, and he wore a grin on his face and shook his head. Ellie smiled involuntarily. Carl was a good guy, and even he was distracted by the young man pounding away at the boards.

Reading and focusing on her book would need to wait for another day. Sighing, she picked up her things and returned to Aunt Penny's. She could work on those socks now.

Four

JOHN – 1969

The reddish, golden brown of amber sea glass is caused by the addition of sulfur when the glass is made.

John was still angry with this morning's argument with his dad. He pressed the gas pedal to the floor of the car and zoomed toward his summer job at the campground. Ahead, a raccoon lumbered across the road, and John slammed on the brakes and screeched to a stop to allow the little thing to live another day. He shook his head askance at the small animal. It didn't seem to notice John and his vehicle waiting impatiently to continue down the road. He careened around it when it was at the edge of the road, albeit slightly slower than before, keeping an eye on the woods on either side for any other errant wildlife.

He entered the campground a few miles down the road and parked near the office and camp store. Carl and Betty Martin owned the place.

"Morning, John," Betty said, smiling at John when he entered. She didn't wait for him to return the greeting before adding, "Carl's out on the grounds. He's pulling trash. He wants you to mow the green this morning before you two get started on other projects." She spoke as she finished a transaction for two scruffy, sandy children buying candy. After handing over their change, they reached into the bag and shoved the candy into their mouths, giggling.

Betty smiled indulgently. She cared for campers' needs and loved selling penny candy to the kids. She was on the edge of being rotund, a grandmotherly type, with iron-gray hair pulled back in a bun at the nape of her neck. She always wore a cotton dress with flowers. At least that's the only type of dress John saw her wear.

"Thanks, Betty," John said as he scooted back to avoid the sticky, sandy children exiting. He held the screen door open as they scooted through, ducking under his arm. He nodded to Betty, plunked a dime on the counter, and chose a Tootsie Pop before exiting to head toward the beach. The green was a large, grassy space just before the beach and marina where children played, families picnicked, and there was music on some evenings. Often, the green was strewn with blankets and folding chairs. Carl had built a small stage at one end for the entertainers.

The sun was warm, and he swiped his hand across his damp forehead. His long hair was wet at the back of his neck. He lifted it to catch the slight breeze. He briefly wished for the military crewcut his father sported. Still, his long hair was also a statement against his father's wishes.

John went to the storage shed near the marina and pulled out the key entrusted to him by Carl. He opened it and got the mower, an old rag, and a gas can out of the shed. After checking the level of oil and gas, he set the choke lever full and pulled the cord until the mower sputtered. When the mower began to put, put, put, he returned the choke to half-choke and let it warm up. The engine purred, and he put the mower to run and began to mow.

Mowing was his Zen. The sound of the mower drowned out

his noisy thoughts and the noise around them. Halfway through mowing the green, he stripped off his t-shirt and tied it around his waist. The green was large, and John mowed deliberately, creating neat, straight rows, his anger still seething within.

His dad was intractable about the Vietnam War. He was a military man from a long line of military men. He couldn't see there wasn't any honor in this war. John didn't understand why it didn't sink into his father's brain when those horrible numbers of lives lost were flashed behind Walter Cronkite each night. "Duty," his father insisted. "Stomp out communism" was another platitude he heard frequently. He saw the haunted look in his mother's eyes because she couldn't take sides. John wondered how she would react if he were a conscientious objector. Or worse, if he was drafted and killed in action. He knew that would destroy his mother. He didn't understand how his father could condone the war. John violently pushed through the grass to the end.

Carl was waiting for him by the shed when he finished. He nodded his approval as John refilled the mower and checked everything before locking it again.

"Next?" John asked Carl, reticent to talk, pushing his damp hair off his forehead. The mowing had helped quell a smidgen of his anger and frustration, but John was still tense. His hands were clenched into fists by his side, and his shoulders were tense.

Carl didn't comment on John's apparent anger. Instead, he told John, "I'd like you to come to the boathouse with me. Some loose boards on the deck need repairing."

Carl wasn't a huge man, but he was a strong one. He was an ex-Marine who served in were World War II and Korea, and his muscles still bulged. Like John, he was quiet but disagreed with the Vietnam War. This was opposite John's father's views, and John was grateful for it. He was honest with John about the 'police action' of Korea. He didn't understand the useless slaughter of American men and women.

John pulled his t-shirt from around his waist and wiped his

forehead again. He climbed into the golf cart beside Carl, and they drove to the boat house. Carl had measured and cut boards. He had even numbered them for John. They pulled up the old boards together, and John laid in the new ones. He had a fistful of large nails and a good hammer and started to nail the boards in place. Some nails were stubborn, and John had to whack at them hard. The action dissipated his anger.

When the hammering stopped, Carl asked drily, "Feeling better?"

John stared at the boards for a minute and then at Carl, realizing Carl's intent with the project. "Yeah."

"Another argument with your dad?"

"He doesn't understand!" John shouted, "On the total uselessness of this war! All I hear from him is 'duty, duty, duty.' He's so freaking scared of Communists taking over. I think he's brainwashed! We have no business being in Nam!"

"I agree, but war is a bigger machine than the two of us. And the protesters. I don't know if there's an easy answer. Like any war, it's more than the fighting. We're pawns for the political machine and fat cats. And I personally don't think we need to worry about communism," Carl stated. "I'll let you work on these boards while I check the campground. This weekend is the start of another summer season."

John nodded and returned to work, pounding the nails in place and feeling better with each strike. Carl drove off, and John paused to watch him putt-putt down the road, stopping to greet campers along the way. John couldn't help it. His image of Carl as a benevolent ruler surveying his kingdom came to mind as he watched Carl interact with the campers.

He returned to his work, hammering the boards in place. As he hammered, he thought about Carl's comments. John agreed with Carl that they didn't need to worry about the threat of communism. He had a hard time understanding the hysterical fear of some people. Carl's thoughts about the political machinations and the ultra-wealthy were eye-opening. He took a moment to stop hammering and gaze at the vista of blue sky and water as he stared down the bay. Suddenly, he felt very small in this world. And he wondered, somewhat bitterly, how anyone could make a difference. And how could he explain this to his father? Every time he talked with him about the Vietnam War and communism, they ended up shouting at one another. He always saw the pained look in his mother's eyes, and that made him stop arguing. Something colorful fluttered at the edge of his vision. He turned to look and hammered his thumb.

"Dammit," John muttered under his breath, cradling his sore, throbbing thumb by holding it close to his chest.

He looked again. There she was, a vision, wearing a short, gauzy dress that was a swirl of colors above a pair of long legs. Her tawny, wavy hair lifted invitingly in the soft breeze. She was leaving the beach. Who was she? Where had she come from?

She didn't notice him; he was glad, as his mouth was agape. She walked toward the campers. He returned to hammering but found it difficult to concentrate as he remembered how her hair and dress seemed to float. And those long, tan legs. He almost whacked his thumb again.

Five

Red sea glass is the rarest form of sea glass. Gold was used to create red in the glass and was extremely expensive.

Louisa descended the stairs to receive a round of scolding from Emma. She hovered around and gave her slippers to put on her cold feet. Louisa traipsed after Emma to the kitchen, appreciative of her efforts. She was chilled and rubbed her arms. Since Grandmama's death, Louisa eschewed the formal dining room. Glancing through its open door, she could almost see Grandmama at the head of the table, teacup in hand, as she read the morning newspaper. Louisa turned her glance away before emotions got the better of her.

The kitchen seemed empty and bereft of the usual hustle and bustle. Betty, the scullery maid, was fighting the Spanish flu at home. Her husband had died two weeks before, and now she had caught the disease. Bertha, their cook, was baking bread and making a large pot of soup. Louisa knew a large portion was going to Betty's family. But, it was warm, not only from the stove, but Emma and Bertha's presence. They were her family now, and Louisa was grateful.

Bertha turned when Louisa entered the kitchen. "Morning, miss," she greeted, giving her a warm, loving smile before she turned back to the soup on the stove.

"Good morning, Bertha," Louisa answered.

"Have a seat," Emma ordered. "We'll get you some breakfast that will stick to your ribs before you go to the hospital."

Emma poured steaming tea for Louisa. Bertha dished up a large bowl of oatmeal adorned with raisins and laced with generous amounts of cream and maple syrup. She set the bowl on the table before returning to the counter, where she sliced a large, thick piece of bread and slathered it with butter.

Louisa didn't feel particularly hungry but did her best to eat as much as possible. Working at the hospital was physically taxing, and she knew she needed to eat well.

"I'll make you a lunch pail, Miss Louisa," Bertha informed her. "It will be ready and waiting for you before you go to the hospital."

Louisa pushed back from the table. "Thank you, Bertha and Emma. That was a delicious breakfast. It will help me get through the day."

Louisa patted her stomach as she left the kitchen and walked up the polished wooden stairs covered with a rich, red carpet. Her steps were silent as she went to the second floor to her room.

Out of habit, she glanced at Grandmama's suite of rooms. Months after her death, she still expected to see her in her sitting room, working on needlework or hearing her call out to Louisa when she walked past. All was silent. Louisa paused a moment, a hand on the door frame, giving a little sigh.

"Be happy, Grandmama. I'm doing my best. I'm doing my duty, too," she whispered to the empty rooms.

Louisa continued down the hall to her bedroom. The tall windows and high ceilings added to the spaciousness. Emma had already been in the room and made the bed. She had even laid out

Louisa's uniform of a gray, broadcloth skirt, shirtwaist, and snowy-white apron.

Louisa took off her wrapper and nightgown and folded them neatly on the bed. Before working as a volunteer nurse, she had the habit of flinging her clothes on whatever surface was available, whether a bed or a chair. Now, she relished the orderliness she'd learned from the nursing staff, and Grandmama's words of "everything in its place" echoed in her head. She hadn't understood before, but now, the orderliness gave her a sense of comfort.

Louisa went to her dressing table, releasing her braid and brushing her long hair. She brushed and brushed, counting to one hundred out of habit. She pulled her hair into a heavy chignon at the back of her head.

As Louisa reached into the small drawer to pull out a couple of hairpins, her fingers met with something cool. She drew her hand back at first and then reached in to pull the piece of cobalt blue glass. Louisa took in a breath. Her heart lurched. It was a piece of sea glass that had formed a heart shape. Willie had found it along the Tolchester Beach shore last summer and had given it to her before he'd left for the war. She absently thumbed the ridges in the heart-shaped glass as memories suddenly washed over her.

Louisa held it up to the pale sunlight through the windows. The piece of glass shone with a deep, blue glow. It echoed the blue from the heavy draperies that hugged the edges of the windows.

Louisa remembered that Grandmama didn't like the small shard of glass when she showed it to her. She trembled and wouldn't touch it. She demanded Louisa get rid of it, calling it trash. Louisa protested. She shared with Grandmama the story Willie had told her that shards of beach glass were the frozen tears of mermaids when they mourned lost sailors. Walking the beaches and finding the sea glass treasures was one of her favorite ways to pass the time. Louisa hid the cobalt blue heart from Grandmama. She loved the mermaid tears story. It was like love crystallized in a small gem. And Willie had told her he was giving her his heart when he handed her the small, cobalt blue sea glass heart.

Louisa remembered that Grandmama had not approved of Willie. She insisted that he was from common stock. Last summer, they stayed in the guest house run by Willie's mother. Grandmama was quite pleased with the clean, tight ship that Willie's mother conveyed in her guest house, but she still didn't like Louisa's friendship with Willie. Likewise, Willie's mother was none too pleased with Willie's interest in Louisa. After all, Louisa was a guest, and what was the slang he used? She remembered Willie's mother called her the slang for someone well-to-do – a 'swell.' As a result, with the feelings of Grandmama and his mother, Louisa, and Willie had to keep their meetings and feelings clandestine. They still met all the same. And they fell in love.

Louisa turned the glass over, thinking of Tolchester across the bay from Baltimore. It seemed hundreds of miles away and far in her memory with Grandmama's death, the war, and the flu pandemic. Louisa wondered how Willie's mother was faring. Willie, her only son, and the handyman around the guest house. To Louisa's knowledge, she was a widow and had no one else to count on for the small repairs Willie took care of. She wondered if Willie's mother's business was still running. Were people still going on holiday with the war and the flu pandemic? Willie had been eager to join and defend the country in the war, leaving his mother alone.

Did she dare write to his mother to ask if she had heard from Willie? Even the thought was foreboding. His mother was a formidable presence. And she wondered if she was still alive. Louisa heard rumors that the Spanish flu had reached the Eastern Shore of Maryland.

Louisa rubbed her thumb on the sanded glass one last time before putting it back in its safe place in the drawer to her dressing table before going to her desk.

Even if it was futile, Louisa pulled out a creamy sheet of stationery and quickly penned a letter to Willie.

Dear Willie,

I will confess that I am very worried that I haven't heard from you in weeks and weeks. I can't help but wonder where you are in France. The mud you described in your last letter sounds dreadful. Please take care and be safe from the Huns.

Autumn is here. Some days are quite warm, but others you can feel the chilly weather, especially in the morning and when the sun goes down.

It's so very strange not to have Grandmama here. The house is empty. That's why I'm so glad to volunteer at Fort McHenry. I love nursing. I think I might want to take courses in nursing at Johns Hopkins when the war and the flu epidemic are over.

In fact, I must close, as I'm running late. I wanted to write as I was thinking of you. I always seem to be thinking of you. I miss you.

Your Louisa.

Louisa sealed the letter and put it on the hallway table to be given to the postman when he arrived. She kissed her fingers and patted them on the letter before stepping out to the hospital.

Fort McHenry had turned into a small city of quickly constructed buildings as a hospital for incoming wounded. It was originally built as a huge surgical center and rehabilitation center. Now over a hundred buildings had been built to help the thousands of men that had been shipped to Baltimore. Some of the buildings smelled like death. Some were cheerier, and Louisa knew most patients would survive in those wards. It had become so crowded that it was difficult to walk between patients. When she volunteered, many men called to her or plucked at her skirts as she walked by. Louisa wished she could attend to each one but knew she had to complete whatever job had been assigned to her on a particular day.

The byways between the hospital buildings were as crowded as on a city street during the holidays. Some people bustle by, laughing and talking on their way to their shift. Others were headed in the opposite direction, weary and yawning after working all night. She passed a group of nurses who looked like a flock of doves in starched white caps and dresses. One of them nodded in greeting as she passed. She checked in at the volunteer desk and went off to find her assignment for the day. It was easy to become lost at this old star fort. Louisa looked at her surroundings, trying to figure out where she was. Eventually, she found where she was to work.

This morning, they assigned her to a building where incoming soldiers had been recently transported to Baltimore for surgery and care from the European front. She walked what seemed like miles to the appropriate tent. She was relieved to see a friendly and familiar face. Nurse Williams was there. Louisa knew her. She was one of the head nurses whom Louisa greatly admired and sought advice from frequently.

"Louisa! It's good to see you!" Nurse Williams greeted her with a smile.

"Good morning, Nurse Williams," Louisa returned.

"It's another lovely day to save lives and to help these men feel useful again," Nurse Williams quipped.

Louisa smiled involuntarily. It was something she said nearly every day. She loved how Nurse Williams was positive she would and could take ravaged soldiers who survived the wreckage of war and bring them back as whole and healthy as they could be. It was a different attitude from another nurse nearby who sniffed at Louisa's volunteer uniform with disdain. Some of the nurses didn't approve of volunteers.

"How can I help, Nurse Williams?" Louisa asked, ignoring the other crotchety nurse.

"I could use your help disinfecting the empty beds," Nurse Williams began, "and I could also use your assistance when we change bandages."

Louisa nodded. Nurse Williams showed her where the

supplies were kept and pointed toward the empty beds. Louisa took a bucket, rags, and antiseptic, then went to work. This was necessary for emptying and cleaning the bedpans or taking loads of bloody and pus-filled bandages to the incinerator. In her heart, she knew those who had been in these beds had not survived. Her eyes filled with tears as she cleaned. These were young men her age or not much older. It was frightening to see the depth of destruction from the war. From the stories the soldiers had told her, Louisa was very grateful she was here in the United States. Willie's letters made France sound like a hellhole filled with mud. He described the land burned beyond recognition and houses shells of what they were. Through his words, Louisa could feel Willie's shock and pain of the conditions he saw in France. The soldiers in the hospital told her the towns had been bombed beyond recognition, and homes were now piles of rubble. They described the squalor civilians lived in and the constant fear the women and children lived through every minute. Louisa's thoughts were bleak as she completed wiping down the beds and returned the bucket and cloths to Nurse Williams.

Next, Nurse Williams loaded Louisa's arms with bandages, salves, and scissors on a large tray. Louisa carefully followed her to the beds on the ward, careful not to drop the heavy tray of supplies. She introduced Louisa to the men as she efficiently changed their dressings. Louisa admired Nurse Williams, undaunted by patients' violent reactions. She always continued to care for the patients and talk in a calm, clear voice. Her steady voice usually helped the patients settle down so that she could continue to care for their needs. Louisa noticed she kept a continual stream of chatter, distracting the men as she worked on their wounds. Louisa spoke when spoken to and offered the men a shy smile. She practiced her poker face when seeing the horrible wounds, deep and ugly, where shrapnel had been removed. Louisa helped to hold down each man as Nurse Williams poured disinfectant into their wounds.

"I know it hurts, soldier," she would say, "but this will keep you alive."

Some of the wounds stank. Those wounds worried Louisa. Sometimes, she would look anxiously at Nurse Williams when she noticed this. Nurse Williams would give Louisa an imperceptible shake of her head. Louisa knew then that they were keeping the patient as comfortable as possible before the end of their life. Nurse Williams encouraged the volunteers to talk with these men, write letters for them, and give general comfort.

Louisa heard a soldier crying loudly as they finished caring for a row of patients. She gave a nervous glance to Nurse Williams, who jerked her head toward the sound.

"Poor dear," Nurse Williams muttered, "the war is still inside his mind. He has a serious head wound. We'll go to him next."

Louisa and Nurse Williams made their way to the crying man. As they walked through the hospital ward, Nurse Williams explained that a shell had injured the man's head. The doctors said his vision had not been affected, but he still couldn't seem to see. Nurse Williams told Louisa that the poor dear still had nightmares that he was in battle. His limbs would shake erratically. "Shell-shocked" was the term Nurse Williams used.

When they drew close, Louisa saw his head swathed in bandages. She helped hold the soldier's head as Nurse Williams removed the bandages but had to look away from the sight of the ragged wounds beneath.

"Louisa!" Nurse Williams said sharply. "Please attend!"

"Yes, Ma'am," Louisa told her superior, turning to grasp the soldier's head more firmly but gently for Nurse Williams to disinfect and dress the wounds. The solder had jumped at Nurse Williams's sharp tones. Louisa looked down at the soldier's face. Recognition dawned as she stared at the familiar outline of the jaw and cheeks.

"Willie?" Louisa said loudly in disbelief. "Oh, Willie!" she cried, tears now streaming down her face. "Willie, it's Louisa!"

Nurse Williams stopped dressing the wound and looked, once again, sharply at Louisa.

"Louisa, do you know this soldier?" Nurse Williams asked.

"Yes! Yes!" Louisa's quiet voice became surer as she shakily stated, "It's Willie. He...he...he is my sweetheart."

Six

WILLIE – 1918

Vaseline Glass was produced from the 1840s until World War II. Its bright yellow-green color glows even more brightly as neon green when a black light shines on it, thanks to the addition of small amounts of uranium dioxide in the glass.

Willie thought he heard a voice that he knew. t was as if he was swimming through the stinking, thick mud of the French Countryside. He could hear the voice faintly as if it were far away. Willie could hear someone calling his name. He turned his head toward the sound. He couldn't see.

Willie felt hands on his head. The comforting tightness disappeared, and the pain returned. Unable to help it, he howled.

More hands. Firm hands were holding him down. He felt a drop of something liquid land on his cheek. Then another. And another.

Someone kept saying his name over and over and over. And the voice sounded familiar. It sounded like Louisa. Was it Louisa? Or was he dreaming?

Louisa.

Willie remembered the first time he'd seen Louisa last summer. Willie was out early, enjoying the cool of the morning. She was sitting on the beach with her hands and hat on her knees, like a living statue. Her bare feet peeped out from her long skirt and petticoat. He remembered the light breeze that had tugged at her hair. The waves on the bay were gentle that day. They made a soft, shushing sound. Louisa was staring out at the horizon where the water met the sky. Something about the look in her eye drew him to her. He'd sauntered over, but when he reached her, his confidence left him.

Willie stopped when he reached her. Unable to speak, he drew small circles in the sand with his bare, big toe. He had stammered a hello. Louisa gave a jerk in surprise when he spoke to her. She looked up at him, eyes wide and as blue as the bay. And then, once she met his eyes, shyly looked down again.

Willie knew he shouldn't be talking with her. She was a guest. Her grandmother was wealthy but not arrogant like some upper-class guests. His mother would be furious to know that he had even approached her.

Willie had walked past her then, whistling. When he glanced back, he saw she was following him with her eyes. He'd turned back, his whistle sounding bright and confident in the morning air, and he had grinned. He knew he fell in love with her that day, seeing those bare toes tucked into the sand, just under the skirts of her blue and white striped dress. She looked earnestly at the line where the sky met the water with those blue eyes. Even though he knew she was avoiding looking at him with his brashness, he knew there was something comforting about looking at that line of sky and water. It brought peace. And those eyes that followed him... he knew he wanted to be in her vision every day.

His memory of Louisa left abruptly when he felt a cold liquid on his head that burned with a white-hot, searing pain as it seeped into the wound. Willie couldn't help it. He screamed. He tried to raise his arms to wipe away the burning stuff, but someone held him down. He continued to thrash about despite the calm voices. The pressure of the bandages quelled some of the pain, and Willie relaxed, sinking back into the bliss of memories.

Seven

ELLIE- 1969

*Sea glass multis are shards with more than one color. Seaham,
England, is famous for multis.*

Ellie found Aunt Penny still caught up in her Shibori pieces when she returned from the beach. Aunt Penny had banded, clipped, and folded the cloth in different patterns. Like the t-shirts, the pieces lay in rows on a table. Later, Aunt Penny would dye the cloth in a deep, blue, indigo dye bringing out rich patterns counterpoint to the bright white of the cloth.

Ellie changed back into her t-shirt and shorts to dye the socks. The socks were pretty easy to create. Aunt Penny had already pre-washed them in a special solution. Ellie only needed to fold and secure them with rubber bands before dying. She loved the bright colors, but as she worked, she wondered if other, more natural dyes and methods existed. They probably wouldn't be as brilliant as the dyes Aunt Penny used. But really, she didn't know. What other ways could she dye cloth and make patterns and designs? It intrigued her.

Aunt Penny came around when she was finishing up,

reminding her they had a potluck for the campground regulars. It was a small celebration before the summer season hit the next day with Memorial Day weekend. Everyone brought a dish to share. Carl and Betty were cooking up hotdogs and hamburgers for the crowd. They were meeting on the large green towards the beach and marina. Aunt Penny told her to finish up and get ready.

She could hear Aunt Penny humming inside the camper as she showered. Ellie grabbed her towel, clean clothes, and her ditty bag of shower things and placed them in a tote bag. She shouted to Aunt Penny over the sound of the water, the radio, and her singing that she was going to the campground bathhouse to take her shower and that she would be back in a few minutes.

Ellie headed down the road toward the property's large communal bathhouse. She could shower quickly to be ready for the community dinner. As she walked, Ellie wracked her brain on what she knew about dyeing fabric and design. She wondered about other ways to add color and design to the cloth besides tie-dyeing and Shibori. She wanted to learn the Shibori techniques, too. But she knew there were other methods. She loved textiles as Aunt Penny did. She was fascinated with the color, texture, and design and how it could be crafted into something decorative or wearable. Perhaps Aunt Penny could tell her or have an old text-book from her old textile student days. There was a lot she could learn from Aunt Penny's expertise.

Ellie was lost in thought when she reached the bathhouse and didn't see the sign taped on the door. She walked in, oblivious and still lost in thought about fabric, dyes, and colors. She realized she was hot, tired, and a little stinky and reached to pull her sun dress over her head.

"Whoa!" a masculine voice interrupted her thoughts as she raised her dress over her head.

"What? Who?" Ellie cried out, confused and panicking. She clutched her towel in front of her as she let her dress drop back into place.

Before her was the young man who had been pounding nails into the boards by the boathouse earlier. What was he doing in the ladies' bathhouse? Instantly, she took in the mop bucket and the mop that he held. Realization hit her. Here, she was practically stripping in front of him. Mortified, she ran out of the bathhouse and back to Aunt Penny's trailer.

Ellie burst through the door and threw herself on the couch, still clutching her towel to her chest.

"What's wrong, Ellie?" Aunt Penny asked, emerging from her bedroom.

Ellie spilled out the story of her humiliating moment in the bathhouse. Aunt Penny made soothing noises.

"I'm so embarrassed! I'll never be able to face that guy again, Aunt Penny!" Ellie moaned. "And he works here at the campground! What am I going to do?"

Penny patted Ellie's shoulder sympathetically. "What you'll do is take your shower here. There should be enough hot water for a brief one. I will go to the potluck dinner, and you will be fashionably late. I'm positive this young man is as embarrassed as you were. And probably worried. Can you imagine facing Carl and telling him what happened?"

Ellie looked at her aunt. She shook her head as she started to giggle and then laugh. It was contagious, and Aunt Penny began laughing as well.

"Poor thing," Aunt Penny said. "I'm sure Carl would take this, run with it, and never let him forget it. Not in a mean way, of course. That man doesn't have a mean bone in his body. But, he'll remind him if he knows about it."

"Let's hope not," Ellie replied in a strangled voice. "Let's keep this between ourselves."

"Done," Aunt Penny replied. "Go shower. I'm heading down to the green to schmooze. I'll see you soon."

Eight

Some glassers find their treasures by exploring old dump sites along waterways.

What had that girl been thinking? Didn't she see the sign on the door? What was she doing coming into the bathhouse and starting to strip before she checked the building or reached the showers?

John's thoughts paused him momentarily from his cleaning. He checked the door, and the sign was still there. He shook his head and proceeded to complete his work, but his mind kept racing back to the beautiful girl who almost stripped in front of him. She left so quickly, obviously embarrassed by the encounter. He wondered who she was. He couldn't get her out of his mind – her long, long legs and smooth, creamy stomach, and...he gritted his teeth as his imagination took over and continued to clean. Cleaning the bathhouses was one of his least favorite jobs. His distraction from the girl's appearance hindered his progress. He kept pausing, thinking about her.

He finished the women's shower room and went next door to the men's. He completed his cleaning duties before stepping in to take his shower. He still couldn't get his mind off the girl. She had pulled up her dress. He saw her bikini underwear and her stomach's smooth, taut skin as she pulled the dress almost over her head. He even caught a glimpse of her lacy bra. He ran out of hot water. A cold blast hit him at the appropriate time as his body reacted to the memory of the girl. He yelped and turned the water off, shivering from the cold blast.

Dried and dressed, John stowed his dirty clothes and towel in his car. His mom had delivered his favorite dessert to the potluck, a tunnel-of-fudge cake. His mouth watered at the thought, and he realized how hungry he was after working hard for Carl. He could smell the grilling of hot dogs and hamburgers.

When he reached the green, he made a beeline to the grill where Carl stood proudly wielding grill tools and wearing a loud, red apron with a picture of a large man in an oversized chef's hat with 'grill cookie' emblazoned on the front. John hid his amusement as Carl looked so silly in the apron, but he looked happy, presiding over the grill with a large spatula in one hand and long tongs in another, the epitome of the cartoon chef decorating the apron.

"Hey," John greeted him. "Do you need help with anything?"

Carl flipped some burgers and turned some hotdogs before turning to John.

"You've worked hard today, young man. Go and get some grub and relax a little," Carl ordered.

John nodded. He filled a plate with potato salad, baked beans, and a large burger covered in ketchup, mustard, and pickles. He carefully placed a slice of his mom's fudge cake on the top. His paper plate was overflowing, and he had to balance it carefully when he went to get a soda. John glanced around the green, looking for someone he knew. But who was he kidding? He didn't know anyone at the campground, not really. Maybe he could find a quiet spot away from the crowd, eat, and go home.

A little kid was screaming bloody murder and ran past John

with what he sincerely hoped was ketchup on his hands and face. Avoiding the child, he pivoted on his heel and teetered dangerously. John tried to right himself, but it was too late. The plate had taken on a life of its own, and it jettisoned out of his hand and landed, food-side, onto, oh-no, on the girl that had been in the shower room.

Her tie-dye t-shirt was now covered in food. It looked like a colorful Christmas tree with ornaments of potato salad, pickles, and garlands of ketchup, mustard, and mayonnaise.

"You!" they both breathed the word.

John was speechless. Red crept up from his neck and into his face.

"I'm sorry!" he cried out, his hands reaching out to wipe off the food, and then he stopped abruptly, realizing what he was doing. "That kid," he tried again. But it was useless to explain. The kid was long gone.

John bent down to pick up the paper plate, but the girl did as well. They bumped heads.

"Oh!" she cried and held her hand to her forehead.

John wished he could sink right into the ground in that spot. His forehead hurt, too, and he rubbed at it, smearing condiments on his face.

The girl looked at him, and John could see she was trying not to laugh at him, biting her lip. He couldn't help himself. This situation was too ridiculous, and he started laughing. She started laughing, too. And soon, they were both holding their stomachs and laughing.

That is until a hippie lady with long, loose gray hair, big hoop earrings, and a tie-dye- sundress with a medley of yellows and oranges in a sunburst pattern approached them, demanding, "Ellie! What's all this?"

The girl, who he assumed was Ellie, worked to stop laughing before answering, "I'm fine, Aunt Penny. Just a small bump."

She turned to look at John, "This is…?" she hesitated because she didn't know his name.

"John," he filled in for her. "John Black."

"John Black," she repeated, trying his name, returning her gaze to the lady. Her Aunt Penny?

"You two need to sit down before you have another calamity. I have a blanket over there." She pointed to a spot. "I'll go and get you some napkins, at least."

Ellie led John to the blanket. They both were flicking pieces of food from themselves, and John clutched the now empty, soggy paper plate that previously held his dinner. Reasonably clear of excess food, they sat on the blanket.

She looked at him. "John," she stated.

He nodded and answered, "And you?"

"Ellie," she replied. "Ellie Ryan."

The hippie lady came up at that moment, and their conversation was interrupted.

"Here," the lady said, thrusting paper napkins at each of them.

"Thanks, Aunt Penny," Ellie replied. "You're a peach."

The woman, Aunt Penny, smiled at Ellie, "You two get cleaned up and get your dinner. I'm hanging with some friends over there." She pointed in another direction.

For a few moments, there was silence, not uncomfortable, just quiet as they sized up one another. Finally, John held out his hand for the soiled paper napkins. Ellie handed them to him. His stomach growled loudly, and he put his hand on it to quell the sound, looking guilty. Ellie bit back another smile.

"Ready for round two?" he asked mischievously.

"Only if you go ahead in front of me so that I can watch out for flying plates full of food," she teased.

He nodded and held out his other hand to help her up. They walked back to the buffet.

As they walked, they started talking. John told her he was a local and worked at the campground. He mentioned he was in college for engineering. Ellie started to tell John she was living with Aunt Penny for the moment, but she was interrupted by John.

"Oh, man!" John said in disgust as they made their way through the buffet table.

"What?" Ellie asked, concerned at his obvious angst. She couldn't see anything amiss. "What's wrong?"

John stood and looked mournfully at a plate with what appeared to be chocolate crumbs and a swipe or two of icing. He looked doleful.

"My mom's cake. It's all gone," he said mournfully.

"Isn't that a good thing?" Ellie asked, a little wary.

"I guess so," John continued in a doleful tone and nearly whined, "it's my favorite."

Ellie had to bite her lip and try not to smile. He sounded like he was four years old and lost his teddy bear.

"What kind of cake?" she asked.

"Tunnel of fudge," he stated,

John saw Ellie's lips twitch. She couldn't help it. She started to giggle. And then laugh. She pointed at her shirt. John saw a smear of chocolate adorn the t-shirt. It was some of the icing on the cake. They both laughed so hard that their plates wobbled dangerously.

"Oh, no, not again!" Ellie moaned.

John was taller than she, and his plate was wobbling dangerously close to her hair. For a moment, his laughter stopped, and he held the plate with two hands to steady it.

"I'm kidding!" Ellie insisted. "Let's go and eat before there are any more accidents."

They sat on the blanket and continued to talk. At first, about favorite foods, and then onto music. Ellie told John she liked folk music and John, rock and roll.

John was mesmerized by the glint of the setting sun on Ellie's hair and the way her eyes crinkled up when she laughed. He wanted to keep her talking.

"How did you end up here?" he asked, wondering if his question was too personal. But he was curious.

At first, Ellie looked slightly embarrassed, but a small triumphant smile crossed her lips when she told John about her defiance with her parents and how their plan backfired.

"I'm so fascinated with color and texture, particularly with fabric," Ellie said, her passion clear in her voice as she described various techniques.

John watched her as she talked about textile arts. She spoke animatedly and with passion. Watching her, he knew he was falling for Ellie in a very good way. John thought it was like a scene in a movie when the camera zoomed out and then zoomed in with an intensity that the background was blurred, and you were hyper-focused on one image. He heard but didn't hear what she was saying. He was mesmerized by the light in her eyes and the way they crinkled up when she smiled, which was often. And, her mouth. His breath hitched. And there was a nuance of a dimple on the right. She moved her hands when she talked. Not frantically, but graceful movements that were like music. John was smitten.

Eventually, they walked to the beach and settled in the sand that was cooling at the end of the day. Someone built a small fire, and someone else put on music. They were on the western side of the bay, and they couldn't watch the sunset, but the colors from the setting sun settled around them like a cloak. A star or two popped out, and they still talked.

When their talking paused, John reached for Ellie's hand and pulled her from the sand. They joined others, grooving and dancing on the beach until the darkness settled in.

John was staggered by the emotions that welled up within him. When he was with Ellie, it was as if they moved in their own bubble of time and place that was astoundingly beautiful. It blew him away.

Nine

LOUISA – 1918

A folk name for sea glass shards is "Mermaids Tears." It is said that mermaids shed tears of glass when a sailor drowns.

Louisa couldn't help herself. She kept calling Willie's name from a whisper to almost a shout. The tears came one after the other, dropping onto Willie's face. She tried to pull herself together.

Willie thrashed, and an orderly came to hold him down while Louisa supported his head, and Nurse Williams applied for the medicine and rebandaged the wounds.

"Come with me," Nurse Williams ordered when they had finished bandaging Willie.

Louisa hung her head and followed Nurse Williams to the curtained area at the end of the building. It was a spare, plain room sans decoration. Sunlight poured through the single window, making the room glow. Louisa's heart thought the sun itself would burst inside her chest. Willie was here. She could be near him and help him heal. Louisa closed her eyes, relishing the thought that he was near her.

And a cloud blocked some of the sunshine, and the sunshine

paled. Reality washed over Louisa. She knew it was against the rules to fraternize with the patients. But this was different, she countered in her head. She knew Willie before he went to war and had been missing. Nurse Williams asked Louisa to sit down in a hard, wooden chair. Its hard back pushed into her spine. Louisa sat up straighter automatically. Nurse Williams stood in front of her, crossing her arms and looking at Louisa.

"Now, tell me about this Willie fellow and how you know him," Nurse Williams said firmly, not sternly.

Louisa swallowed. First, she twisted her hands and then looked down at her toes. She noticed some spots of blood on her shoes and wondered if it was Willie's blood from when he was thrashing around. She glanced at the curtain that separated Nurse Williams and herself from the rest of the hospital ward. She glanced down the rows of beds through the crack in the curtain. Willie was out there.

"Louisa," Nurse Williams pressed.

Louisa's voice softly confessed, "It was last summer at Tolchester Beach. Willie is the son of the guest house proprietor. We weren't supposed to talk. Grandmama didn't approve. Willie's mother didn't approve. But we found ways to meet at the beach and amusement park. When the summer was over, he joined up. He joined the military when they called up all the men over eighteen. We've been corresponding, but the letters stopped about two months ago."

She looked down at her hands. "I was wondering, and I was worried. We hear all of the horrid stories from the men who come here. I can't think of life without him. I didn't think he had died. I thought I would feel that." Louisa looked sheepishly up at Nurse Williams. "I suppose that sounds silly."

Nurse Williams acknowledged with a strangled whisper, "Not at all."

"I wanted to write to his mother, but I couldn't," Louisa continued. "We had promised to keep our love a secret until he returned from the war. And I couldn't tell Grandmama. Then Grandmama got sick with the flu and died, and here..."

Her voice trailed off. Louisa's mind raced to a memory of her Grandmama just before she died. The tangle of emotions welled up. Louisa pulled herself together before continuing, "And here we are. I can't believe he's alive!" Louisa's voice was filled with joy before she sobered. "Nurse Williams, what is wrong with him? His head wounds didn't look too damaging."

Nurse Williams sighed. She looked through the curtain and peered at the rows of men lying on cots. She watched the orderlies and nurses bustle around the ward, tending to the wounded.

"He'll recover from the wounds outside his head," Nurse Williams began. "But I think he has more wounds inside his head from the horrors he saw at the front. He seems to be blind, but his eyes are fine, the doctors say. It's the horrors that he's trying to stop seeing inside his head that are causing the blindness."

"Oh." It was all Louisa could say in a small voice.

"Would you like to go home?" Nurse Williams asked. "After all, you've had quite a shock."

"Oh, no!" Louisa insisted. "I want to be here!"

"Will you be able to attend to the other soldiers and give them the attention they need? You won't be tempted to stray from your duties to see Willie?" Nurse Williams questioned.

Louisa paused before she answered. "Of course, I want to be near him. But I will be all right and attend to the men. Would it be all right if I took my breaks and lunch to sit near Willie?"

"That would be fine," Nurse Williams answered Louisa. "It would be good for you to sit near him and talk to him about your lives. Bring him out of his nightmares, Louisa. I will make sure that you have ample time to sit near him. After all, our purpose here is to heal the soldiers and make them clean and healthy. That includes their minds. It's one more win for us in this war if you can save Willie's mind."

Louisa was grateful for her words. Timidly, she asked, "May I have a moment?"

Nurse Williams nodded. "Give yourself a few minutes to get yourself together. Walk about in the fresh air. The sunshine is glorious today."

"Thank you, Nurse Williams," Louisa said. She stood shakily to go outside. Trembling hands smoothed at her skirt and then her hair. Before she turned to go, she smiled a hopeful smile.

Louisa stepped out of the hospital into the autumn sunshine. The sky was a crystal-clear blue, and the air was fresh, with an autumn crispness. t was a perfect balance of cool air and warm sunshine. Louisa took a deep breath and walked through the buildings to the edge of Fort McHenry. She rested her hands on the wall and looked at the rippling water. The ripples were coming toward her, so the tide was coming in, bringing good things.

Ten

WILLIE - 1918

Early spring is one of the best times to find sea glass.

"It's a long way to Tipperary. It's a long way to go. it's a long way to Tipperary, to the sweetest girl I know." The lyrics started quietly in the hospital ward and were sung almost fervently. Part of the lyrics seeped into Willie's brain. He would sing that song with his buddies and comrades in the trenches. He would think about Louisa with her beautiful brown hair and shining, shy eyes that looked at the world as a wondrous place. She was the sweetest girl he knew.

A clumsy orderly dropped a tray. It banged on the floor, reverberating with a clanking noise that took Willie right back to the front. It was so very real to Willie. He could smell the stinking mud, the men, and the smell of gunpowder. In his mind, he heard the sergeant shouting, "Over the top! Over the top!"

The first wave of men climbed up and out of the trench, scattering dirt everywhere from their boots sliding as they scrambled over the top. He heard a volley of gunfire. Ping. Ping. Ping. Ping. He winced at the sound. Kaboom! A shell exploded behind him. Bits of dirt rained down on them.

"Over the top! Over the top!" the sergeant shouted and ordered his men.

It was his turn, and there was no time for fear. His rifle and bayonet were at the ready. He scrambled over the sandbags and up over the dirt wall of the trench. He saw the barbed wire up ahead. The booms of mortars echoed through his head. A constant stream of soldiers kept coming, but men kept falling. There were more pings of ammunition. They whizzed past Willie's ear. The scent of gunpowder filled his nostrils. The smoke from the battle hung low to the ground. Bitter clouds from the steam from the 30-caliber machine guns moved across the land. Willie watched his comrades fall. Willie saw Danny fall. He watched Tommy's arm get blown off. It was time to fight or to die. Willie dropped to his knees. Then he dropped to the ground. He had to get closer to check on Tommy to stop the bleeding. Willie crawled on his belly toward his friend when he heard the whistle of an incoming shell. Willie looked up and saw the blue sky. It seemed surreal. And then the shell hit the earth and exploded. Everything exploded around him. And the world went dark for Willie.

Willie thought he heard voices. No, it was one voice. He couldn't determine who it belonged to. He thought he recognized the voice. The tone was light and soothing, like cool, running water. He wondered if he was dead. If so, was it an angel speaking? He didn't know where he was. He didn't know when he was.

The voice stopped. Willie dozed. For once, the nightmares didn't come.

The voice returned. Willie wished he could see who it was. All he could see was the dazzling brightness. He remembered the shell blasting with a brilliant flash. Now, blinding white light was the only thing that filled his vision.

The voice. He remembered the voice, and Willie wished he

could remember the person behind the voice. He could not make out what they were saying. He turned his head to see if he could hear more clearly. The voice became excited.

Another voice joined the light, angelic voice. It was a low, rich voice, like a contralto that had visited the rooming house a few years ago. She performed on stage at the park and warmed up her voice at the rooming house. He had been younger then, and that woman's voice filled him with ecstasy.

Unfortunately, he couldn't understand what that low, beautiful voice said. Willie equated this voice with firm, strong hands. They cradled his head as they wrapped the thick bandages around and around. The other voice, the voice of the angel, had a gentle, light touch.

The voices went away. Loneliness assailed Willie.

Eleven

ELLIE – 1969

The white glass that has turned a light purple is sometimes called "sunglass," from the manganese added to the glass, which turns purple in the sun.

Ellie crept into the trailer, opening the door ever so slowly to keep it from squeaking loudly. Penny had left one light on, and Ellie assumed she was in bed. What had started as a disaster ended up being a wonderful evening? Ellie relived the details as she hugged herself in bed. The conversation was so easy with John. It seemed to Ellie as if they had been old friends, parted for years, and now had to catch up on their lives. They couldn't stop talking and laughing and talking more.

A little shy at first, Ellie would glance at John, taking in his tan skin, a few freckles, and the myriad of colors that made up his hair. And his eyes. When he looked at her, his eyes softened as if taking in the whole of her, cherishing each moment together, making her feel as if she were his entire world. His glance filled her. There was an indescribable comfort in that glance. It was as if time and space had moved heaven and earth to bring them together.

And here they were, together. It was as if they had been apart for a long time and were finally meeting up again. Twilight fell, and the backdrop of the trees at the campground was a lush green smote with charcoal. The setting sun glinted in a rainbow of color on the water, briefly lighting up the windows on the opposite shore like colorful fireflies beginning their blinking dance as night fell.

When John took her hand to pull her to her feet to dance, it felt like her hand belonged in his. They danced and danced until they dropped into the sand, laughing and giggling. Ellie was almost too tired to sleep. She hugged herself in bed, replaying the evening over and over until finally, sleep came. A smile played on her lips as she dreamed about the fire on the beach, the music, and dancing under the stars with John.

Seemingly moments later, someone called her name, pulling her out of her dream. Aunt Penny shook Ellie's shoulder. Ellie groaned.

"Ellie! You need to get up! We're at the Farmers Market today. We need to get there early to set up. People start arriving at seven." Aunt Penny's voice was insistent.

Ellie opened her eyes and squinted at Aunt Penny, "What time is it?" she croaked.

"Five a.m.," Aunt Penny told her.

She was already dressed. Ellie blinked and woke up a little more before stretching and leaving bed.

Aunt Penny handed her a cup of coffee and ordered, "Super-quick sea shower, now. I'll get your clothes out. We're leaving in fifteen minutes."

"Did anyone ever tell you that you should have been in the military?" Ellie teased her aunt. She sipped her coffee and headed to the bathroom. The shower helped wake her up a trifle more. Quick ablutions and Ellie returned to the bedroom where Aunt Penny had laid out a new tie-dye dress in gorgeous blues, greens, and purples.

"Ooh! Aunt Penny! I'll feel like a mermaid in this dress!" Ellie cooed as she popped the dress over her head and admired it in the mirror.

She loved Aunt Penny's creations. Her floaty, gauze, tie-dye sundresses felt as light as a cloud. Indeed, the green in the dress gave the appearance of a kelp forest, with a swirly blues and purples background.

"Okay, let's go." Aunt Penny pushed her niece.

"Let me brush my hair, and I'll be ready," Ellie assured her.

"I'll warm up the Beast," Aunt Penny said.

The 'Beast' was Aunt Penny's older VW bus. It was packed with Aunt Penny's wares, a table, chairs, and a tent. They headed out of the dark campground. The sun was beginning to rise, giving the morning a glowing backdrop as they headed down the road. The Farmers Market in Havre de Grace was only a few miles from the campground, on the other side of the Susquehanna River. They traversed the Hatem bridge, and Ellie could see the lights of a tug boat out in the mouth of the Susquehanna. The water beneath them rippled darkly. Havre de Grace was still asleep, too. Aunt Penny drove through quiet streets to a small waterfront park that was bustling with activity under the glare of streetlights brighter than the twilight of the morning. Ellie squinted in the harsh lights. Aunt Penny pulled up behind several tents and parked where there was an open space.

"Here we are," Penny announced and ordered, "Now it's time to get to work."

She greeted the others at the park with a hello and wave before giving Ellie instructions on how they would set up the tent.

Ellie helped Aunt Penny set up their tent and put out their wares to sell. Their colorful creations looked lovely as the morning sun rose over the water. Ellie looked around, counting two dozen vendors whose tents dotted this section of the park. Ellie's stomach ached when the smell of cooking food wafted from the food trucks. Her stomach grumbled.

"I heard that," Penny teased Ellie. She handed Ellie some cash. "Go find us some breakfast."

Ellie meandered down the row of vendors, greeting them as she looked at their wares. At the Amish bakeshop, the huge cinnamon buns slathered with cream cheese frosting interested her but seemed too big and sweet. She shook her head, smiled at the pretty, young Amish woman, and moved on.

Further down the row was a wizened, older woman with yarn-filled baskets. Her thin, gray braid was wrapped around a knot at the back of her neck, with wisps of hair that had escaped and were lifted in an invisible little breeze. She wore a serviceable denim jumper over a floral cotton blouse. The sign on the baskets of yarn stated they were hand-spun and dyed naturally. There were other baskets filled with clouds of wool in ivory and tan. The sign labeled it as wool rovings. Ellie was in awe. She touched the yarn and its kitten-like softness.

"Do you knit or crochet?" the woman asked.

Ellie shook her head. "Sadly, no," she answered, "but I'm learning tie-dye from my aunt. I'm interested in the natural dying process. It's something I would like to learn."

"Let me give you my card," the woman said. "Give me a call if you want a lesson or two."

"Really?" Ellie exclaimed, so excited at the thought.

"Really," the old woman answered, a twinkle of amusement in her eyes.

"Thank you!" Ellie enthused. "I will take you up on the offer! I'm down the row there with my Aunt Penny."

"I know, Penny. You can tell her that Dora said hello."

"Thank you, Dora. I will give you a call in the next couple of weeks."

"The shearing's been completed. I'm working on foraging for dye materials, making the dye, and spinning the yarn. It's a busy time. Your help would be welcome."

"I would love to come, and I would love to learn the techniques," Ellie breathed. "Let me get our breakfast, and I will talk to Aunt Penny."

She could barely contain her excitement and backed out of Dora's booth, bumping into someone.

"I'm so sorry!" she cried without looking up.

"We need to stop meeting like this. At least you don't have a full plate of food for revenge," John's amused voice said in her ear.

"Oh!" Ellie replied, surprised, looking up to see John's smiling face.

Ellie was delighted and a little confused. "What are you doing here?" she asked.

"I thought you might be missing me," he teased.

Ellie blushed. "I...I..." she couldn't speak.

"Don't worry. I won't hold you to an answer. I'm here with my mom. She loves coming to the market," he explained. "And what are you doing? I thought you would be at the booth with your Aunt Penny."

Sheepishly, Ellie answered, "I'm to be getting us some breakfast, but I was side-tracked by Dora's yarn."

"Where are you headed to get breakfast?" he asked.

"I don't know. This is the first time I've been here. Probably one of those food trucks," she replied, nodding toward two food trucks that flanked the end of the vendors' tents.

"What if I walk with you to save you from distractions?" John suggested.

"That would be nice," Ellie agreed.

John *did* distract her. She could feel him next to her elbow. As they walked through the market, Ellie remembered the magic of the night before with the stars, the beach, the rhythmic waves, the music, and the bonfire. The combination was powerful, and she remembered how the night passed, dreamlike. She felt a connection with John but wasn't sure she could admit it to him or herself yet. When he walked her home last night, he took her hand at Aunt Penny's. He didn't kiss her, but she knew he wanted to.

And here he was today. Odd that. Did his mom come here regularly? She wondered.

They reached the end of the vendors' tents. One food truck had waffles with yogurt and fresh fruit. Aunt Penny would like that. She was vegetarian, and even the whiff of bacon on the food from the other food truck would turn her stomach. Ellie paid for the bowls, and they headed back toward Aunt Penny's stall.

A woman approached the booth and lightly touched the shirts and socks. She wore a neat, cotton shirtwaist dress. John, who only had eyes for Ellie, was surprised when the woman tapped him lightly on the arm.

"Mom!" he exclaimed when he turned to see who it was.

"I wondered where you had gotten to," the woman stated, looking up at her son. Her hair was carefully coiffed and sprayed into place, but she had the same dancing hazel eyes that John had. There was no doubt she was his mom.

Ellie tried not to stare, surprise evident on her face. She looked at John, then his mom, and finally, Aunt Penny. She smiled nervously, and John's mother smiled back. His mom began asking questions about their products. Ellie answered as best she could and sent a pleading look to Aunt Penny for help. Penny stepped in and answered the questions while Ellie backed away, inadvertently moving closer to John.

Twelve

JOHN – 1969

Brown sea glass, primarily from beverage bottles, ranges from golden amber to a deep, earthy brown.

John wasn't sure where to look, at his mom or Ellie. He glanced up and saw Penny's amusement and blushed deeply. Penny took over, explaining her dying process and the designs to his mom. She pointed to the tie-dye and then at the Shibori pieces.

John couldn't help it. He leaned toward Ellie. He was like a moth to her flame. His mom was busy listening to Penny. He smiled at Ellie

His mind drifted back to last night with the bonfire and dancing on the beach under the stars. He wanted to hold her close last night, to bury his nose in her hair, but he didn't. That would come later.

"Aren't you going to introduce me?" his mom eventually asked.

John nodded and introduced Ellie to his mom. Ellie reached out her hand.

"How do you do, Mrs. Black?" Ellie asked, holding out a slim hand to John's mother.

"I'm just fine. It's Ellie, isn't it?" Mrs. Black returned, her eyebrows raising at Ellie's cultured tone. Penny stood up and introduced herself. John wasn't sure what to say or do and looked sheepish in some ways. He looked at Ellie and then at his mom.

After some small talk, John's mother announced, "We must be going. John has to be at work in a short time." And she turned to John, "And you can carry this back to the car." She turned back to Ellie and Penny, "It was a pleasure meeting you."

John mouthed to Ellie, "See you later.

Mrs. Black handed the vegetables to John and hooked her arm through his.

His mother remained quiet until they got into the car.

"Nice girl," she commented while driving towards the campground.

"I think so," John said.

"You'll have to bring her around for dinner," his mother suggested.

"Mom! We barely know one another! Don't start jumping to conclusions, okay?" John reprimanded his mother, his beet-red face belying his words.

His mother said nothing more but only smiled. She pulled into the campground and dropped John off at the campground store.

"I'll see you later," he said as he exited the car.

John had hoped his day would be like the day before when he could mow or pound nails and have a chance to think about Ellie. But fate didn't favor him that day. Carl asked him to help the holiday campers get settled. Carl greeted each camper and had John assist with campers backing into their spaces, chocking wheels, helping with hook-ups of water, electricity, and sewer, and getting firewood. At the end of the day, he managed to squeeze in the bathroom and shower room cleaning and trash removal. He was wearily walking back towards the campground office and store when Carl pulled up in the golf cart.

"Busy day, eh?" He handed John a cold soda dripping from an icy bath in the cooler.

"Thanks," John said, raising the can like a toast. He nodded to Carl in answer to his question as he slugged back the soda.

"Hop in," Carl offered.

John didn't hesitate for a second. His body ached in weariness. He jumped in the golf cart beside Carl.

Carl took off in the golf cart.

"One last check for the evening. Everyone's settling in," he commented to John.

He looked over the campground as he drove around, waving, nodding, and greeting everyone. He surveyed the campground as a rancher, surveying his land and livestock. He was proud and pleased, John noticed. As well, he should be. The campground was bustling. Happy children swarmed the beach and the playground. People were lighting grills and campfires. The smell of charcoal and woodsmoke, mingled with steaks and hotdogs, filled the air. Transistor radios played pop hits at some of the campsites. The campers looked relaxed and happy.

"Looks like we have a fine group this weekend," Carl commented. He turned to John. "You get a wild card now and again. Those are the ones you need to look out for. Yeah, we always get one or two of them each summer." He shook his head, remembering.

"Betty's going to take you home tonight. She needs a bit of a break from the store and has to head to the grocer," Carl told John. "I already called your mom."

"Thanks," John replied.

They drove up to the camp store that had quieted down at the beginning of the dinner hour. Carl parked next to the store, and

Betty emerged. Carl gave her a peck on the cheek and told her to be careful before he and Betty entered the station wagon parked near the store.

"See you in the morning, John," Carl said as he entered the store.

John waved in reply as Betty seemed anxious to get on the road.

"Busy today?" he asked her to start a conversation.

"Unbelievably so," Betty commented. "I'm glad for a little break. I must pick up a few things at the grocer and return to the campground. Someone always needs something."

Betty continued to prattle about the campground, the weather, and missing the Memorial Day parade. She pulled into John's driveway. He thanked her and told her he would see her tomorrow. Betty waved gaily as she backed out of the driveway and went on her errands.

John walked to the back of the house and entered through the back door to the kitchen. His mom was bent over, checking something in the oven. It smelled like meatloaf. His mom's meatloaf was the best.

From the living room came the voice of Walter Cronkite. John knew immediately that his dad was home and watching the news. He cringed as he listened to the number of men killed that day.

"Hi, son," his mom greeted. "How was your day."

"Good. Hot. Long," John stated succinctly as he snagged a celery stick and a couple of olives from the small relish tray on the table.

His mom glanced at the clock above the kitchen sink. It was a subtle warning. He knew his dad expected dinner on the table moments after the news ended.

"Dinner will be in about fifteen minutes. Will that give you enough time to clean up?" his mother asked.

"A quick shower would be great."

"Make it quick," she warned. "I still have potatoes to mash but not much else. I'll turn down the meatloaf."

He saluted her with his pilfered celery stick. "I'll be lickety-split," he assured his mom and went to the stairs. He barely greeted his father except for a quick, 'hi' and a wave.

"Shower," he announced and pointed upstairs.

His father, glued to the television, nodded and grunted an acknowledgment, his eyes never leaving the screen.

He showered and dressed quickly, barely beating the end of the newscast. His mom beamed at him and asked for help to put the dishes on the table.

The news ended. The television clicked off. His dad sat at the head of the table, and John and his mom slid into their places. His dad bowed his head for a quick prayer, and they passed around the food.

"How are things at the campground, son?" his father asked.

John swallowed his bite of meatloaf and mashed potatoes drenched in gravy before answering. "Really well, Dad."

"What did you do today?" his father pressed.

"Today was really busy. Campers were pouring in for the Memorial Day weekend. Carl had me help the campers get set up with backing into the spaces, chocking wheels, and setting up the utilities. I also did my usual chores of trash and bath-houses. It's going to be a busy weekend. Carl and Betty seem pleased."

But, John answered his father stiffly. The numbers of the dead echoed in John's mind with Walter Cronkite's deep voice. And there was his father, relishing his mom's meatloaf and mashed potatoes as if he didn't have a care in the world. John realized that this wasn't his father's care or worries. He made a disgusted sound as he pushed the food around his plate.

"What's wrong?" his mother asked concerned. "Are you all right, John? Are you getting sick?"

"Just sick of this war," he muttered, his anger changing from simmer to a boil.

"What's that, son?" his father asked.

John exploded, "I don't know how you can sit so casually eating dinner after watching the news! All those men! They're dead now, and for what? What business do we have being in Vietnam?"

His father sighed, put down his fork, and looked hard at John before stating, "It's our duty, son. It's our duty to stomp out communism. Without this war, we could be overtaken by the Reds."

John made a derisive sound, "You're unbelievable! How can you believe Americans would put up with Communism? This war is only lining someone's pockets with dollars. It's not about Communism taking over the United States! Dad! How can you be so blind?"

His parents sat in stunned silence at John's outburst.

"You have some good points, John," his father answered him evenly, "but Communism is a threat and has been since before you were born. You weren't even born with when Hitler was around with his evil. And you were just a small child when we were terrified during the Bay of Pigs conflict. But you're welcome to your beliefs. This is America, after all."

"Maybe," John replied sullenly. He toyed with the food debris left on his plate.

His mom tried to change the subject and make peace, "Do you need the car tomorrow, John? Maybe I can talk your father into taking me to the Memorial Day parade in North Bay and possibly out to lunch?" She looked hopefully at her husband.

"I would love to take the car, Mom," John replied, his anger melted when he talked with her.

"You'll have to save money for your own set of wheels," his dad commented.

"I will, Dad. That's the plan this summer. I'm saving every

penny to get a set of wheels before I go back to campus." John tried to keep any attitude out of his voice.

They finished their dinner, and after a dessert of Jell-O, John offered to clean up. He knew his mom enjoyed watching some of the evening programs.

"If you're sure," she hesitated.

"I'm sure," John answered.

"Our boy is growing up," he heard his father say sotto voce to his wife.

His mom murmured something in return, but their quiet conversation was drowned out by a laugh track on the television.

John filled the sink with hot, soapy water and plunged the dirty dishes into soak for a minute while he put the leftovers away. Already, his mouth was watering for the meatloaf sandwich from the leftovers tomorrow. He cleaned the kitchen area, washed the dishes, placed them on the rack, and put the food away. Cleaning had displaced some of his anger toward his dad, and his mom would be pleased with the result of the clean kitchen. All at once, he realized how tired he was and told his parents he was going to his room and going to bed early.

"Night, son," his dad and mom told him.

In his room, he finally had a chance to think about Ellie. He lay on his bed, his arm behind his head, remembering how beautiful she looked today in that colorful dress, almost what he envisioned a mermaid to look like with the swirls of blue and green color and her hair, soft and wavy, curling around her shoulders. Last night, the firelight glinted off her hair. He loved her hair. It looked so soft, and he itched to stroke it. And he thought she was beautiful.

John had never met anyone like Ellie before. She was fiercely independent but soft and vulnerable in so many ways. He felt a need to protect her, but he also was awed by her determination and independence in defying her parents and making her own way.

He realized he hadn't seen her for the rest of the day. Surely, the Farmers' Market didn't last all day. Then he remembered she was setting up for the art and garden fair at the big church in North Bay. It was too bad he had to work tomorrow, or he would go to the parade and visit her.

He drifted to sleep, dreaming about Ellie's hair and her smile.

Thirteen

LOUISA – 1918

Some people feel that sea glass is a metaphor for life and a symbol of renewal and healing.

Louisa stepped out of the cab in the growing darkness. The gas streetlamps looked like dull, orange stars in a linear constellation lining the streets.

Stars. Louisa remembered a night with Willie under the glittering canopy of stars in Tolchester last summer. They were beautiful. She wished she could see the stars in Baltimore. The city's lights muted most of the stars in the sky as she craned her neck, squinted, and concentrated on the deep blue of the heavens. It took a moment, but there was a faint twinkling point of light in the darkening sky. Fervently, Louisa made a little wish about Willie.

Willie! She couldn't believe that he was here, in Baltimore. She didn't know how he made it from France's front lines to the Baltimore hospital, but she was grateful. Her wishes turned to a fervent prayer that he would be all right. She had seen several victims of shell shock in her short time as a hospital volunteer.

Many of them did not recover, not well, at least. She hoped Willie would come back to her.

Louisa opened the door to the townhouse. Its emptiness echoed in the silence, and Louisa remembered Bertha and Emma were delivering food. She didn't have anyone to tell her good news to, at least not right away.

Bertha left a plate in the warming oven, and Louisa sat at the kitchen table staring at a plate overflowing with roasted pork, carrots, and potatoes. Her thoughts turned to Willie as she ate her dinner. Her heart ached as she could only imagine the ghastly horrors Willie and the other soldiers saw on the front lines of the war. Those horrors were partly why he had lost sight and made his limbs tremble erratically at the slightest noise.

"The mind can only take so much violence," Nurse Williams had told Louisa. "These boys are on overload from the terrors of war. Some can return to us. Some cannot," she added grimly.

Louisa hoped Willie's mind would heal and he could return to the present and return to her.

For once, Louisa was glad she was alone in the house, left alone with her thoughts instead of being fussed over by Emma or Bertha. She toyed with the food on her plate and remembered the previous summer. The memories were still sharp and fresh. Louisa sank into her daydream, thinking of when Grandmama had planned a surprise for Louisa.

A little over a year ago, they had left Grandmama's stately townhome to find a cab at the curb. The cab was loaded with luggage. This was a turn of events! Grandmama stepped into the motorcar like an elegant horse and carriage. The cab took them to Light Street Station.

The station was all hustle and bustle. The wharf was a mass of horses, carriages, and motor cars. Trunks and cases were stacked about, pulled, and rolled along to the steamships. Louisa gaped at the sight of the regal-looking steamship. It seemed like hundreds of people were boarding in all shapes, sizes, and manner of dress. Louisa couldn't help but stare.

"Louisa! Come along, girl!" Grandmama snapped.

Louisa started at the sound of her grandmother's sharp tone.

"Yes, Ma'am," she answered automatically.

Louisa gulped and hurried after her stately Grandmama, who walked spritely, even with

a gold-topped cane to assist in keeping her balance. The steady stream of passengers turned from a crowd to a throng as they headed up the gangplank to the boat's deck. Louisa noticed that some passengers gave Grandmama's imperious aura a wide berth. Louisa tried to model Grandmama's graceful stride. She wasn't disdainful nor aloof, but what Louisa thought of as a "queenly grace."

They found a small space along the railing. Louisa felt she could jump up and down and up and down like a small child instead of an almost grown girl of eighteen at the sight of the water meeting the horizon as they looked away from Baltimore. Louisa turned to her grandmother with sparkling eyes.

"Oh, Grandmama! I've never seen anything so beautiful," Louisa cried.

Her grandmother patted her shoulder, and as the crowds dwindled to the salons, she put up her parasol and sat in a deck chair, watching Louisa's delight as they pulled away from shore.

Once on their way, Grandmama led Louisa into the large reception area. Sunshine poured through the skylight, lighting up the creamy, white arches of carved wood graced with gilt. The towering open windows that cooled the elegant room with the breeze called Louisa to gaze out on the bay. Louisa wanted to leave the reception area and hang over the railing, but she knew Grandmama would never permit this. Grandmama sat with a circle of women. Louisa turned her chair slightly away to keep her eye on the line where the water met the bright, blue sky. She could get lost in that view, and she almost was, until a gloved hand patted her knee and caused her to jump.

"Oh!" Louisa cried softly.

Another older, elegant lady patted her knee and held a lace-edged handkerchief to one of her eyes.

"I am so sorry, m'dear," the woman murmured.

Still lost in the magic of the view, she stared at the woman.

"Pardon me?" Louisa asked, confused.

"I am so sorry you lost your parents," the woman repeated sincerely.

"Thank you," Louisa replied demurely. She lowered her eyes.

When she looked up again, she sought Grandmama's face. A look of approval and a subtle nod from Grandmama indicated that Louisa had acted appropriately.

Louisa tried to pull herself into the conversation with the women seated in plush chairs, but she wasn't interested. The conversation went from the noise and mess of Baltimore's rebuilding from the 1904 fire to the latest fashion in hats, dresses, and hairstyles. Some thought it was scandalous that skirts had risen above the ankles. They looked disapprovingly at a lovely, elegant woman who wore a butter-yellow silk gown that was definitely above her ankles. She had a chiffon wrap that looked light as air and shorter, smartly styled hair. Louisa sighed. She thought she was one of the most beautiful women she had ever seen.

A few of the ladies made snide comments. Louisa heard the woman being referred to as "fast." She didn't know what that meant, only that it wasn't a good thing. It was something looked down upon by the society ladies. Louisa remembered her mother drilling into her that she should never, ever talk badly about a person. He remembered her mother saying that the people who said bad things about others were likely only doing it to make them feel good about themselves. She had urged Louisa to be careful in what she said, always. Louisa wished her mother were here. She wondered how she would have handled the gossip. Louisa looked at her grandmother. Grandmama's face was grim.

"If you will excuse Louisa and me," Grandmama said to the gathered ladies, "I would like to show Louisa more of the steamship.

Grandmama rose gracefully from her seat and turned to Louisa. "Come, child."

She led Louisa to the railing. Grandmama rarely liked outbursts, but Louisa could not help herself. "Oh, Grandmama! It's like a beautiful dream!"

Louisa loved the feeling of the wind in her hair that had escaped her long braid. She held her straw hat tightly to her head. The wind tugged at her shirtwaist, skirt, and petticoat. It whipped the wide tie knotted around her shirtwaist's wide collar. When Louisa turned back to look at Baltimore, all she could see was a dark line on the horizon. In front of her loomed a large pier where another steamship was parked, buildings, and what looked like an amusement park.

The shoreline grew closer with every moment. She did not want to blink for fear she would miss something. Birds wheeled about in the sky. She saw seagulls, and she thought she saw an eagle.

"Look, Grandmama, look!" Louisa cried.

"Yes, child, I see," Grandmama replied with patience. "We'll be landing within the hour."

Louisa put her hand above her eyes to shade them to see more detail. She heard Grandmama chuckle and came closer, holding her parasol over their heads. She began to see buildings on the shoreline. As the steamship cut through the water, the buildings rose magically from the green shoreline. Grandmama pointed to a splendid, white building up on the hill, a bit above and away from the buildings that crowded the shoreline.

"There, Louisa darling. That's where we'll be staying," Grandmama told her.

Louisa drank in every detail of the landing. She hoped their rooms looked out upon the bay. There was the hustle and bustle when everyone departed the ship. As eager as everyone was to get on the steamship in Baltimore, they were more eager to depart and begin their holiday.

Grandmama held Louisa back. There was a crush as the mass moved almost as one from the ship to the pier to the archway, welcoming them to Tolchester. When the majority of the crowd dispersed, Grandmama led Louisa down the gangplank, parasol held high. She was a stately figure that Louisa followed carefully.

Louisa broke from her daydream and found her food cold on her plate. She picked up her fork and ate a bite, but it no longer tasted good.

Last summer's dreams. They had filled her head and her heart this last year. Willie had filled her head and her heart. And, now, he was here in Baltimore. Despite his injuries, she was so relieved he was on home turf and near her. She sent another fervent prayer for his recovery before discarding the food on her plate and heading to bed.

Fourteen

WILLIE – 1918

Much sea glass on the Chesapeake Bay is found near towns where ships were docked. The ships would discard their trash over the sides of the boats.

Alone. Willie's heart sank. He wanted to hear that beautiful, angelic voice that had talked with him moments ago. He wanted to see the person behind the voice. Of all the voices in the past few days or weeks, this was the voice he wanted to hear. Was it possibly Louisa? Or was it a dream?

He seemed to have been asleep for a very long time. He felt he was beginning to wake from the nightmares. Those nightmares of ravaged, bloody faces and bodies of his comrades in arms filled his vision. He could hear their cries of pain and moans of anguish. He could hear the bullets whizz past his head and the explosions of rockets. It happened over and over and over again. Nightmares without end. He cried out involuntarily. What was happening? His arms and legs trembled without volition. He had no control. He couldn't see. And he couldn't remember things clearly. This was hell orchestrated by his mind.

It was an ongoing film of hell on earth, the battlefield, and the suffering of war.

Vaguely, he remembered a large, bright, white flash in front of him and a very loud boom. His ears were still ringing. In his mind, he saw soldiers flying through the air as if they were on a trapeze. But they didn't land gracefully and bow. They landed hard, crumpling on the ground, lying still and not moving. Their bloody faces and uniforms were the final act in the macabre circus of the war. A war that didn't seem to end.

Willie couldn't remember what happened after the explosion. He didn't even know where he was. He wondered who had that angelic voice. It sounded like Louisa, but how did she get to France? Her grandmama would never have approved.

Louisa. He had fallen hard for her last summer. No, he loved her. Her letters kept him going. He sometimes wondered if his desire to return to her was what kept him alive. Willie wrote her dozens of letters and waited eagerly for her letters in return. Letters from home kept Willie and his fellow soldiers alive more than the rations and occasional bunk. Exhausted most of the time, they slept sitting up in the trenches. They never seemed comfortable. There was never a place to rest their weary bodies. Depending on the weather, they would either feel burning hot or freezing cold. And they were always hungry. But, those letters. They brought memories and a taste of home that filled their hearts with hope.

When the bullets weren't volleying, and the bombs weren't flying, the soldiers played cards and sang. Willie remembered the tune 'Keep the Home Fires Burning' and hummed. He couldn't quite say the words out loud, but inside his head, the lyrics played over and over as if on a gramophone.

Willie's voice was weak and wavering, but he broke out of humming and into song. He could barely hear his voice through the bandages. His wounds burned, but the singing made him feel happier. Somewhere beyond the blindness and outside the bandages, he heard more voices take up the song. The music calmed him. It calmed his limbs.

He felt at rest, and he felt at peace. When he opened his eyes this time, he began to see blurry shapes in the bright light beyond the bandages. The light was astoundingly beautiful.

Fifteen

ELLIE – 1969

Yellow, orange, and red pieces of sea glass often come from decorative ware.

Ellie and Penny watched John and his mother walk away from their table.

"You did that well," Penny remarked as she watched them go.

"What?" Ellie questioned.

"The meeting of the mom," Penny intoned.

Ellie looked at her aunt askance. "You're reading far too much into this," she scolded. "It was just a picnic and dancing on the beach."

"If you say so," Penny responded in a sing-song voice. She turned away from Ellie, smiling a knowing smile, and greeted customers who came to the table.

Another customer approached, and Ellie couldn't ruminate on Penny's words. The market was a bustling hive of activity. The morning passed quickly with steady sales. When it was time to pack up again, Ellie remembered telling Aunt Penny about Dora's greeting and invitation.

"You will love visiting Dora's little farm," Penny agreed. "I'll just run up to see if I can catch her. Can you please get these boxes into the Beast?"

Ellie nodded and began packing up the van. Penny returned a few minutes later with a satisfied smile.

"We're all set," Penny told Ellie. "We'll call Dora on Tuesday morning to see which day is best for us to visit."

"That's fantastic, Aunt Penny!" Ellie cried, wanting to jump up and down in anticipation.

"C'mon now, climb in. We need to head to North Bay next to find our spot for the craft and garden show this weekend."

Ellie dutifully got in the van. They drove to North Bay, a small town at the top of the Chesapeake. It was a little further north on the bay's eastern side than Aunt Penny's campground on the western shore. Traffic was heavy, and Aunt Penny swore lightly under her breath as she maneuvered the Beast through the small street of two-way traffic. The town was bustling with store-keepers hanging out red, white, and blue bunting, and parking spaces were filled with cars towing boats. Near the end of town, a small church was purported to exist before the Revolutionary War. The grounds around the church were bustling with people. To Ellie's astonishment, Aunt Penny drove right into the grave-yard. A man in khakis and a wide-brimmed safari hat carried a clipboard, pen, and walkie-talkie. Penny stopped to give him her name. He consulted the clipboard, looked at her, and then pointed.

"Talk to Jim down there," he advised. "You're in J-8. He'll tell you where to park and set up."

Penny thanked the man and moved slowly. Vendors were in all stages of set-up. Aunt Penny had briefed Ellie that this was one of the tri-state area's most well-attended garden and artisan markets. Penny pulled close to the next man holding a walkie-talkie. He pointed to a spot near the wall around the graveyard. It was adja-cent to a small parking area for the church.

"This is fabulous!" Penny breathed. "We can set up the tent and tables today. We'll come early tomorrow morning to snag a parking spot and set up the textiles. We can keep the extra stock in the Beast and take turns refilling when needed. That way, we won't have to lug box after box of stuff for backup stock."

Aunt Penny pulled the Beast off to the side, and they repeated the drill earlier that day of setting up the tent and tables. The sun was directly overhead, and they were glistening with sweat by the time the tent and tables were in place.

Ellie wished she had pulled her long hair into a ponytail. She flapped her gauzy dress to get a bit of breeze. Aunt Penny laughed when she saw this.

"Come on. You've worked hard this morning. Let's go to an air-conditioned restaurant to have some lunch."

Ellie didn't pause for a second and went to the car. Aunt Ellie drove back through town, maneuvering carefully to the sole stop light and restaurant on the corner. The Lighthouse Diner was a town icon. Ellie didn't care where they ate as long as it was air-conditioned.

The smell of coffee and fried foods greeted them as they opened the door to the restaurant. Stepping inside the restaurant, the cool air washed over them, and the clatter of cutlery, dishes, and conversation filled the air. The conversational noise paused when they walked in as diners viewed the newcomers but settled back into a rhythm of talk and laughter. The waitress, who looked ancient, sat them at a small table for two under a nautical stained-glass window with a lighthouse and sailboat and took their drink order.

"It's a small town," Penny whispered as she sipped the ice water the waitress delivered to the table. "All the best gossip is here."

Ellie looked around and stirred the fresh lemonade the waitress had brought. Its sweet-tart flavor slid down her hot, dry creek bed of a throat. There were conversations about the upcoming parade at many tables and comments on the current political climate and the Vietnam War. There was also a low buzz about something else, something fervent. Penny tried to look casual, but her body was taut, listening. Carefully, she shook her head at Ellie, followed by a wink.

The waitress interrupted their eavesdropping by coming to take their order. After the waitress left, Penny seemed intent on listening, so Ellie kept quiet. It was fine. She could finally think about the morning with the customers, meeting Dora, and John's surprise visit. She was lost in thought and startled when the waitress brought their food and slid a plate in front of her.

Ellie jumped. "Oh! Thank you!"

"Not a problem, dearie. Enjoy."

"When we get back this afternoon, I need to order more supplies," Penny told Ellie. "If you can, wash up some of the remaining stock to cure. We can tie things up and get ready to dye them on Sunday."

Ellie nodded vaguely.

Penny continued, "And we'll want to pack lunch and bring a thermos of ice water for tomorrow. I understand it's to be hot and humid. We're lucky we don't need to unload the Beast. We're all set for tomorrow's festivities."

Ellie ate her sandwich slowly. Now bored with her eavesdropping, Penny said to Ellie, "What about you?"

Ellie paused, sandwich halfway to her mouth. "What do you mean?" she asked, a little trepidatious.

"You've been here a few weeks. Are you in for the long haul, or do you want to go home?" she asked bluntly.

"Aunt Penny, I love being here!" Ellie responded, "As long as I'm not a burden to you."

Penny gave a small harumph. "Burden? Ellie, you have been an amazing help to me. But do you like the work? What about college?"

"Aunt Penny, I do not want to go to college to become a

"Mrs." College is fine, but I'm not interested in the general curriculum. Mom and Dad's plan is for me to go to college to find a husband or settle down with a safe job as a secretary, a nurse, or a teacher. Gah." Ellie made a face. "With you, I am learning stuff I can't learn anywhere else. I'm fascinated with the fabric and colors! I wish I could go to school to learn more about textiles."

Penny's eyes twinkled at this comment. "Well, you can do that. If you're interested, you could begin looking at art schools. You probably can't get in for the fall semester because you'll need a portfolio. We could explore that, and I can work with you on putting one together."

Ellie gave Penny a brilliant smile. "That would be amazing!" Then her expression clouded, "But what about Mom and Dad? They would never approve. How can I pay for college? Why, I think I'm already a disappointment to them."

"Nonsense. Your mother is probably concerned that you are more like me than her ultra-conservative self. You and I are like two peas in a pod. We're creatives, and there's nothing wrong with that. I stepped away from the norm. It bothered your mom more than it bothered your grandparents. Your mom is probably concerned you'll turn out like me."

Aunt Penny sighed, "One step at a time, Ellie. I will speak with your parents. And there are scholarships available. We'll figure it out, one step at a time."

Ellie nodded, dazed at the possibility of going to art school. Her art explorations were pushed to hobby status by her parents. To really explore different mediums, especially textiles, would be a dream come true.

"You've always had an affinity for art, right?" Penny asked.

Ellie thought about the question before answering. "I think so. Mom and Dad chalked it up to being 'crafty.' I could explore art at camp and such, but not really at home."

"Well, I know you've always liked textiles. I remember fabric shopping with you and your mother. We had to practically drag you out of the store."

Ellie nodded. "I remember. I loved the textures and colors of the fabrics. I kept imagining different clothes to make from the fabric. I wanted to touch every bolt and absorb every color."

"As I remember, you were quite talented at making doll clothes."

"And I nearly cut off my finger in fifth grade. I was punching scissors through a neckline, trying a shortcut, and ended up with a few stitches in my finger. Mom and Dad quelled the sewing after that until Home Ec, and then I could learn to sew on a sewing machine."

"And you've been making clothes ever since, right?" Penny questioned. "Have you designed them?"

"Sometimes," Ellie admitted. "I find the tissue paper patterns frustrating, so I've learned to make my own patterns with butcher paper."

The waitress interrupted them, asking if they wanted dessert. They shook their heads, and she brought the check.

"We'll talk more of this later," Penny promised.

Sixteen

JOHN – 1969

"Pirate glass" looks black but reveals a color when it's held up to the light. Usually, it is very old and sometimes has air bubbles inside."

Carl leaned heavily on the store counter, clutching a cup of hot steaming coffee, when John walked into the store the next day.

"Morning," he greeted John in a weary tone.

John nodded in return, unsure what to make of Carl's mood.

"A cup of coffee for you, John?" Betty asked.

John shook his head. "No, thank you."

Carl took another swig before telling Jon drily, "You missed some fun last night."

Startled, John asked, "Why? What happened?"

"Some fool decided it was a good night to set off fireworks on the beach at about eleven last night. He violated the fire code and could cause me to lose my campground. He also disturbed the other campers. There were crying children and dogs barking all over the place." Carl sighed heavily.

"People are funny," Betty told Carl, kissing him on the cheek and rubbing his arm, which was stiff with annoyance.

"Harumph," Carl expostulated and muttered, "Idiot."

"It took us most of the night to get him off the grounds. He had been drinking and was slightly belligerent. I had to bring out my old Military Police skills," Carl informed John. "And fortunately, the local constabulary are supportive. They came and assisted with getting that guy out of here." John could only mouth a stunned 'wow.'

"I'm going to go catch some shut-eye, and you're in charge of getting the new campers in their places. Betty will help you."

John gulped.

"You'll be fine, John," Betty assured him.

Carl nodded in agreement. "I have every confidence in you, son." He gave a large yawn. "And, on that note, I am heading to bed."

John nodded and stood quite still, processing the situation. Betty, all business now, pointed to the campground map on the wall. The day flew by. By the time Carl got up in the late afternoon, John had had his fill of campers. He spent the day as he had the day before, guiding people to their campsites, chocking wheels, and assisting with hook-ups. The difference between yesterday and today was that the campers who arrived today were in a hurry. Some were short-tempered, snapping at John as if it was his fault they came on Saturday instead of Friday for the holiday weekend. They wanted to get set up and get to the water or start their campfires. The little beach was packed, and boats whizzed up and down the bay.

John didn't argue when Carl told him to go home a little early. He even offered to take care of the bathrooms and bathhouses. John thanked Carl for the reprieve and high-tailed it home.

When John arrived home, the smell of spaghetti sauce and baking pasta wafted through the kitchen screens. But the house was very, very quiet and still. He glanced back, double-checking that his dad's car was in the driveway. The mower was out, and the yard was only partially cut. Odd.

"Mom? Dad?" John called out, a little worried.

He heard his father clear his throat and gruffly replied, "We're in here, son."

John entered the living room to find his mom sitting on the sofa beside his dad, red-eyed. She clutched a handkerchief in one hand and his father's hand in the other.

"What's wrong?" John asked.

"You'd better sit down, son," his father said.

John sat, mystified.

"P-p-peter Hol-Holbrook," his mom started, but she stopped and sobbed.

"He was killed in Vietnam, John," his father finished.

John sat back, his body rigid. Peter was a couple of years ahead of him. They were friendly, though not close friends due to the age difference, but Peter had been in Boy Scouts with him. Pete was tall and lanky. John used to tease him and call him Daniel Boone. He looked a little like Fess Parker, the star of the television show with dark hair and smiling eyes. He loved hunting and fishing. He always felt at home in the woods when they went camping. John learned a lot from him about wild creatures, tracking, and archery. He remembered Pete's easy grin, belly laugh, and how his eyes crinkled when he smiled. He was one of the happiest people John had ever met. And now he was gone. Dead. Dead because of this stinking war. John clenched his fists.

"I'm going to their house in a few minutes when the pasta bake is done," his mom told him. "I can't imagine how Paula is feeling."

John found words stuck in his throat. All he could do was nod at his mom.

"I have another pasta bake for you and your father," his mother continued. "I don't know if I'll be a few minutes or several hours."

"You do what you need to do," his father told his mother gently. "You let Paula and Kevin know we will support them in any way we can."

His mom leaned against his father and closed her eyes. The timer in the kitchen dinged.

"I'll get it," John said, and he hurried to the kitchen to take the pasta out of the oven.

He took hot pads and removed the pasta bakes from the oven. They looked perfect with the melty cheese and a light, golden-brown top.

"John, can you please put foil on both?" his mother called from the living room. "One can go in the oven to stay warm for you and your father."

"No problem," John called back and followed his mother's directions.

A few minutes later, his mother left with the casserole, a green salad, and a bottle of Italian dressing. He set the table for his father and himself, and they sat and ate in silence. John kept his anger at bay but viciously stabbed at the pasta. He wondered what his father thought and felt but didn't ask.

"It was a shame to hear about Pete," his dad commented.

John nearly choked on his food at the comment, his anger peaking. He looked at his dad through narrowed eyes, "A shame?" he asked rhetorically, sarcasm biting into the tone. "Dad! It's another useless death! Pete won't be coming home. And for what?"

"He died for our country. For our freedom!" his dad expostulated. "If one country falls to communism, others will fall like dominoes!"

"What? Tiny little Vietnam will be an influence on our democracy? Or is it just foreign policy? We've invaded a third-world country, Dad, forcing our belief system on them. Of course, they're going to fight back."

"You don't know the half of it, son. This cold war, the threat that we'll be blown to smithereens by a nuclear bomb, isn't a fairytale. There's a reason why we still have a bomb shelter in the backyard."

"And do you think Vietnam will be the one to press the freaking button?" he asked unbelievingly. "I don't. There's a bigger picture; we're all pawns in their war game." He shook his head. "Look, I don't want to fight with you. I'm done. I'll wash up," John said curtly to his dad.

His father nodded stiffly, his body taut with anger. He didn't retort. They had a temporary truce.

He thought he heard his father mutter, "You think you know so much," as his father went outside, slamming the door in his wake to finish the mowing. John assumed they received the news about Pete when his dad worked on the yard that afternoon. John didn't engage. He put the leftovers away. His mom always washed as she cooked, so there was little to do except the plates and glasses. But he scrubbed the dishes much harder than he intended and splashed water on the front of his shirt. He swore, grabbing a towel. When the dishes were done, he took the dishcloth and scrubbed the countertops and stove, scrubbing away his remaining anger. The kitchen gleamed, and John was worn out.

He realized he felt numb and went upstairs to take a long, hot shower. He stood under the needle-like spray until it turned cold before drying off and leaving his room. Pete was the first person he knew who died in Nam. He was afraid it might become the norm. Niggling his psyche, he wondered if, or rather when, his draft notice would arrive.

Seventeen

To some, sea glass is trash. To others, sea glass is beautiful.

Nurse Williams pulled Louisa aside before she could reach Willie's bedside the next day. Trying not to panic, Louisa stood before the matron to listen to what she needed to say.

"There's been a change in Willie," Nurse Williams began.

Louisa closed her eyes tightly. A knot of fear settled in her stomach. Her interlaced fingers gripped her hands tightly.

"No, no!" Nurse Williams said sharply. "Louisa, it's not bad news, it's good news! Willie started to sing yesterday."

Louisa couldn't believe her ears. "Sing?"

"Sing," confirmed Nurse Williams. She smiled at Louisa. "He sang, 'Keep the Home Fires Burning.'"

She gaped at Nurse Williams and then smiled a broad smile.

"I would love to see him before I begin my shift."

"Go right ahead," Nurse Williams told Louisa. "Talking to him yesterday helped him tremendously. I'm sure of it."

Louisa barely heard what Nurse Williams said. All she could

think of was Willie. She hurried down the ward as fast as she could walk, as running anywhere in the hospital buildings was verboten. He was lying there. His eyes closed, his pale face against the snowy white bandages and heavy cotton sheets. Louisa took his hands in hers.

"Willie!" she called to him. She willed him to look at her. "Willie!"

He turned his head.

"Please, Willie! It's Louisa! Please tell me you remember me. Please tell me you remember us!" Louisa pleaded.

"Lou...Lou...Louisa?" It was barely a whisper, but he had said her name.

"Yes! It's me, Willie."

Louisa sat beside the bed and took Willie's hand in hers. Last summer, she had marveled at Willie's strong, tan hands and how it enveloped hers protectively. With a sense of wonder, she realized how much could be communicated by holding someone's hand. Words weren't needed.

And now, she was the one with the strong hands, holding Willie's pale, weak one. He had lost so much weight in the war. She held his skeletal hand firmly but gently, afraid tears might fall again. She tried to communicate all the love in her heart through their clasped hands.

"Oh, Willie," was all she could say for several minutes. But then, she remembered Nurse Williams's directions and began talking to Willie about her days at the hospital and that she would come to see him every day.

"You must get well, Willie. You must!" Louisa told him vehemently.

Willie visibly relaxed, with Louisa holding his hand. He had a smile, and he drifted off to sleep. Gently, she loosened her fingers, went to Nurse Williams, and told her the good news that Willie had said her name.

Giving Louisa a broad smile, Nurse Williams took her arm,

almost crowing with delight, telling her, "I think we'll be saving this one. This is such a good sign."

"Yes! Yes!" Louisa cried joyfully.

Nurse Williams gave her tasks to stay about the ward. Louisa made beds, helped with medications, and with changing bandages. She did her tasks with a light heart and a smile. Near the end of her shift, she assisted Nurse Williams with the rebandaging of wounds. Once again, they worked as a team, Louisa holding and soothing the soldiers and Nurse Williams treating the wounds and bandaging. They saved Willie's bandages for last so that Louisa could stay to visit with him.

Willie's head turned toward her when she spoke to him this time. Louisa flashed a triumphant smile to Nurse Williams. When they changed his bandages, one of the wounds near the edge of the bandage was purulent and puffy red. Louisa looked worriedly at Nurse Williams.

"Willie, I'm going to put some antiseptic on your wound," Nurse Williams directed. "It's going to sting, and it's going to burn. I need you to hold as still as you can. Louisa is here to hold your hand."

Nurse Williams motioned for a couple of orderlies to assist in holding Willie down in case he moved while Nurse Williams was treating him. Louisa clasped Willie's hands tightly.

"Willie, I have ever so much news to catch you up on," she told him. "You see, I was quite worried when I didn't receive a letter from you recently. It's a miracle that you ended up at the Baltimore field hospital. I guess they know your home is the Eastern Shore. Have you heard from your family? Do they know that you are here? Do you want me to write them a letter?"

Louisa waited after each question for a response. Today, the only response was a moan of pain when the antiseptic seeped into the wound. Willie tried to move his hands to touch it, but Louisa held on tightly.

Willie's wound made Louisa nervous. She had seen pus-filled

wounds turn gangrenous in a matter of hours to a few days. Willie wasn't responding now, and she touched his forehead, praying there wasn't a fever.

She took his hands in hers and, out of nervousness, started prattling. "Willie, I wonder what your life was like before I met you. I wonder what it was like to grow up with your mother. She is an amazing and formidable woman. Grandmama loved her. Did you know that?

"Did you know, Willie, that coming to Tolchester was my first vacation? I had never been on a steamship or an amusement park. I was so amazed by the rides and the little steam engine. I wanted to swim in the bay and ride every ride at the amusement park every single day. I dreamed of dancing in the dance hall in a beautiful dress. Grandmama was so very strict. Your mother's guest house was so perfect. It was perfect for Grandmama because it was a serene place amongst the "honky-tonk," as Grandmama put it. She commented so often last summer that she wished we had gone to Betterton Beach, where it was quieter. I couldn't tell her the truth that I loved every moment in Tolchester. It was the very best summer of my entire life. And you made it that way, Willie. Did you know that? It wasn't all the honky-tonk. It was you. You made me come alive, Willie. And you made everything real and right. I don't know how to explain it other than that. It would be best if you were with me, and I need to be with you. It sounds like something out of a motion picture, but it isn't. It's true, and it's real. Please, Willie. Come back to me."

Nurse Williams completed the bandaging while Louisa chatted. She nodded to Louisa as she went to the next bed, giving her permission to stay.

"Keep talking," Nursing Williams mouthed to Louisa.

Louisa nodded and turned her attention back to Willie. The noise in the hospital ward faded like an old memory as she continued to remind Willie about their lives together last summer.

Louisa didn't know if Willie had heard anything or not. His eyes were closed. She hoped he was taking it all in.

"And Willie, you were the best thing that happened to me last summer. I will never forget when we met. You came to the beach early in the morning. I had escaped from the guest house and wanted to stare at the water and the sky. I'm not sure where I was or what I was thinking about, but suddenly, a big toe made circles in the sand beside me. It was you! You scared me a little bit. Did you know that? I had never met so forward a young man. And then you left. And you whistled! I couldn't believe it. I watched you walk down the beach. Something about you struck me..." Louisa trailed off.

Louisa noticed that Willie was holding her hands now, not vice versa. She squeezed his fingers. She hoped he heard what she had babbled. She wanted him to engage with her, to turn his head or squeeze her hand. She wanted the bright-eyed boy she knew back. Louisa wondered if it would ever happen. Would his outer and inner wounds heal?

Eighteen

WILLIE – 1918

Two out of three pieces of sea glass you find will be white.

Willie heard the angelic voice. He now knew it belonged to Louisa. He didn't know how she was where he was, but he was happy. Willie was surprised he didn't hear more French voices, thinking he was in an outpost hospital in France. But then, Louisa had said he was in Baltimore. How had he gotten there? It didn't make sense to him, and he was too weary to figure it out. Louisa was here, and he was here, and that was all that mattered.

His head hurt. It hurt badly. And a small part of it itched. He hoped the lice had not returned. At the front, they seemed to be everywhere. He would burn them off to get rid of them. It wasn't just Willie. It was everyone, every soldier. He hated lice.

When Louisa talked to him, it calmed him. When Louisa spoke, a peacefulness came into his mind, and the horrors of the battlefront faded. When she spoke, his stiff, trembling limbs no longer had a life of their own. He could feel his arms and legs and control them. She spoke in soothing tones and told him about happy things. Some words from this sweet, calm voice made sense to Willie's addled brain.

She talked about their summer together. Willie could get lost in the dream of her voice and remembering her beautiful hair and small hands that he liked to hold. He remembered how shy she was, not wanting to talk to him at first. But he was persistent and smiled and said hello every chance he got.

He remembered Louisa quietly slipping out of the boarding house and going to the beach early in the morning. He was always up early, starting small chores around the boarding house before going to the amusement park. He fed the chickens and gathered the eggs for breakfast. And last summer, he slipped away from his chores to follow the pretty girl who went to the beach. He watched her from a distance and marveled at how she settled into the sand to watch the water and the sky. She was like a pebble, comfortably sinking into the sand, reveling in the quietude of the morning. He couldn't remember meeting anyone who held the tranquility of the water and sky inside of them as Louisa did. He marveled at her and couldn't help but stare.

He became bold one day, walked down to the beach, and stopped to say hello. She ignored him, but he knew he had caught her eye. When he went further down the beach, he looked back, and she watched him. There was something in that glance of hers that he fell in love with at that very moment. Strands of her hair glittered in the early morning sunshine, and her deep blue eyes matched the water's color. He thought her eyes were a lighter blue-gray, but they were a deeper blue that morning. As he got to know her, he learned that her eyes would change shades depending on her mood. But he loved the deep blueness of that day. It was an indicator that she was supremely happy. He wanted to make her happy to see that deep blue every day, especially when she looked at him.

Memories. They were funny things. They grabbed you by the gut, like a shot of whiskey, and burned in your soul before they warmed your limbs and made you lightheaded in grief, joy, or other emotion. His memories of Louisa filled his head, his heart, and his gut. The memories of last summer with Louisa were one of the things that got him through the war.

And more than anything, Willie wanted to see Louisa again with his eyes. He silently cursed his blindness and the bandages. He wanted to gain control over his shaking limbs and forget the war. He wondered if this would ever happen and if they could return to Tolchester and sit on the beach together.

Nineteen

ELLIE – 1969

Sea pottery is well-worn shards of ceramic or porcelain dishes.
Collectors prize many.

The artisan fair was hot and humid, just as Aunt Penny had predicted. Ellie thought longingly of the breeze from the bay at the campground. The walls of the churchyard seemed to hold in the heat and humidity. Ellie knew that wasn't true, but she had become used to the open space at the campground.

It was busy. Incredibly busy. Her respect for Aunt Penny grew in leaps and bounds as Ellie assisted her with customers. Aunt Penny wasn't a pushy salesperson but had a knack for reading people. She looked people in the eye and listened to what they said.

They made a good team. Aunt Penny talked about her artistic process and made subtle suggestions to customers while Ellie handled the cash and bagged the items.

The sales and crowds died down during the parade. They took a small break and ate their sandwiches, glimpsing the tops of the band and the upper half of the floats as they went by. Aunt Penny took a walk and returned with tall glasses of freshly squeezed lemonade. It was a welcome treat.

When the parade ended, it was as if the gates were let loose as people poured into the fair.

Ellie had bent down to retrieve more t-shirts from a box when she heard Aunt Penny say, "Hello, Mrs. Black. How lovely to see you again."

John's mother? Ellie stood and smoothed her colorful dress. It was John's mother, in her neat shirtwaist dress and snappy black eyes. Beside her was a tall man who looked faintly like John, except he had a crewcut, glasses, and a militaristic air about him. Mrs. Black introduced her husband to Aunt Penny and Ellie. She introduced Ellie as "John's girl," which made Ellie blush deeply. Recovering, she held her hand to Mr. Black, saying, "How do you do?"

Mr. Black's return handshake was firm. Ellie felt his eyes could bore right through her, but Aunt Penny's brief touch to her shoulder made her straighten and meet his eye.

"Pleasure," Mr. Black returned.

Mrs. Black bought a T-shirt and a pair of socks. As they exchanged products for cash, she told Ellie, "I hope you'll come around the house soon."

Ellie replied politely, "That would be lovely. Thank you for the invitation."

And with that, they were gone. Ellie felt a little dazed. But the swell of customers couldn't leave her mulling over the encounter for long. She assumed John was at the campground and wondered briefly how he was making out with the influx of campers. The afternoon wore on, and the crowds began to dwindle after two. Vendors began packing up a little after three.

They packed a much lighter Beast at the end of the day. Aunt Penny told Ellie that they deserved a treat. She stopped at a small pizza place about a block from Main Street and on the way back to the campground.

"Stay here," she ordered Ellie. "This is a surprise."

Ellie didn't argue. It felt good to sit in the air conditioning of the van. She put back her seat and closed her eyes. She remembered Mrs. Black referred to her as "John's girl." Was she? Ellie wondered why she had commented. His father was so stoic. Ellie couldn't read him, but she liked John's mother.

Her thoughts were interrupted by a bang on the car door. Startled, Ellie's eyes flew open, and she saw Aunt Penny grinning and holding a pizza box and a small bag. Ellie rolled down her window.

"Can you open the side door?" Aunt Penny asked Ellie.

Ellie slid the side door of the van open, and Aunt Penny arranged the pizza box and bag on top of the boxes of T-shirts. A delicious aroma oozed from the pizza box, and Ellie's stomach rumbled. It had been a long time since they ate their sandwiches.

It was only a few miles back to the campground. When they returned to the camper, Ellie started a small fire in the fire pit, and Aunt Penny went inside to fetch a bottle of wine and glasses.

"Cheers, luv," Penny said, handing Ellie a glass of wine. "It was an excellent fair. We'll need to take inventory tomorrow and see what we need to restock. Tonight, we relax."

Aromas of seafood mixed with tomato sauce and cheese emanated from the large pizza in the box when Aunt Penny opened it.

"It's a seafood pizza with crab, shrimp, and calamari," Aunt Penny explained. "It's a delicious treat."

She handed Ellie a large slice on a paper plate, and they sat under the camper's awning, catching a breeze from the water. Ellie took a bite of the pizza. Aunt Penny was correct. This was a wonderful treat.

As they were finishing their dinner, Carl drove up, putting along in the golf cart on one of his checks of the campground.

"Hello there, Carl!" Penny called out. "Care for a drink or a slice of pizza?"

"I would love both, but Betty would never forgive me if I spoiled my dinner and missed her latest casserole creation. But I will take that drink!"

He climbed out of the golf cart and came to the awning, pulling up a chair near the firepit. He settled in with a groan.

Ellie had run inside for another glass, and Penny poured a generous amount of wine and handed it to Carl.

"Thank you," he said to Ellie, sighing, "What a day."

"Why? What happened?" Penny asked.

"You didn't hear the rabble-rousing last night?" Carl asked.

Ellie shook her head, puzzled, while Penny responded, "Our fans were on. I didn't hear anything."

"Oh, my. We had drunk, disorderly, and belligerent. We had to evict one of the campers for his actions. There were barking dogs, children, and the cops," Carl moaned.

"And I missed it!" Penny crowed, upset but delighted at the same time.

"So, I slept all day, and that young man, John, ran things along with Betty. I don't know what I would do without him." Carl turned dour. "And I hope we can keep him for the summer before they draft him."

Ellie's head jerked up at this. She hadn't thought of John being drafted. A shudder went through her. At Aunt Penny's, she could put the war out of her mind without watching television regularly. The thought of John being drafted sobered her. Aunt Penny noticed.

Carl finished his wine and handed the empty glass to Penny. "Thank you, Penny. I'm off to my Betty after I finish my rounds. You ladies have a good night."

He nodded at Penny and Ellie before climbing back into his golf cart and tootling down the road on his rounds through the campground.

"I hadn't thought of it," Ellie said quietly and soberly.

"What?" Penny asked, pouring more wine.

"John. About John being called up," Ellie said. "What do you think?" Her voice had a desperate edge.

Penny paused with her drink to her lips. "Ellie, you can't think about it. It will eat you up from the inside. What's that saying, "Carpe Diem"? You need to seize each day and live it to its fullest. Words that might seem didactic now may haunt you later. Try, my dear. You've started living by leaving the establishment and coming to live here. I feel you need to keep up the good thing you started."

Ellie looked at her aunt. She agreed but felt rather tipsy on her second glass of wine in the heat. Her thoughts were tipsy, too. She nodded to her aunt and got up from her chair carefully. She wanted some time to herself. She didn't feel steady enough to walk or swim. The camper was close quarters, but she could shower, lie down, and close her eyes. It was one of the few times she thought longingly of her spacious bedroom in her parent's suburban home. It had been an oasis many times when she needed escape. The little beach here was the closest thing to an oasis for her, and she wasn't up to it tonight.

"I think I'm tired. I'm going to take a cool shower before bed," Ellie informed Aunt Penny.

Penny nodded. "I picked up fresh cannoli for dessert. We can save them for tomorrow," Penny commented.

"I'm going to sit here and enjoy the evening," she told Ellie, raising her glass in a salute. "I'll see you in the morning."

Twenty

JOHN – 1969

Areas near old glass factories where slag or broken glass were dumped are good sea glass hunting grounds.

John woke up feeling discombobulated. At first, he didn't know why, but then he remembered the news about Pete. He remembered hearing his mom sobbing last night and his father comforting her. His emotions were a jumble of grief, anger, disgust, and frustration. The house was quiet. His parents must still be asleep.

Carl said he could come in later Sunday morning, but John was restless. He needed to *do* something. At the campground, he could work on the grounds and even do his hated job of cleaning the bathhouse and bathrooms. He made breakfast and left a pot of coffee on warm for his parents.

He was surprised that neither Betty nor Carl were up. Betty usually had a pot of coffee for campers, but it was still early. He paced around the campground office and store. He didn't want to go to Carl and Betty's house and rouse them. Carl had the keys to the golf cart, but John could get the trash bags from the little storage area, walk from trash can to trash can, pull the trash, and pick up the full trash bags when Carl was up and about. Walking around the campground would help his restless energy. At least he was *doing* something.

He was about a third of the way through changing trash bags when Carl pulled up in the golf cart.

"You're up early," Carl commented.

"Yup," John answered. "I thought I would get a jump-start on the day."

"Climb in," Carl ordered. "You can help me pick up the full trash bags and get them to the dumpster, and then we can work together to complete the rest."

They drove to the trash cans John had already visited, loaded the golf cart, and made several trips to the dumpster. Then, they worked as a team to pull the trash from the rest of the trash cans.

"We ran out of firewood last night at the store. After we finish the trash, I need you to chop and stack the wood into bundles for campers. We still have another day on this holiday weekend. We sold out of marshmallows, too," Carl told John.

John nodded, and Carl looked at him, giving him a sidelong glance before he asked, "Everything all right, son?"

John felt furious tears fill his eyes, and he clenched his hands. He had to swallow hard not to let his emotions get the better.

Finally, he croaked out, "Last night, we learned that a family friend died in Nam. He was a couple of years ahead of me in school. He was in my scout troop. An Eagle Scout. Pete was a good guy, and now," John hesitated, trying to regain control of his emotions, "he's gone. Just like that. He's gone because of this stupid, stupid war!"

Carl was quiet for a few minutes before answering, "That's rough. I'm sorry, son."

"I never knew anyone who died," John said disbelievingly.

"And it's something you don't get over. It's not that you get used to it, but once you experience someone dying in your life, it's an undercurrent that haunts you. Your mortality seems to hit you full in the face. You begin to question everything," Carl told John quietly.

John glanced at Carl. His face was a mask, but his eyes swam with memories. John remembered Carl had been in the Korean War. He wondered whom Carl was remembering.

Carl snapped out of his memories and said, "Let's take a little break and then get to chopping wood. You can jump in the bay to cool off if you get too hot. Summer's here with all of her humidity."

Carl wiped his forehead with a handkerchief and took them back to the store, where he popped the top off a bottle of Coca-Cola and handed it to John. He raised his bottle and toasted, "To your friend, Pete."

John clinked the bottle with Carl and took a swig. The icy-cold soda bubbled down his throat, quelling the hot rise of emotions. He managed to say thanks before downing the bottle.

Carl left John to chop and stack wood. John found it good to balance the wood and strike it hard to get clean, straight pieces. He tossed the split wood into a large pile with a vengeance. John gathered armload-sized bundles and took a couple to the store, pushing the door open with his hip. Betty was there, saw him, shook her finger, and then pointed to the sign on the door: "No shirt, no shoes, no service." John groaned. He had stripped off his t-shirt in the heat while chopping wood. She opened the door, and John exited, placing his two bundles just outside, and went to fetch his shirt that lay crumpled on the ground. He shook the woodchips out of it and put on the shirt before picking up more wood to go into the store.

Campers were purchasing small items when he entered with more wood. Betty took one look at him and mouthed, 'Thank you.' John smiled and nodded to Betty in acknowledgment. He continued to bring in stacks of wood until they were neatly lined up on a rack inside the door. When finished, he brought the ax inside and returned it to the store room.

Betty was alone when he returned. She smiled sympathetically at him.

"Carl told me about Peter. I am so sorry, John," Betty said. "Carl thought you should take the rest of the day off."

"I, uh, thanks, Betty," John replied hesitantly.

John appreciated the sentiment, but he wasn't sure how to feel. His physical activity in the morning made him feel less confused. But he didn't want to go home, not yet.

"I think I'll cool off with a swim before I go home," John told Betty.

She nodded and told John, "Good idea."

Now, he was free for a few hours. He didn't want to face the reality of Pete's death, which would be forefront when he got home. John grabbed his swimsuit, towel, and flip-flops and changed in the bathroom adjacent to the store. He walked toward the beach and veered to the road where Ellie and her Aunt Penny lived, wondering if she might join him swimming.

There they were, at the mini-van that Penny called 'the Beast.' Penny had a clipboard and pen in hand. Ellie was inside the van, crouched over some of the boxes. She looked hot and brushed a strand of hair away from her face.

Penny noticed him as he approached and greeted, "Hi John, perfect timing!"

He looked at Penny, puzzled. She laughed.

"We just finished taking inventory and are ready for a break. Do you want something to drink?" Penny offered.

John shook his head and replied, "I wondered if you wanted to go for a swim?" He looked pointedly at Ellie.

"Sure!" Ellie responded. "That sounds fantastic! That is if we're done here?" She looked at her Aunt Penny questioningly.

Penny nodded, and Ellie said, "Give me five minutes." She raced into the camper to change.

John stood awkwardly for a minute before Penny waved for

him to sit in the chairs under the awning. She waved her clipboard like a fan.

"Summer has arrived right on time," she commented. "And sometimes, I think, Eastern Shore Maryland has the same weather as the tropics. At least, it seems so today. We could use a little breeze!"

John nodded in agreement, but before he could say anything, the door to the trailer

squeaked, and he looked up. Ellie was a vision in a bright pink, yellow, and orange floral two-piece swimsuit with a short terry coverup around her shoulders. She held her towel in her hand. John stood up and tried not to stare. She flashed him a brilliant smile.

The tiny beach was crowded, but John found a place for them to put their towels. They stepped into the water and maneuvered around small children in the shallows until they could both stand, chest deep with swells from boats lifting them gently off their feet and the bay grasses tickling their feet and legs. The water was warm, with occasional cool pockets from the natural springs.

"Mmm, this is nice," Ellie said.

John was quiet. He nodded in agreement but didn't say anything.

Ellie looked at him sharply, picking up that something was wrong. "Something's bothering you?"

John didn't answer. He violently shoved a piece of seaweed out of his way with a huge swoosh. Ellie's eyes widened at John's violent splash at the seaweed. She didn't say anything. John threw himself on his back so that he could float. He squeezed his eyes shut in the sun's glare, tumultuous emotions, and grief.

Finally, he opened his eyes, filled with pain and anger as he stated haltingly, staccato pauses between each word. "Peter. Pete. A friend. Died in Vietnam."

Ellie's head jerked towards him as she heard the news. She

visibly shuddered. John nodded, acknowledging her reaction. But he continued in a flat tone, "Death. Pete's death was senseless. And I haven't seen him in a couple of years. We weren't close, but his death feels like a hole has been ripped out of my universe. It's surreal."

A large motorboat whizzed down the bay. Large, rippling swells lifted them in the water like a gentle roller-coaster. Children squealed in delight as larger waves crashed at the shoreline. One little boy, swamped by a wave, howled.

He continued, "And I don't understand my dad's fear of communism. He and his cronies all fear communism will take over our country. I don't understand! How can they believe that our democracy is so weak? I understand defending our country, but Vietnam? Why are we even there?'

Another boat went whizzing by. They jumped when large swells came near, not to be swamped by them. John missed one and spluttered as the wave hit the back of his head. He shook his wet hair like a dog, scattering droplets everywhere.

"Maybe a leftover from Korea? I know that I feel completely stupid about the war," Ellie admitted, "I've ignored a lot of it while in school. My parents don't talk about it. I'm sure that my dad is like yours, though. I'm not sure they believe communism threatens our democracy or if it's sociable to believe in right now, and therefore, follow the pack like lemmings." Her voice held a bitter note.

"You shouldn't feel stupid. Maybe you're the smart one, avoiding the sickening news every night of how many lives were lost. Pete is one of thousands of men. And I'll probably be called up sooner than later, the way we're liquidating the men of this country. I can't lie and say I haven't thought of being a conscientious objector," he admitted.

Ellie's head whipped around to look at him. "Really?"

John shook his head, "I don't think I could do that to my parents – especially my mom."

A pall stalled their conversation as a cloud drifted across the sun, making a shadow on the water. Ellie shivered.

"You're cold," John said, "Let's go in."

They walked back to the camper to find Aunt Penny gone.

"I can't stay. I gotta get home and see what's happening," he told Ellie.

John had been holding Ellie's hand. He pulled Ellie closer to him. He gave her a slow, sweet kiss that left them both breathless and then walked away.

Twenty-One

LOUISA – 1918

*Black Amethyst sea glass comes from glassware. It's a beautiful,
deep purple when held up to the light.*

When the letters had ceased coming from Willie, Louisa had forced herself to think about their relationship. Last summer, Grandmama and Willie's mother made it quite clear that they were both from extremely different backgrounds and that any liaison would be forbidden. This ultimatum motivated Louisa and Willie to seek more clandestine meetings.

It had started on the beach. As much as she loved Grandmama, Louisa felt she needed some space, and the early mornings were peaceful in Tolchester. She remembered the visitors slept later as the workers busily prepared for their day. There was no one to notice or to bother her when she slipped to the beach, grateful that no one noticed her. She was barefoot and barelegged, loving the feel of the silky sand between her toes. Louisa settled on the upper beach's cool, softly rippled sand. Louisa had pulled up her knees and hugged them, resting her chin on her knees. She could stare at the bay and the sky's hue of soft blue and think of nothing. It was a little cloud of happiness until a big, hairy toe interrupted her dream. The owner of the toe said hello. He traced small circles in the sand that seemed to get nearer to her skirts. Louisa thought it rude and felt a bit compromised. She ignored the toe and its owner, and eventually, he went away, whistling.

She looked at his retreating back as he whistled down the beach. She remembered thinking what a forward young man he'd been. He'd looked back to see if she was looking at him, and she'd caught his glance for a moment before she'd cast her eyes down, concentrating on the fabric of her skirt. Before she did, Willie had grinned. Unable to help herself, Louisa grinned back before she looked away, hoping she would see him again.

After that, Louisa seemed to bump into Willie everywhere she went. She didn't know, at first, if it was on purpose. Willie helped run the carousel at the amusement park, and Louisa was drawn to ride the carousel frequently, where she could smile and exchange brief greetings with him. It was after a ride where Louisa became stuck on one of the horses, and Willie helped her descend that he introduced himself.

After their introduction on the carousel, Willie would join her on the sand in the mornings after he finished his chores. At first, they were shy together, unsure of what to discuss. Once they started talking, it was as if they would never stop. Willie's life in Tolchester was worlds away from her life in Baltimore. Willie liked to hear about the motor cars and ships in the city. Louisa told him about her grandfather's business at the warehouse when he was alive. Willie told Louisa funny stories about summer visitors and the winters in Tolchester when it was stark and silent. He told her the amusement park was almost ghostly during the winter, but he liked it as much as he liked the busyness of summer. His mother kept him busy, working on repairs on the boarding house and preparing for the next summer. He also kept the carousel in good shape, repairing and painting the animals to prepare for riders for the next season. He told her of quiet evenings of reading and playing cards and checkers with his mom. He was teaching himself chess, and he told Louisa how he liked thinking about the strategies of possible outcomes of one simple move.

Louisa asked Willie if he would teach her to play chess. He brought the chess board and pieces and taught her the game basics. They spent many happy hours with the board and pieces.

Louisa wasn't sure, but she thought Grandmama had an inkling of the meetings with Willie. Of course, she didn't approve of him for a relationship, but she seemed to appreciate that he taught her to play chess. Upon their return to Baltimore, Grandmama soon pulled out a chess board and would play with Louisa. She never asked how Louisa knew the game, but she applauded her efforts. Grandmama was quite good. Louisa thought she would likely beat Willie. Grandmama told her that her Grandpapa had taught her to play chess, and they wiled away many hours playing the strategic game.

Her other favorite time was when she sat with Willie on the steps to the beach in the evenings, just out of sight of the boarding house. It was their secret spot to watch the sunset over the water and the western shore in a blaze of color and glory. They were nearly invisible in the twilight as their individual shadows turned into one. It was here that Willie first took her hand. Her hand felt small in his large, calloused one, but Louisa had never felt so safe. She found that she never wanted to let go.

Louisa sat by Willie's bedside, holding his hand while he slept. She was lost in memory of those summer days together. Grandmama was gone. She couldn't protest their future now. Louisa wondered about Willie's mother. How would she feel if she knew Louisa was by his bedside? But that didn't matter right now. The important thing was the need for Willie to heal in his mind and body. She knew it was only a matter of time. She brought Willie's hand to her lips and kissed it gently. He continued to sleep peacefully. She withdrew her hand and went home, holding the memories in her heart and wishing fervently for Willie to get well.

Twenty-Two

WILLIE – 1918

*Some great sea-glassing beaches in Maryland are Tangier Island,
Terrapin Beach Park, and Smith Island.*

Willie found himself remembering Louisa. She'd said last summer. Had it been that long since he had seen her? In his dreams, it felt that it was only hours ago. He had been smitten by her shy smile and deep, blue eyes from the moment he saw her.

In addition to helping his mother, one of his jobs was to run the carousel at the park. Willie took pride in keeping the gears running and the calliope music going. He polished the brass and kept the animals in good shape. It was a fairly new merry-go-round built by Dentzel. It had a menagerie of animals. Willie liked to climb aboard the animals as much as the park visitors. His favorites were the lion, the giraffe, and a beautiful white horse with a red and gold saddle. Carousels were magical and seemed to bring happiness to the riders with the simple pleasure of riding around and around with the music and the beautifully decorated steeds. He also liked the steam engine's mechanics and kept a good supply of wood chopped and ready to keep the engine running. He took pride in his work and kept the steam engine in tip-top shape.

He remembered watching as the usually stern face of Louisa's Grandmama relax for a moment and smiled as she went round and round. Carousel magic again. He caught Louisa's eye, smiled, and nodded at her, touching his cap.

On another visit to the carousel, without her grandmother, Louisa was stuck when the horse landed in the tallest position after the music stopped. She needed help descending, and Willie was more than happy to oblige. Louisa had stammered her thanks. Willie introduced himself. Louisa did as well. He offered her a free ride on the carousel and offered to take her for ice cream during his break in a few minutes. Surprising to Willie, she agreed.

Louisa sat in the gondola car for the next ride, her eyes shining. He gave the guests an extra-long ride to see her smile. George relieved him at the end of the ride, and Willie went straight to Louisa.

"I shouldn't be doing this," Louisa murmured as they walked off the Carousel and into the park. "You're a bold one."

"And so are you," he returned, grinning.

The midway was packed with summer visitors. Children with sticky candy, ladies with parasols, mothers herding children, gentlemen, hot in suits, looking about. People jostled them as they walked along. The crowd knocked Louisa into Willie, and she thought she might fall. Willie caught her by the elbow, and he didn't let go. He guided Louisa to the ice cream stand, where they stood in line for a cone of vanilla. Once they had their ice cream, Willie led Louisa to the beach, where they could stroll.

It was warm, and their ice creams were melting quickly. They couldn't talk as they licked the quickly melting, sweet, white drops that stickily ran down the sides of the cones.

"Walk a bit?" Willie asked.

Louisa nodded.

"I've seen you at the boarding house," he commented, "with your grandmother?"

Louisa looked at him, surprised that he knew where she was staying. Willie laughed at her expression.

"My mother owns the boarding house," he confessed to Louisa.

"Oh," Louisa replied softly.

"So, you're from Baltimore?" he asked Louisa.

She nodded again shyly.

"Do you like Tolchester?" Willie asked.

Louisa brightened. "I love it! I wish I could live here. It's so exciting!"

"Not all the time," Willie replied ruefully. "It's pretty desolate in the winter. The park is a little creepy with the stands closed and the rides like ghosts."

"But you still have this view," Louisa commented, looking out at the bay. "I don't think I would ever be tired of looking at the water."

"There is that," Willie agreed and remarked. "And it's not so filled with two-legged fish in the winter." Willie nodded at the bathers playing in the bay.

Louisa giggled.

A young girl of about ten came up to them. Their giggles stopped.

"Patsy!" Willie exclaimed, "What are you doing here?"

Patsy gave a quick bob in Louisa's direction. "Miss, your grandmother is looking for you. She says to come quickly."

Louisa blanched, "Grandmama!" she said in a panicked whisper. "I must go!"

She turned and walked away as quickly as she could without running, her braid bouncing down her back and the large bow looking like it would fly off, taking Louisa with it. Willie was left alone on the beach. He stared after Louisa and grinned.

Willie was shaken roughly from his dreams by a nurse who was not as kind and gentle as Nurse Williams. This nurse had rough hands and a rough voice. The medication she gave him tasted foul.

Twenty-Three

ELLIE – 1969

Opalescent glass is usually from decorative ware. A relative of milk glass, the opalescent glass gives off a blue or orange sheen.

Ellie stood speechless after John kissed her. Her lips tingled, and she touched them involuntarily as if to preserve the kiss. Her reaction to John's kiss was different from other boys she had kissed. This one fizzed, and she felt as if her emotions and sensations would shoot into the sky like a rocket. She watched him retreat, admiring the swing in his step and his tan muscles, which rippled in the afternoon sun. He was her Apollo, she thought, her own god of sun and light. She went inside to shower and wash off the water from the bay before changing into comfortable denim cut-offs and a tie-dyed t-shirt of Aunt Penny's creation.

It was an anomaly to be in the camper on her own. It was quiet and peaceful without Aunt Penny's bustling energy. She sat outside, under the awning, thinking about her grandmother.

Her conversation with John brought her grandmother's memory to the forefront. Aunt Penny was indeed like her, with a bubbling personality and someone who was content with herself.

Once, when recuperating from a painfully shy episode, her grandmama had assured Ellie that she had been the same way for years and years. Grandmama confessed that she hadn't always been outgoing. "It took your grandpapa to bring me out of my shell," she confidently told Ellie. "That man! He could charm the skin off a snake. He was always kind, he had a great sense of humor, and he would work to make me smile in whatever mood I was in. Lord, I miss him! I wish you could have known him, Ellie. He would have loved you so much and spoiled you rotten."

That conversation with her grandmama was clear in her mind. They had been sitting in the formal living room in Grandmama's Baltimore townhouse. Ellie loved the feeling of coolness and security inside its brick walls. In some ways, it reminded her of a church with its feeling of peacefulness. The house had been in the family for a long, long time. Grandmama reminded her that her great-great-grandparents once lived there. Grandmama had worked to keep its historical beauty as it was updated, and the furnishing were mostly antiques. Grandma had shown her the secret place she loved to escape growing up. It was a garret that looked out over the city at the top of the stairs past servants' quarters and attic. Ellie had been enchanted and, often on visits, would head to the garret to read or to draw.

Aunt Penny pulled in, and Ellie broke from her daydreaming.

"You looked a hundred miles away," Penny commented. "I have a few things that I picked up at the grocery store. "Here," she said, handing Ellie some paper bags, "you can take these inside." Penny picked up two more bags, and they trooped into the camper to put them away.

Penny glanced at Ellie while they put the food away. "Everything all right?"

"Mmm hmm, I think so," she responded. "I was thinking about Grandmama. And I was missing her."

"She was something," Penny agreed. "I liked how she respected how your mother and I differed. I was the wild one who loved the freedom of the Eastern Shore, where we spent our summers. Your mother loved the city. She was always the proper one and went to college to become a Mrs. And, she succeeded."

Penny's eyes took on the dream look of memory as she reminisced, "Perhaps that's why your mom and I turned out so differently. Your grandmother was a dichotomy. She was a *very* proper lady in Baltimore. But on the Eastern Shore, she would wander barefoot and hatless. She loved to explore and sat quietly on the beach, watching the sky and the water. Your mom is the proper Baltimore lady, and the freedom of the Eastern Shore influenced me."

Ellie thought about this and agreed with her aunt. She remembered going to the Eastern Shore as a child and loved the beaches and the amusement park. But the resort they visited at Tolchester became derelict and sold to developers who put in a housing development. The house they used to stay in was razed along with the amusement park. She hadn't been there in many years.

Penny's eyes cleared of memories, and she stood up to go into the camper to get lemonade.

When she returned and settled, she asked Ellie, "How was your swim? Did you have fun?"

Ellie took a long drink of her lemonade before answering, "Fun. It wasn't exactly fun."

Penny raised an eyebrow, "Oh?"

Ellie went on to explain what had happened with John's friend Pete. Penny visibly stiffened.

"That poor boy," she murmured.

"Aunt Penny, I feel so incredibly stupid about this war!" Ellie cried out. "I feel as though I've been kept in a bubble."

"Don't be silly!" Penny expostulated, "Your parents kept you in a bubble and completely naïve about the Vietnam war!" then she became more serious, "Growing up isn't easy, Ellie. Death coming near your door is difficult. It's not easy for anyone, but death hits you in the gut the first few times. Mortality becomes a reality, and it is a bitter pill to swallow. You're a bright young woman. You are out from the shroud of your parents. You can think and feel and learn what you want to under my roof. It's definitely time for you to live a little."

Ellie was stunned by Aunt Penny's diatribe. She appreciated Aunt Penny's urgent plea for her to live a little and to learn. Today's conversation with John about Peter and the Vietnam War, as Aunt Penny said, punched her in the gut. Ellie vowed to learn more and follow Aunt Penny's words to 'live a little.' Now, she would just need to figure out 'how.'

JOHN – 1969

Sources of aqua sea glass came from fruit jars or canning jars.

John didn't bother showering at the campground but put a towel beneath him as he drove home. His house was quiet when he entered the back door, and his dad emerged from the living room and put a finger to his lips.

"Shh," he said, "your mom is resting. The news about Pete has been quite a shock."

John nodded before telling his dad, "I'm going upstairs to shower. I'll be down in a few minutes."

When he returned, he found his father in his easy chair with the television on very low, watching a golf tournament, the host whispering in the background. He also was reading the current issue of *Popular Mechanics*. He looked up when John entered.

John sat on the couch, and his father spoke. "Services for Pete will be on Friday, son. Will you check to see that you can get off from the campground?"

"Of course," John replied. "I can probably switch my day off or something. Carl and Betty will understand."

His father nodded before stating, "We'll get a pizza for dinner tonight. Save your mother from cooking. Will you go and pick it up?" He reached for his wallet to pull out some cash. "I'll call in the order."

"Sure," John replied before heading to the kitchen to take the keys from a hook.

John was pensive driving to the pizza parlor in North Bay. Pete had loved pizza, he remembered, and he would often hang out at Bellissima Pizza. Pete liked their Gramma pizza, a thin-crust pizza with plum tomatoes and cheese. It was crispy due to a generous amount of olive oil. The owner's grandfather, who spoke only broken English, was a master at making this pizza.

They greeted John when he entered the pizza parlor with a cheery "Buon Giorno!" The pizza parlor was redolent of garlic, tomato, cheese, and flour. His stomach grumbled, and John remembered he had forgotten to eat lunch. Their pizza wasn't ready, so John settled into a red leatherette booth with an ice-cold Coca-Cola to sip. A noisy bunch of teenagers that John assumed were in high school sat in a booth in the back corner. They were laughing loudly and jibing at each other. John remembered similar times after the scout meetings when they gathered here. Suddenly, John felt old. It had only been three, no, four years since he hung out with the other scouts here, but now it seemed a lifetime ago. Three or four years ago, he, Pete, and the other scouts were clueless about Vietnam. At that time, they never considered being drafted. They felt like they would live forever and weren't terribly anxious to be adults. They liked to goof off at scouts and let off some steam there and here at Bellissima. Pietro, the owner, was a little like a benevolent uncle. He lost himself in the memories of good times and didn't hear them call his order.

Pietro was at his elbow, pizzas in hand, asking John if he was all right. "What's the matter? You look so sad, son."

John broke the news about Pete. Pietro crossed himself, murmuring, "Mio Dio. That poor boy."

John nodded in agreement. And suddenly, John felt very bitter towards God.

John shook his head, "I don't know if I can believe anymore," he told Pietro, pointing to the crucifix Pietro wore.

"But, you must, son. That is what will get you through this," Pietro advised.

John shook his head. He was afraid his emotions would take over. He picked up his pizzas and took them home.

Twenty-Five

LOUISA – 1918

Artificial sea glass is created by a machine that tumbles it until it is well sanded like the sea glass tumbled by waves, sand, and wind. Artificial sea glass is too smooth and doesn't have the "C" markings of real sea glass.

Louisa hoped desperately that Willie would be able to see and walk again. She didn't know enough about the treatment of shell shock victims. She had overheard some of the doctors discussing treatments. One very scary suggestion was electro-shock therapy. She hoped that Willie wouldn't have to undergo something like that. Another therapy was hypnosis, which had varying results. Supposedly, after the hypnosis treatment, many had been healed of their tremors, tics, and some of their fears. That didn't sound too bad and much better than the electric shocks. She also knew that some men were sent to farms to work. There was a belief that working the land helped the shell-shock victims. She would ask Nurse Williams her opinion.

Willie seemed to be on the mend. His limbs calmed when she

talked with him. And now his face turned toward her when he spoke. She had hope. And that was good.

Over breakfast the next morning, she shared her news with Emma and Bertha. Bertha wiped her eyes with the corner of her apron.

"Bertha!" Louisa asked, surprised. "Are you crying?"

Bertha sniffled. "I'm just so happy for you, Miss," Bertha's voice was muffled through her veil of tears.

"Oh, Bertha, thank you," Louisa agreed, patting Bertha's plump hand.

Louisa took another bite of Bertha's homemade toasted bread and spread it with butter and jam. "I think if Willie were here, he would get better in no time with your good cooking," she commented.

"Oh, Miss, that wouldn't be proper!" Emma was scandalized. "You two aren't married or anything."

"I know, I know," Louisa said. "But I would love to get Willie out of the hospital and in a place away from the flu. I don't want him sent far away."

"What about his family?" Bertha asked.

Louisa looked down at the table and traced a vein in the polished wood. She hesitated a moment before she answered, "No word yet."

"Flu's bad in Tolchester," Emma stated flatly.

"That's what I'm afraid of," Louisa admitted. She had taken it upon herself to write a letter to Willie's mother, but she had not received an answer. That worried her.

Louisa described some of the therapies for shell shock victims to Bertha and Emma. Bertha shivered in horror at the electro-shock therapy Louisa described. "That doesn't seem right, messing with people's brains."

"I'll agree with you, Bertha. It's a new thing they're trying. I don't know enough about whether it would be right for Willie. I think it would be better for him to be at home or to work on a farm," Louisa said. "I agree with Nurse Williams, who believes they need time to rest their brains and bodies and stop reliving the horrors they saw in the war."

Louisa had a shock when she arrived at the hospital. Nurse Williams pulled her aside before she could get to Willie.

"Louisa," she said, "Willie's mind seems to be going again. I don't know why. He had been doing so well." Nurse Williams's eyes were filled with sorrow and sympathy.

Louisa wrenched her hands. "I must go to him," she said.

"Yes, yes, you must," Nurse Williams agreed.

Louisa handed her cloak to Nurse Williams and hurried down the ward.

"Willie! Willie!" Louisa called desperately as she neared his cot.

He didn't turn his head toward her. He just lay in bed. But now, his limbs trembled.

"Oh, Willie! It's me, Louisa," she cried and clasped his hands in hers.

Willie was lost in his world of nightmares again. He couldn't see her or respond to her. Louisa's tears inadvertently fell onto their hands and the coverlet.

Willie!" she sobbed. "Oh, Willie! What's happened? Come back to me, please!"

Nurse Williams did not let her cry long. She asked Louisa to return to the office area and prepare for the day. Louisa sniffed and gulped and blew her nose. When she got herself together, Louisa spoke with Nurse Williams about the hypnotherapy for Willie. Nurse Williams promised she would look into it. But in the meantime, she ordered Louisa to smarten herself up and assist her with bandages. "Work will help."

Louisa shuddered, took a deep breath, stood straight, and nodded to Nurse Williams. And they got about their business. Nurse Williams was correct. Work was distracting. When they reached Willie, Louisa was calmer and could assist with Willie's wounds. They looked much better than the day before. But Willie had retreated to his unknown world. His limbs shook. His legs raised and lowered themselves on the bed of their own volition. Louisa spoke soothingly, hoping to calm Willie's mind. It didn't help this time, and she looked helplessly at Nurse Williams.

"I know you want Willie released to recuperate at home, Louisa, but you know as well as I do that isn't possible. Not when he's in this state," Nurse Williams advised.

"But he was getting better!" Louisa cried. "I don't understand!"

"We know very little about the workings of the brain. We're learning more and more each day. If Willie regained his vision, we could work on physiotherapy to help his limbs. Continue talking with him, Louisa. Your reminiscences seemed to help soothe him," Nurse Williams urged Louisa.

Louisa sat next to Willie and took his hand. She stroked his hand and spoke soothingly to Willie. Did he remember eating ice cream together? Did he know that she rode the carousel repeatedly just to see him? She reminded him of their walks on the beach and how he told her about his goals for the guest house. Louisa talked with Willie until her voice grew hoarse and her hand numb from clutching his. Nothing changed. There was no response. Louisa gently kissed him on his head and left to go home.

It was late now, and dusk had fallen. Louisa felt as gloomy as the gathering dusk. "What had happened? What went wrong with Willie?" The questions turned over and over in her mind. Weariness assailed her. It had been a long day, and she was despondent over the change in Willie. Louisa knew Willie's recuperation could take years, but she wanted him to be better sooner than later. She wanted to see his twinkling eyes and his smile. It took a lot of effort not to begin to cry. She was weary of crying. There were too many tears of grief over her grandmama and Willie's situation. She thought of her grandmama's resolute spirit. Louisa knew if Grandmama were alive, she would find a way to help Willie. Louisa wanted to cling to the positive thought that Willie would get better. He had been doing so well. The change perplexed her. She wondered if she could speak with the doctor. Surely, Nurse Williams would vouch for her as a friend of Willie's. Perhaps she would write another letter to Willie's mother. Grandmama always used to say, "The squeaky wheel gets the grease." She thought that no matter what Willie's mother thought of her, she should be grateful Willie had someone to look after him in the hospital. She reached her door as the streetlights came on, giving her a bit of light as she entered the house. She climbed the stairs eagerly to her room to write another letter to Willie's mother, pouring out her heart that she felt it would be good for him to return home to heal. She hoped she received an answer to this missive.

Twenty-Six

WILLIE – 1918

Some of the best sea glass can be found near sites of old Landfills.

The hospital ward was different after Nurse Williams left. Her beautiful, contralto voice kept the ward tranquil. After she was gone, things changed. The other nurse, Nurse Johnston, marched into the ward at the beginning of the shift and delegated tasks to her staff. Her low, gravelly voice seemed to penetrate every corner. Nurse Johnston had an odd sense of humor.

Nurse Johnston was new to the ward and didn't seem to like or care for the men. She liked to flout her authority. Involuntarily, when Willie heard her voice, he tensed. His eyes might not work, but his ears made up for this. Her gravelly voice reached his ears, even when she whispered nasty things to the men, calling them cowards or stating, "I hope you die." When someone dropped something or there was a loud noise from anywhere in the ward, soldiers reacted, but Willie could hear her break into a laugh when she saw the men's reaction. He didn't understand. And he couldn't see. He fought to see. Fuzzy blobs began taking shape in the brilliant white that filled his vision. The effort of seeing was exhausting.

Willie dozed after supper. A loud clatter of a tray of metal instruments was dropped near his head, waking him. Startled, the jarring clatter took him back to the front. He trembled, and he couldn't control it. His arms and legs flailed. In his mind, he could clearly hear, "Over the top! Over the top!" Underneath it all, he heard a low, gravelly voice and accompanying laughter.

The low, gravelly voice insidiously and scornfully said, "You lily-livered white feather." And the voice laughed.

Willie was embarrassed about how his body reacted. His limbs and his body couldn't control themselves. His legs raised themselves up and down on the bed and contracted as if he were running. Willie panicked. His arms trembled. And all the while, a nasty laugh played like a bad melody in his head. Even though they were nightmares, the nightmare seemed safer than the outside world. He closed his eyes and retreated to the front, remembering the smells, the mud, and the miles and miles of trenches. Willie hated the rooms dug into the ground like caves. He would rather sleep out in the open air where earthen walls didn't pen him in. The trenches were filled with unwashed men where smoke from cigars and cigarettes masked only a portion of their scent. Boxes of supplies and munitions were piled around, and sometimes, it was a maze to find one's way. On those crates, Willie propped himself up to sleep, ready to fight at a moment's notice. And on the occasional, rare, peaceful night, Willie could watch the stars in their dance in the sky. The stars were a constant comfort for him, for these were the same stars he saw from the beach in Tolchester.

Twenty-Seven

ELLIE – 1969

Shippersea glass is known as dragon glass because the glass slag looks like a dragon's egg.

Ellie was astounded by the noise of the exodus of the campers. There were shouts as parents corralled their children and more shouts and grunts as campers unhooked their trailers and prepared to leave. More shouted farewells, and people climbed into their trucks and station wagons and pulled their trailers out of the campground. Ellie assumed John was busy assisting and cleaning up after the campers left. She didn't see a trace of him. Aunt Penny had taken her three-wheeled adult tricycle with a large basket contraption on the back filled with their dirty laundry and t-shirts to be prepped for drying at the community laundromat. She told Ellie that she liked the white noise of the washers and dryers and found it the perfect place to read. She had packed two books along with the laundry. It was Ellie's job to fix lunch and dinner. She hard-boiled eggs to make egg salad for lunch, wanting to copy the egg and olive salad from the diner. She chopped fruit for a fruit salad and thought of a simple salad her mom created for hot summer days of lettuce, tuna, olives, celery, and a little oil would be refreshing and light.

She wrapped the egg salad sandwiches in wax paper, walked to the laundromat to eat lunch with Aunt Penny, and hoped to glimpse John. Penny was deep into her book when Ellie arrived. She didn't even hear Ellie come into the laundromat, but that didn't surprise Ellie. There were fans, and the noisy, circular motion of the washers and the dryers created a comforting background whooshing noise. Aunt Penny sat in a tattered armchair, legs crossed and thrown over the arm so she saw in a cock-eyed position that looked suspiciously comfortable.

"Hi there," she called to Aunt Penny.

Penny sat up with a start. "Oh!" she exclaimed softly when she saw Ellie, "I was caught up in my book."

"I can see that. What are you reading?" Ellie asked.

"*Two Under the Indian Sun*," Penny responded, and with a dreamy look in her eyes, she said, "It took me back to my memories of Asia. I studied there for a short time. It was glorious! The rich colors, the smell of spices in the air, and I lived on practically nothing. I was one of the many starving artists, but I wouldn't trade the memory for anything."

"You'll have to tell me more sometime," Ellie requested.

Penny nodded but responded with a "mmm" as she bit into her sandwich. "Very good," she commented to Ellie before saying, "You just missed John."

"Oh?" Ellie responded, a little disappointed.

"Yes, he's working on trash collecting around the campground. He'll be at it awhile, I think."

Ellie bit into her sandwich thoughtfully. Maybe John would stop by after work, and they could go for a walk or a swim. She hoped so. She had come to expect him after he finished working. There was something whole about their time swimming. It was as if they were the only two people alive. And she liked it. She hoped he might kiss her again. That thought brought butterflies to her innards. She knew she blushed and hoped Aunt Penny wouldn't notice.

They finished their lunch. Ellie had brought a small package of chips to share and a banana for each of them. Penny asked Ellie to take back a sack of clean laundry, and Ellie toted it back to the camper and began putting it away when John's voice called to her.

"Ellie?" he called, a little hesitantly.

"In here!" she called back. "I'll be right there."

Hurriedly, she stuffed the remaining clothes in drawers and went to see John. He looked up at her and smiled when the door squeaked open.

"Hi," she said softly, surprising herself at the hitch in her breath when he smiled at her.

"Hi yourself," he said.

She joined him in an adjacent ancient aluminum folding chair with faded nylon strips. It was old but comfortable, and it squeaked lightly when she sat.

"How are you today?" she asked.

John was quiet and thoughtful for a moment. "I guess I am okay. Busy here. We had a lot of cleanups today. The majority of the campers are great, but some are just pigs," he said disgustedly.

"The exodus this morning was unbelievable," Ellie agreed, shaking her head at the memory.

"And now, we need to get ready for the next batch, from what I understand," John said. "It'll probably be like this all summer with another big push at the 4th of July and Labor Day weekend."

He hesitated a minute and then said sheepishly, "I forgot my swim trunks today. I wondered if you wanted to go for a hike or maybe some ice cream?"

"Sure," Ellie agreed. "Let me leave a note for Aunt Penny."

"And you'll want to put on sneakers where we're going," he advised.

"Oh? Where are we going?" she asked.

"Near Elk Neck State Park, to the clay cliffs," he told her.

"Oh, okay," Ellie responded, but she didn't have a clue to where that was.

She went inside the camper, pulled out a small notebook, and left the information that she was with John, and they were hiking to the clay cliffs. Then she put on socks and sneakers and returned to John.

They walked up to the parking lot adjacent to the store where John had parked his mom's dark blue Ford Fairlane. He opened the door for Ellie, and she climbed in, wincing as her bare legs burned on the hot seats. They opened the windows, and John drove them through North Bay and kept heading south on the Peninsula. It was hard to talk with the air whooshing in through the windows, but they were comfortably quiet together. Houses were spottier here, and the forest was near the road. After about twenty minutes, John pulled into a small parking area alongside the road.

"Where are we?" Ellie asked.

"Just north of the State Park beach. Come on," he motioned for her to climb over the guard rail. It was there that Ellie noticed a narrow, steep path. She followed John, feeling like an explorer through the primordial forest. Quiet settled over them except for the swish of plants as John pushed through the undergrowth. It took them several minutes as they zig-zagged down the slope on the narrow path.

"Coming back up is a bit more challenging," John told her.

Ellie privately thought going down the slope was challenging, but she didn't say anything to John. She frequently grabbed onto plants and young trees, fearing she would topple down the steep slope and break a leg or something worse. Despite her trepidation of falling, Ellie began to enjoy the forest's peace with the tall, thick trunks of trees and deep green canopy that permitted scattered sunlight to penetrate the forest floor. Ellie heard woodpeckers tapping and squirrels racing among the branches with indignant squeaks. As they neared the bottom of the slope, she heard other sounds, the sounds of waves hitting the shoreline and voices. But the voices seemed rather far away. The path ended, and she found them at the edge of a beach. She didn't see anyone nearby and was puzzled. Where were the people?

"Good," John breathed. "We're lucky it's low tide."

John went to the water and scooped some up to put on the back of his neck before sitting on the sand. Ellie joined him. They sat on the sand, the sunshine striking them full and hot after the climb through the cool trees. Ellie discovered that the voices she heard earlier were from boats anchored not too far into the water. The boat people were laughing, drinking, and jumping into the water to swim. On Ellie's right were stunningly high cliffs of clay in white, tan, and bronze. It looked like someone had taken a huge paintbrush to create the large swathe of warm colors and then dragged the brush through to create vertical patterns on the cliff face.

"It's stunning," she said.

"Yeah, this is a pretty cool place," John agreed. "I love coming here. It's worth the climb."

He took her hand and held it, not tightly, but firmly. He used his other hand to shade his eyes and look at the sparkling water that shone like thousands of diamonds as the sunlight rippled on the small waves from other boats.

"How's your mom doing?" Ellie finally asked. "You said she was struggling with Pete's death yesterday."

"She's pretty upset. I think it hits a little too close to home," John admitted.

"What do you mean?" Ellie asked.

"That I could be next," he stated.

"What?" Ellie asked, aghast. "You won't be called up, will you? Don't you have a college deferment?"

He nodded, "I do have a deferment, but Lady Luck is seldom on my side," John said. "It's literally the luck of the draw with the draft."

Ellie shivered despite the heat of the day. "Are you scared you'll be called up?"

"Terrified, actually," John admitted vehemently. "I hate this damn war with a passion!"

He picked up a rock and threw it into the bay with a splash. Further out, a fish jumped, surprised that something else invaded the water.

"I need to confess," Ellie admitted, somewhat sheepishly, "That my parents have kept me smothered. I know about the war, but I don't know about it. I'm embarrassed."

"Maybe you're better off," John replied bitterly. "It's such a stinking, useless war! We have no business being in Vietnam! My dad thinks it's all about communism. I'm afraid I have to disagree. I think it's about the money. We're spending millions, maybe billions, on this war. And what for? Just for thousands of young men to die? I don't see any benefits."

He shook his head in disgust. He noticed Ellie look stricken, possibly guilty about not knowing much about the Vietnam conflict. He wondered how she felt about his diatribe. But he didn't ask. Instead, he pulled Ellie to her feet. "Come on, let's walk a little while it's low tide. We won't have too long, and then we'll lose most of the beach."

They strolled the beach. John would bend down and pick up interesting rocks and a shell here and there. Ellie saw something glittering brightly in the sun.

"Ooh! What's that?" she asked.

John plucked it away from a wave. It was a small piece of green glass, well-sanded and pitted.

"Beach glass," John informed her. "It washes up on the shore here."

"It's beautiful!" Ellie cried. "It's like a little jewel."

"Some people call it 'mermaid's tears,'" he told her.

"Why?"

"Because when a sailor dies, the mermaids cry, and their tears become beach glass, or so the story goes," John explained.

Ellie was enchanted. And now the treasure hunt was on. Instead of looking out at the water, her eyes were glued to the beach and rocky shoreline. They found glass here and there in green, frosted white, and brown. Ellie was delighted to find a light, bluish piece of glass.

"That's from an old Coke bottle. The brown pieces are from a beer bottle or maybe an old Clorox bottle," John told her.

"How do you know about all of this?" Ellie asked.

"My mom. She loves beach glass. She has a big jar of it in our house. Dad grouses that it's trash, and she says, "One man's trash is another's treasure." John laughed. "Anyways, Dad hates it, but Mom loves it.

"I'm with your mom," Ellie said. "It's so pretty!"

They wandered the beach, filling their pockets with bits of beach glass.

"How did you find this place?" Ellie asked.

John nodded at the water. "Friends of the family had a pontoon boat, and we came down one summer's day. We swam to shore and wandered the beach. Mom loved finding all the glass."

The tide was coming in, and they were losing valuable beach real estate. They turned and walked back toward the path they had come down. Out of the blue, John stopped, pulled Ellie to him, and kissed her. Surprised, she gave into his kiss, reaching up to put her hand on his shoulder to steady herself from the headiness of kissing John. The kiss deepened and became more insistent. But whoops and hollers from the water interrupted them. Ellie realized that the people on the boats were watching, and she blushed deeply. John just waved.

They headed up the slope with handfuls of beach glass in their pockets. The climb back to the top was indeed more challenging. John took her hand and helped by pulling her over roots and areas that were extremely steep. Ellie was huffing and puffing by the time they reached the top.

"Whew!" she said when they made it, holding her stomach and taking deep breaths. "I can't believe we made it!"

John grinned at her. "What?" he teased, "Don't you trust me?"

"It's not that," Ellie protested, turning red again.

"Let's get some ice cream," John suggested. "We've earned it."

He drove her to a small ice cream stand on the outskirts of North Bay. They ordered twisted ice cream cones dipped in chocolate and covered with sprinkles. It was a challenge to eat in the hot sun without dripping everywhere, and they were both laughing at their attempts to keep from spreading the stickiness all over their chins and hands. John retrieved a paper cup of water and a bunch of napkins to clean themselves up. She had liked other boys, and dated a few casually, but her feelings for John were something different entirely. Her stomach was filled with butterflies that teased all of her nerve endings when he touched or kissed her. It was as if her essence had merged with his. Even though she had known him only a short time, she knew in her heart that they belonged together. She was awed by this revelation. Ellie was falling in love with John. She knew it.

John caught her staring at him, and he looked at her quizzically at first but then bathed her in his smile that filled his eyes and her soul. He kissed her again. And the butterflies loosed themselves with wings of joy.

Twenty-Eight

JOHN – 1969

Sea glass from Coca-Cola bottles is a lovely seafoam blue.

What was it about Ellie? One minute, he was tongue-tied around her. She was so beautiful and so nice, but he really didn't know her. Not yet. But, his feelings for her eclipsed his feelings for other women.

She was enchanted by the sea glass they found on the beach. Just like his mom, little things entranced her and caught her imagination. He liked that about Ellie. And when he kissed her, his body and mind warped into a primal state. He wanted to kiss and run his hands through her honey-colored hair and kiss her gorgeous skin and...and he needed to stop. He was astonished at the connection he felt with her. It was one without words. He wasn't brave enough to ask if she felt the same way. Not yet, at least.

He woke up Tuesday morning to the beat of a steady rain. His mom told him Carl had called and said not to come in today. Frustrated with himself, he realized he didn't have a phone number for Ellie and didn't have any way to reach her. Besides that, his mom went off to her ladies' circle, so he didn't have a car to visit her. He watched television, laughing at *I Love Lucy,* *Bewitched,* and *The Beverly Hillbillies.* When the soap operas came on, he turned off the television and worked on the chores his mom assigned him.

His mom came home pleasantly surprised that he had completed his chores, and he hung out in the kitchen with her while she prepared dinner. She made homemade macaroni and cheese, and his mouth watered at the thought. His mom's mac and cheese was the best. He helped her by grating the cheese for the cheese sauce and told her Ellie was enchanted with the beach glass.

"You'll have to invite her over sometime," his mom offered, "or maybe we could picnic at Betterton? Sometimes you can find really nice glass there. I would love to go to Tolchester, but I don't think we can go on the beach unless we have a boat at the marina. I've heard that's an amazing place to find glass and pottery."

"You are obsessed," he teased his mom.

"You bet!" she agreed. "Ask Ellie. Maybe we can go this weekend."

"She has the Farmers Market on Saturday," he reminded her.

"Well, what about Sunday?" his mom asked. "Let's talk with your father when he gets home."

And as if on cue, his father came in, holding a newspaper over his head.

"It's raining cats and dogs out there! Driving was the pits," he told them.

"I know," his mom agreed, "I was out in it because I had ladies' circle today. And, guess what, our son was home and did all the chores I assigned him."

"Good man," his father praised him.

His mother told him, "We were just talking about taking a picnic to Betterton. Maybe this Sunday?" she asked her husband. "And we'll invite Ellie too. Apparently, John has introduced her to beach glass. She loves it!" she ended with a grin.

"Oh no!" His dad moaned in mock dismay. "Another one."

"I told you I liked this girl," his mother said smugly.

"Me too." John grinned.

"Okay, okay! A picnic and beach glass it is," his father acquiesced.

After dinner, and after his dad watched the news, they sat around the kitchen table and played gin rummy. They hadn't done that in a long, long time. It was nice, just being a family. After observing the families at the campground, he wondered if he yearned for that happy time with his mom and dad. It was a good family evening. John was relieved he and his dad didn't get into an argument about the war.

Twenty-Nine

LOUISA – 1918

There's a beach just outside of Okinawa, in the southwestern corner of Japan, covered in glass.

The next day, at Willie's bedside, Louisa took Willie's flaccid hand in hers.

"Willie," she told the still form on the bed, "I remembered a funny story from last summer. Do you remember the first time you bought me ice cream?"

Louisa told the story of how she was out of breath, hurrying back from their encounter, walk, and ice cream.

"Oh, Willie, if I could count the number of times Grandmama would say, 'Louisa! Ladies, don't run; we hasten!' And then she scolded me, saying, 'Look at you! Your hair is a mess,' and 'What's that on your dress? Where have you been?' And I considered lying for about half a second. You know Grandmama! She had the eyes of an eagle, and she could spot a lie miles away. I was such a mess from running back to the boarding house. And that ice cream spot stood out like a beacon on my dress. So, I told her that I was on the carousel. And then I had ice cream on the beach."

She looked at Willie to see if there had been a reaction. She hoped he might return the squeeze of her fingers, but nothing today.

Louisa continued with her story. "I told her, Willie. I told her I was with you, the guest house proprietor's son. I told her you worked on the carousel and that we walked, talked, and had ice cream. She was aghast, Willie! She was worried that I might get a 'fast' reputation. I insisted we were fine and that we just walked and talked. She was insistent that we have a chaperone. She said, 'But you should walk and talk with a chaperone if he's courting you. And I don't like the thought of that!'"

The memory of that day in Tolchester struck Louisa in so many ways. It was bittersweet. As strict and gruff as Grandmama was, Louisa knew she loved her dearly. Louisa missed her Grandmama and her elegant ways, snappy dark eyes, and dry sense of humor. She loved that first time she and Willie walked the sand and enjoyed the conversation and ice cream. They always seemed to have much to discuss once they started. She would have to work to get Willie to talk again. They had much to catch up on since they had been apart for over a year.

Louisa stopped talking and looked at Willie. He looked peaceful. His limbs weren't moving, but he wasn't responding.

"Oh, Willie, where are you? Please come back to me," Louisa whispered to him.

She vowed not to cry today. Louisa hiccoughed a little, taking deep breaths so as not to cry. It was getting late, and she needed to get home. She stood up and nearly bumped into a nurse she wasn't familiar with.

The nurse wasn't happy. "Now look what you almost made me do!" she snapped. "I almost lost this tray of instruments." She shook the tray for emphasis.

"I beg your pardon," Louisa said. "I didn't see you."

"Next time, look around before you act like a lout," the nurse told her with a nasty edge to her voice.

"I'm sorry," Louisa apologized again, but only to the swishing hips of the starched uniform of the nurse.

Rattled, she moved away, saying quickly, "I'll see you tomorrow, Willie."

Thirty

WILLIE – 1918

Bonfire glass is sea glass that has gone through the fire, usually at a high temperature. The fire molds the glass into interesting shapes, and often, the glass has inclusions of sand, debris, or water inside.

Willie heard Louisa's voice and story as if they were a dream. He remembered the evening after he and Louisa had walked and had ice cream. His mother was furious with him. How could he approach a young woman improperly? It looked bad on him, and she said it also looked bad on her.

The boarding house guests were everywhere, so Willie's mother didn't shout. She pulled him into the office and spoke to him in an angry, terse whisper. Willie hung his head while his mother railed at him.

Finally, when she seemed out of breath, Willie interjected, "Mama, I'm sorry. How can I make this better? I still want to see Louisa and talk with her. I want to court her."

"Oh, Willie!" His mother's voice rose. "She's a guest and a swell," she said, returning to her whisper. "You can't offer Louisa what her grandmother wants for her in marriage! You don't have the money or education. Girls like that are different."

"Louisa is different, Mama. But not different in the way you think. She's wonderful," Willie insisted.

"You're cow-eyed! Go and get some supper and do your chores. I don't want to hear anything more about this!" his mother said.

"I'm going to talk to her grandmother," Willie was determined.

His mother threw up her hands and stalked from the room, muttering, "What am I going to do?"

The next day, Willie cleaned himself up, put on his best britches and shirt, and held his cap in his hand. He went in search of Louisa's Grandmama. He found her sitting in a rocking chair on the porch. Her eyes were closed, and Willie didn't think she was asleep as she rocked softly. He cleared his throat. Her eyes flew open as she had not heard him approach.

"Excuse me, Ma'am," he started, his voice pitching high in his nervousness. "Ma'am, my name is Willie."

"I know who you are," Grandmama stated flatly, her eyes boring into Willie's.

He almost faltered. Willie wanted to look down at his feet. Instead, he straightened up and looked Louisa's Grandmama in the eye.

"Yes, Ma'am. You see, Ma'am, I came to ask permission to court your granddaughter, Louisa," he said.

Silence. There was silence. Louisa's Grandmama looked him up and down and up and down. Willie stood uncomfortably. There was a breeze, but he couldn't feel it. He tried not to appear nervous, but a sweat trickled down his back. The toe of his shoe traced a line along with the board on the veranda. He paused long before broaching his plan with this strident woman.

"Ma'am?" he finally questioned.

"And what do you have to offer, my boy?" Grandmama asked.

Willie cleared his throat again before he answered. Nervously, he swept one hand to indicate the boarding house.

"Someday, this will all be mine," he told her. "Someday."

"And until then? What would Louisa's life be like if she married you?" Grandmama asked haughtily. "Your mother runs a lovely establishment. I have seen you helping out around the place. You are an industrious young man, and I like that. But it's not appropriate. If Louisa were to marry you, she would become a servant. There's nothing wrong with that, young man, but I hope Louisa aims higher. I'm getting older, you see, and I want her taken care of in the best possible way."

Willie was twisting his hat. Ma'am, I would do my best to see that she didn't want for anything."

"Your thoughts on 'anything' quite differ from mine," Grandmama said drily. "The answer is no. You may not court my granddaughter at this time."

"Yes, Ma'am," Willie said miserably. He gave the nod to Louisa's Grandmama and turned away.

Willie remembered his disappointment that day. He felt sick and dejected. He didn't see Louisa anywhere. Near the end of his shift, she came down to the carousel and rode on the giraffe. When the ride ended, she seemed stuck on the carousel animal. Then he went over to assist and saw that she was pretending.

Louisa loudly called, "Can you help me, young man?"

"Certainly, Miss," Willie replied automatically.

He helped Louisa down from the giraffe. As he did so, she whispered to him. "I'm so mad at Grandmama I – I could spit! I'm so sorry she spoke to you that way. What does your mother think?"

Willie whispered back, "My mother agrees with your Grandmama."

"What are we going to do?" Louisa asked.

"We'll think of something," Willie said.

"Thank you for your assistance, young man," Louisa

announced. You saved my dress from being torn. I thank you."

"Anytime, Ma'am," Willie told Louisa. He tipped his hat to her and whistled as he returned to the carousel's center to start the ride again, his eyes never straying far from Louisa.

Willie was the epitome of industriousness at the boarding house. Rumor said they would call younger boys to go to the front. Willie wanted to make sure that things were ship-shape for his mother. The business had dropped off with the war, and profits were low. His mother could not hire the staff she usually did, and the chores fell to Willie. Willie also wanted to impress Louisa's Grandmama. He was positive she was keeping an eye on him. And he wanted every opportunity to steal a word with Louisa. Her Grandmama made it extremely difficult, but they found ways to speak a word or two, passing in the hallways, on the porch, or in the garden. They had become very good at clandestine meetings. On the steps leading to the beach, there was a spot just out of sight from the boarding house. Willie and Louisa had taken to meeting there and chatting for a few minutes.

It was difficult for Willie to remember that it was a memory. The damned war kept creeping in. Where was he now? He remembered Louisa's voice penetrating through the fog of his nightmares. Her voice transported him to the memories of last summer. He was confused. Louisa was here now. Where was his mother? Where was her Grandmama? What hospital was he in, and in what country? Somewhere beyond the hospital smells, he smelled the brackish water of the bay. It was faint, but he could smell it. That confused him more.

He heard a loud bang, and all the fears and confusion of the war were at the forefront of his brain. The smell of blood, mud, and gunpowder assailed him. They were under attack! He would have crawled under this hospital bed if he could, but his body wouldn't permit him. He tried. His limbs wouldn't cooperate. He couldn't see. He screamed in terror. And beneath the horrors, an insidious laugh penetrated through the nightmare.

Thirty-One

ELLIE – 1969

Hawaii is known for its pastel sea glass.

Ellie overslept and woke to a steady rain, making a lovely, steady percussion sound on the camper's roof. It was soothing, and she drifted in and out of sleep for a long while. Finally, she woke to the smell of coffee from the kitchen and wandered out, yawning, to find Aunt Penny already dressed, coffee in hand.

Ellie yawned heavily. "Good morning, Aunt Penny. What time is it?"

"Believe it or not, it's after nine," Penny told Ellie.

"What?" Ellie started with a gasp. "That's not possible."

"Relax," Penny assured her. "It's the rain. We'll get to dyeing in the shed in a few minutes. Throw some clothes on and come out and have breakfast."

When Ellie returned to the kitchen, dressed and ready for the day, Penny gave her a mushroom and cheese omelet and toast.

"Wow, I need to sleep in more often. What a treat. This is yummy, Aunt Penny," Ellie told her. "My tummy is warm and full. I could go back to bed."

"Not on your life!" Penny threatened good-naturedly. "We have a lot of dyeing to do for the Farmers Market this weekend."

"Okay, okay, just teasing," Ellie insisted. "I'll clean up the kitchen while you set up the t-shirts. Deal?"

"Deal," Penny agreed.

A few minutes later, Ellie traipsed under the awning and scooted into the shed with minimal contact with the pouring rain. They had a system worked out with the dyeing process. The only bad thing about the rain is that they would need to wait until tomorrow to set the t-shirts in the sun to cure.

Ellie looked out at the steady stream of rain pouring down. "I doubt John is working today."

"Probably not," Penny agreed.

"And the sad thing is, he doesn't have your phone number," Ellie mourned.

"Ouch," Penny said. "And tomorrow, we're heading to Dora's."

"And his friend's funeral is Friday," Ellie reminded her.

"Busy week," Ellie quipped.

Ellie nodded. She wanted to finish the T-shirts. The rain didn't look like it would let up.

"If you can package up the shirts in plastic bags for tomorrow, I'll double-check with Dora that we're still on," Penny said.

"Sounds good," Ellie answered. Her tongue was between her teeth, and she focused on the colors. After talking with Dora, she had bound the t-shirts in different patterns today and was anxious to see them tomorrow.

It was quiet for the remainder of the day. Aunt Penny worked on a couple of Shibori pieces. She shared the technique with Ellie, who tried the Shibori technique on a couple of scarves. They turned out beautifully, and Ellie loved the contrast of the blue-dyed patterns and white cloth.

"On a sunnier day, we'll gather some plants, and I will show you how to hammer patterns into cloth with plants," Penny told her.

"What? How is that possible?" Ellie asked.

Aunt Penny laughed and explained the technique of pounding out the plant's natural dyes to color the cloth.

"I think I need a notebook to keep track of these different techniques and directions," Ellie commented.

"We can take care of that tomorrow," Penny told her. "That's a great idea. It will be a good resource for art school."

They climbed into the Beast after breakfast the next day. Aunt Penny drove them through flatter terrain that turned into southern Pennsylvania's low, rolling hills. Here, old stone and clapboard houses were bordered by many crumbling stone walls, reminiscent of Ellie's visit to New England years ago. The Beast groaned a little on the hills as a gentle, bucolic roller coaster bordered with hedgerows and tunnels of mature trees instead of railings.

"It's like another world out here," Ellie murmured.

"More like another time," Penny corrected.

At the bottom of a steep hill, Penny turned into a small farm. A babbling creek wound its way through a pasture, and the pasture rose in a sunny swathe into another gentle hill bordered with trees at the top. Ellie counted three sheep grazing in the pasture. The farmhouse was fairly unremarkable. Ellie could tell that it was very old and painted in the dull, mustard-yellow color so often associated with colonial times. The door was bright red. It was like a miniature carpenter Victorian without the center peak and had an extension out the back. To the left of the house was an enormous flower garden blooming in a riot of color. Dora was in a rocking chair on the porch. She stood up when they got out of the car.

"Welcome!" she called.

Dora was once again in her serviceable denim jumper that fell below her knees, and her blouse was a brilliant yellow with blue flowers embroidered on it. She wore a pair of fisherman's sandals on her feet. Her wide smile smoothed the quilt of wrinkles momentarily.

The day was already becoming warm, and Dora offered them iced tea from a pitcher sitting on a tray on a side table with glasses. Tall sprigs of mint peeped out of the top of the pitcher.

"Be a love and grab a chair from the kitchen, will you?" she asked Ellie.

Ellie went inside to find a small living room and the kitchen at the back. Its pine cabinets had been painted, and its large, enameled apron sink was spotless. The dinette must have dated back to the forties. The table was a rounded square of red and silver with a design of red leaves down its center. Red leatherette chairs sat snugly beneath the adorable table. Ellie picked up a chair and took it out to the front porch. Penny and Dora were drinking iced tea and discussing Farmers' Market politics. Ellie's glass of tea was sweating in the morning sun. She picked it up gratefully. It was warm here in the foothills of Pennsylvania but not as humid as at the campground.

"So, you're here to learn about natural dyeing?" Dora asked.

Ellie nodded. "I love the colors of your yarn. You spin, too, correct?"

Dora sipped her iced tea. "I do. I shear the wool, but I don't card it any longer or process it. I send it out to a mill for that. Unfortunately, I started dating Arthur, that's Mr. Arthur Ritis, and he has hold of my hands. I can't manage some of the tasks any longer," Dora chuckled acerbically. She went on, "I still dye and spin my yarn myself. That's what I sell at the Farmer's Market in Havre de Grace and in Newark. If I can, I go to the wool festival up north in the fall."

"Wool festival?" Ellie asked.

"Yes, there are a variety of sheep and wool festivals, mostly in the fall. It's overwhelmingly wonderful, and it's a good place to pick up supplies and to pick everyone's brains about their art," Dora relayed.

"Are you ready to go find some colors?" Dora asked.

"Absolutely!" Ellie answered.

Dora led them to the large garden bursting with blooms. "I love the natural dyes. Nature gives us many colors– through the roots, leaves, berries, and flowers. This shirt's colors are thanks to the Coreopsis plant, and the embroidered flowers are a hank of wool that I died in blackberries."

"Beautiful," Ellie murmured.

They wandered among the garden. The flowers nearly glowed in the sunshine. Joyous bees buzzed about and were busy amongst the blossoms. It was sublime. Ellie thought Dora's life on the farm was idyllic. It reminded her of Aunt Penny's life. Both women were fiercely independent and happily living their creative lives.

Dora went on to explain. "Many of the plants give us yellows and greens. These lovely Hollyhocks that are about to burst into bloom will give reds and purples. On the other hand, Bedstraw," and she pointed to a lower growing plant with yellowish flowers, "yields creams, reds, and rusts. The Hardy Hibiscus yields some gorgeous purples. Mostly, I grow or forage for my dyes. Sometimes, I am tempted to purchase some materials like Logwood. It gives a gorgeous matte cobalt bluish-purple color."

Ellie's feeling of peacefulness was replaced with a feeling of being overwhelmed. She scribbled notes in the composition book they purchased on the way to Dora's. Dora led them to the back annex of her house.

"And this is my dye house. You never want to mix the dyestuff and chemicals in the kitchen where you cook," Dora advised.

They walked into a bright area close to a traditional kitchen. There was a long, antique farm table along one wall, a stove, a full sink, and large cabinets that held pots of all shapes and sizes. Plants were drying from a rack hanging from the ceiling. Dora showed them a cabinet filled with paper bags neatly labeled with each plant and the date it was stored. She warned Ellie not to store dye plants in plastic. Ellie continued to take notes frantically.

Dora led them into the house, where a spinning wheel was adjacent to a woodstove set into the bowels of the fireplace. Baskets of dyed wool and yarn were all around and on a bookshelf behind the spinning wheel. Here, Dora had them sit and explain the plant and plant part she used to get the color.

"I don't know if I'm impatient, lazy, or both," she told Ellie and Penny. "I mostly use Alum as my mordant."

Penny and Ellie looked puzzled, and Dora chuckled.

"A mordant sets the dye. Alum is easy as I can let the wool sit in a cool bath for twelve hours if I am lazy or heat it up to pre-mordant wool more quickly. It depends on what kind of mood I am in.

A black cat came into the room and stretched and yawned. "And this is Indigo," Dora introduced the cat.

When he heard his name, he walked over to Dora, bumped his head against her hand, and rubbed his cheek against her legs before jumping in her lap and purring. Dora petted him absent-mindedly.

"The real indigo plant is tropical; we can't grow it in Pennsylvania. So, I'm always after the elusive deep blues. There's Japanese Indigo, which is different from the tropical plant. It's considered an annual plant here, and I've had difficulty finding the seeds and the plants and not having too much luck growing them. I have one more room where I store the wool I sell at the Farmers' Markets," she paused as if to catch her breath.

"What do you think?" Dora asked Ellie. "Is this something you would like to pursue?"

"I'll be honest, I'm a little overwhelmed, but I am interested. I'm fascinated with how you can color cloth and create designs," Ellie told Dora. "When can I come back?"

"Next week?" Dora proposed to Ellie. "Would Wednesdays be good days to come?"

"That would work. I can drop off Ellie in the morning and pick her up in the afternoon," Penny assured her.

"Wear old clothes," Dora advised Ellie, smiling. "We'll be making messes."

"Thank you for your time today, Dora. I'm looking forward to learning more," Ellie told her.

"It's an addictive hobby," Dora warned.

"Sort of like tie-dye and Shibori!" Penny laughed.

"And I want to explore it all!" Ellie burst out.

And they all laughed, feeling a kinship with the love of color, texture, and textiles.

Thirty-Two

JOHN – 1969

*Small, Victorian porcelain dolls called "Frozen Charlottes" are
popular among beachcombers.*

John's tires swooshed on the wet pavement as he traveled to
the campground. He was looking forward to seeing Ellie.

Stepping out of his car at the campground, he noticed
everything seemed freshly scrubbed and clean from the
rain. The strong scent of pine from the campground's perimeter
permeated the air. He took in a deep breath, enjoying the strong,
spicy scent.

Carl stepped out of the store with his coffee cup in hand. "It's
still too wet to mow this morning," he told John, "but you can
check the trash, make the bathhouses sparkle, and chop more
wood today."

John nodded. It would be a busy day preparing for the next
round of weekend campers. His day was busy with the tasks Carl
assigned. When work was finally completed, he went to Penny and
Ellie's camper. Neither the Beast, Penny, nor Ellie were home. He
vaguely remembered she was going somewhere. Where was it?
The wool lady's farm? Disappointed, he went home. He wanted

to ask her about the picnic planned for Sunday. He hoped that she would come. He would have to try again tomorrow.

And the next day, he was just as busy as the day before as they prepped for the incoming flux of weekend campers. John felt guilty for taking Friday off for the funeral and offered to Carl to come later in the day.

"You're not going to want to work," Carl told him. "You and your family will need some time."

He went straight to Penny and Ellie's camper the minute he had finished work. Knowing they would likely be tie-dyeing, he went around the back of the camper to their studio area. He found Ellie checking the shirts curing in the sunshine. She called them the "rainbow mummies," John found this hilarious. Indeed, they looked like little mummies inside their plastic casings.

"Hi, you!" he greeted Ellie.

She whirled around at the sound of his voice, "Oh! John! You startled me!"

"Interested in going for a swim?" he asked. "I didn't forget my trunks this time."

"I would love to take a break. We've been working all day. Let me get my suit on. Give me five minutes," Ellie told him.

Ellie almost bumped into Penny as she rounded the corner.

"Oops!" Ellie cried, "Sorry, Aunt Penny."

"No harm, no foul. Where are you off to in such a rush?" Penny asked.

But then she spied John in his swim trunks and guessed.

"It's a gorgeous day for a swim! The water may be a little chilly after that rain yesterday," she warned.

"Cooler, but clearer," John said. "By the way, I need to ask Ellie, but is it all right with you if she comes with my family on Sunday for a picnic at Betterton Beach?"

"That sounds fabulous! Of course, it's all right with me," Penny said.

John smiled at Penny's reaction. Before he could say anything else, Ellie was coming out the camper door in her swimsuit with her beach towel. They walked to the little beach, which was virtually empty now that the bulk of the campers had gone.

"Penny warned me it might be colder today from the rain yesterday," John said.

"I wonder why that is?" Ellie asked.

"Because we're swimming in the shallows of the bay. The sun hasn't had time to warm the water again," John explained.

"Oh!" Ellie replied. "Interesting."

"Is it?" he teased, splashing her with water.

"You beast!" she cried and countered with another splash.

They were soon laughing and completely soaked.

"You know what they need here, don't you?" John asked.

"Nope, I don't have a clue," Ellie admitted.

"One of those floating platforms that you can climb onto," John said.

"Ooh, those things creep me out," Ellie admitted. "I'm always afraid of getting stuck underneath one or having something swim out from under it that's scary."

She shivered, not only from the thought of the swimming platform but also because she was getting cold.

"Your lips are turning blue," John said. "Let's go sit in the sun to warm up."

"You'll have no argument from me," Ellie replied, teeth chattering.

They sat in the sun, and John put his arm around Ellie. She leaned into him to warm up. Her teeth chattered for a few minutes until his body heat helped warm her up. John heard her sigh almost unperceptively. He tightened his arm around her. She sighed contentedly, and he couldn't help but smile.

"I almost forgot," John started.

"What?" Ellie replied, a little sleepy. She felt so relaxed with John, and she liked the feeling of his arm around her protectively.

"Can you come for a picnic and glassing on Sunday? Mom

wants to take you to one of her favorite beaches to find sea glass," John explained, "and I already asked Penny."

"I would love to! What can I bring? I'm not a good cook, but Aunt Penny could help me," Ellie told John.

"I'll get the details and let you know. I need to get your phone number," he said.

"And I need to get yours," Ellie returned.

They both laughed.

When he stood outside the camper to say goodbye, Ellie threw her arms around John at the last minute, holding him tight.

"Good luck tomorrow," she said, looking into his eyes.

His face, which had been carefree, was now scored with grief and pain.

"Come by after if you need to. Maybe we can go for a walk, swim, or drive. If not, I'll see you on Saturday?" Ellie asked hopefully.

Emotions had caught in John's throat. He had been able to put Pete's death behind him for a few hours, knowing that it would hit him in the face tomorrow. The emotions welled up, but he worked to push them down. Instead, he held onto Ellie. She was an anchor for him, and he didn't want to let her go. She had picked up on his grief, no matter how deeply he buried it. He gave her a slow, sweet kiss and then said goodbye.

Thirty-Three

LOUISA – 1918

Kelly green glass has been popular for soda bottles since the 1960s.

When Louisa visited Willie, she reminded him how they made their clandestine relationship work. Often, Willie and Louisa would pass notes like school children, using one of the neighborhood children to secret notes back and forth and laughingly vowing to tear them to bits after reading. Louisa turned up where Willie worked daily and made excuses to take rides on the carousel. Her favorite times were when they had a chance to sit close on the steps that led to the beach. The weather was typical, Eastern Shore Maryland summers. The hot, humid days sat heavily, and the occasional lick of wind from the bay was heavenly. The sunsets across the bay were glorious, and Louisa thought she had never seen anything so beautiful with the sky on fire with coral, red, and orange brilliance. They often sat side by side on the steps. Willie took her hand, and Louisa permitted this. They watched the drama of color that overtook the sky, changing moment to moment, like dancers weaving colorful scarves in the sky.

Louisa reminded Willie of his plans for the boarding house.

"Do you remember, Willie?" Louisa pleaded to the man who lay still on the bed. "Do you remember what you said? You told me about your dreams of turning the boarding house into a year-round resort and reaching out to Philadelphia and Baltimore to find guests. You talked about when the war was over, people would want to come to relax by the bay. You told me that you wanted to walk through life with me by your side. We still don't know how to do this, but we will. I want to see your eyes again, Willie. I want to see my love reflected in your eyes. And you kissed me, Willie, right on the steps to the boarding house from the beach. I wondered if it was a proposal, but I wasn't bold enough to ask. Kissing you was like tasting some of Grandmama's wine. Grandmama would never approve. She had already indicated so."

Had she imagined it? Did she feel the pressure of his fingers pushing into hers?

Beyond the flush, fluttering, and joy of their new love, there was something deeper between them. It was like a great, strong, invisible rope bound them together. She didn't know how they would get together, but she knew, in her heart, that it would happen.

"We need to bide our time, Willie. We can make things happen. You can make your dreams come true about the boarding house. I know it. But I need you to get better. Please, Willie," she pleaded again.

"I love you," she whispered against his bandaged head, kissing him quickly.

Thirty-Four

WILLIE – 1918

Glass with smaller bubbles or seeds dates back to the 1700s. Glass with large bubbles is likely from the 1800s.

His sweet daydreams and memories about Louisa and last summer were interrupted by the nasty voice of Nurse Johnston. He didn't understand why she called names. He wondered if she was the culprit of the loud noises. His head itched, and he wished for his vision to return. The doctor said it would, but it would take time. The one doctor told him his loss of sight happened because of all the horrible things he had seen in France.

Footsteps were coming closer. Willie listened as well as he could through the gauze. They were getting closer. The footsteps walked past his bed, wafting the sharp scent of lye soap. They stopped, and the steps shifted.

Bang! Something crashed to the floor. Willie threw his hands to his face, and his limbs started trembling with their own volition.

He barely heard the whispered comment. "Coward," it said.

The footsteps moved on with an evil chuckle accompanying each footfall.

Willie worked to control his trembling limbs. He took a deep breath. He tried to think of Louisa. He grasped memories like fleeting thoughts. He remembered their precious time together. along with her letters, they held him and kept her close when he was at the front. He could almost feel her presence some days.

And now, she was here. He closed his eyes. When he thought of Louisa, his limbs calmed.

The footsteps walked further down the ward and stopped—another crash. There was a cry from a man. The nasty laugh continued to make its way through the hospital ward. Footsteps. Crash. Laughter. He heard men cry out. He heard the banging of limbs against the bed.

Thirty-Five

ELLIE – 1969

18th-century clay pipes and pipe stems are treasured finds by Eastern Shore glassers.

Ellie was restless. She couldn't settle herself knowing John was at Pete's funeral. Her heart ached for him.

Aunt Penny seemed to sense this. She assigned tasks for Ellie to prepare for Saturday's Farmers' Market. They also discussed what she could take on Sunday for the picnic. Aunt Penny suggested a pasta salad or a potato salad with vinaigrette.

The potato salad intrigued Ellie. She had never had a potato salad without mayonnaise and wondered what it would taste like. So, Aunt Penny took her to the Amish market to buy fresh young potatoes, onions, and dill. They made a test salad on Friday, with Penny guiding Ellie on the steps to put together the dressing and how to prepare the salad.

"The beauty of this is that you can serve it warm, room temperature, or cold," Penny told her. "You don't have to worry about the mayonnaise turning bad."

Ellie loved the salty, tart taste of the lemon, dill, salt, and herbs. The potato salad was a winner in her eyes. She just hoped

John's family would like it. She also dithered on what to wear, with different outfits strewn over the couch, driving Aunt Penny a little crazy. "I should probably wear something conservative. His dad seems super conservative, Aunt Penny. Should I wear knee-length culottes? Pedal pushers? Definitely not short shorts. What should I do, Aunt Penny?"

"Calm down, Ellie. It's a picnic. Pedal pushers will be fine. Those nice blue chambray ones will work. They would look lovely with a crisp white shirt. I have just the thing in my closet. And Betterton has a washroom, so take your swimsuit and towel," Aunt Penny advised, "and a hat."

"Okay, okay," Ellie agreed. And she turned to Aunt Penny, "Why am I so nervous? I just have a feeling, you know? I have this weird feeling today that I can't shake. I hope John and his family are doing all right at the funeral. "

"Stop worrying. The funeral is going to be a madhouse. Peter was the first young man from the county to die in Vietnam. There are going to be bags of people," Penny said, referring to the British colloquialism. "You'll see John after the Farmers' Market tomorrow, or maybe he'll come down again with his mom. You never know."

Ellie worked out her restlessness by loading the Beast with the latest shirts and socks. Later, she went down to the beach, where she paced in the sand. Campers were returning, and the little beach was filling up. Ellie was in her own world, staring at the sand as she walked along and kicking at some of the small waves that made it to shore. The warmth of the sun seemed to sink inside her. She began to relax as she looked for beach glass. She found one piece of white that was obviously old. It was well-rounded and sanded from its time in the water. Aunt Penny told her that winter was the best glassing time at their beach, around February or March. She didn't know why. She also told Ellie to keep an eye out for arrowheads. Apparently, they were quite common in Kingstown. Her treasure hunt passed the time.

More campers moved in during the day. Off and on throughout the day, she watched the veritable parade. She was sure Carl was missing John. Carl pulled up in his golf cart when they sat around their campfire for dinner. He looked bone-tired.

"Hi ya, Carl!" Penny greeted him as usual.

"Hi, Penny and Ellie," he said, nodding at them.

He climbed off the golf cart, and Penny waved him to a chair, asking how his day was going.

"To be honest, 'I'm too pooped to pop,' to quote an old song."

"Beer? Wine? Lemonade?" Penny asked him sympathetically.

"I wouldn't say no to a beer," Carl responded.

Ellie went inside the camper to get a cold beer for Carl. She handed it to him, and he popped it open gratefully.

"Ahh," Carl sighed after a long swig. "That hits the spot right now. I've sorely missed your young man today," he directed at Ellie.

She blushed and protested, "I don't know if he's my young man."

Carl barked a laugh at her comment and told her, "I'm glad I wasn't taking a drink when you said that. That young man is cow-eyed for you. And he's a good one."

"I know," Ellie said quietly. She missed John today, too.

"And I think he will need your support in the coming weeks as he works through that young man's death. We've had many conversations about the war. This didn't help. And, that young man, what's his name?"

"Pete," Ellie interjected.

"Pete," Carl said emphatically. "He's the first of what I fear to be many not coming home. We've already had an avalanche of deaths over the years. Now, it's hitting home. Maybe, just maybe, people will begin to sit up and take notice of the insanity of this 'police action.'"

"Maybe," Penny replied dourly. "But I doubt it. Rich, old,

white men have run this country since the dawn of the American Revolution. I don't know when it will change. Possibly not in my lifetime."

"Is that the wine talking?" Carl teased.

In a serious tone, Penny replied, "Maybe. But maybe not. Progress is infinitesimally slow. And, there are days, like when Peter dies, when I doubt some of the good."

Ellie had never heard Aunt Penny talk like this. Perhaps it was the wine, as Carl suggested. Once again, the war was at the forefront of thought and conversation. It had slipped insidiously into her life, and she wasn't sure how she felt about it. Pete, Carl, and Aunt Penny were giving her new insights. She was cracking away at the shell that had surrounded her and finding the outside world. What a small world she had lived in before. This new stretching of her mind and consciousness was exhilarating and terrifying at the same time. But she didn't want to go back inside of the shell. She wanted to stretch, breathe, and learn more.

Thirty-Six

JOHN – 1969

Hanapepe Bay Glass Beach in Kauai, Hawaii, is popular for glassers.

John stood stoically beside his parents at the church. His eyes kept straying to the flag-draped coffin at the front. John couldn't believe Pete was inside. The number of people at the church swelled until it was standing room only. John had overheard one woman stating that Pete was the first Vietnam casualty in the county. People had turned out to support his parents.

The minister droned on. One of Pete's cousins gave a eulogy. John felt the entire service was surreal until it was time to go to the graveyard. At the last minute, Pete's mom had asked him to be a pallbearer. At a signal from the minister, Pete's cousin John and some scouts in full uniform went to the front of the church. They lifted Pete's coffin on their shoulders and walked to the graveyard. They walked in slow, measured steps.

John's thoughts were as heavy as the coffin on his shoulder. As hard as it was to believe, Peter was inside, and would never be around again. It was a heavy, empty shell of a body they carried.

Peter, with his easy smile and wicked sense of humor, wouldn't be a part of his life anymore. Those had dissipated along with Pete's soul, wherever that went. John wasn't so sure about what he believed any more. The thought of heaven was a comfort to some people. He couldn't believe that you died and then stood around in robes singing all day long. He wondered what other religions thought about death and your soul. Peter was now lost to his memory. His heart wrenched as they placed the coffin with a small jolt on a trestle outside a gaping open grave.

The outside portion of the service was mercifully short. John found it difficult to see the coffin lowered into the ground. Tears pricked his eyes, and his father put a steadying hand on his shoulder. Someone, a guy from the army, played a haunting rendition of Taps. Other army members folded the flag from the coffin and gave it to Pete's mom with a bow. She hugged it to herself as if she would never let it go. Tears streamed down her cheeks in silent rivers of pain.

Everyone returned to the church parish hall, where there were tea sandwiches and other finger foods. The ladies from the church served. John nearly gagged on the lukewarm, sweet punch. He just wanted this afternoon to be over.

His dad had always drilled it into him to find something to do if he was bored or at odds. So, John made himself useful to the ladies in the kitchen. He worked at cleaning up the debris from the guests. The sooner the reception was over, the sooner he could get home.

John and his parents were silent on the way home until his mom said in a wavery voice, "He had a nice showing."

His father agreed, but John wasn't sure. He loosened his tie and sat back, wondering what to think. He stared out the window, not really seeing anything. "A nice showing." The words echoed in his head. Death was so useless. What did it matter how many people showed up? Funerals, he decided, were an unnecessary show. He preferred to grieve in private.

Once home, John put the kettle on to make his mom a cup of tea. She was sitting at the kitchen table, rubbing her temples. His dad went out to get the mail. When he returned, he stood in the doorway and cleared his throat.

"Son," he croaked out.

John, who had been waiting for the kettle to boil, turned at a note he heard in his father's voice.

"Son," his father said again, and he held a letter to John in his shaking hand.

John walked over and took it from his father. "Selective Service" was on the return. His mother saw it and paled visibly.

"How can this happen?" she asked in a panicked whisper. "You have a college deferment."

John smiled wryly. "Mom, you know Lady Luck doesn't follow me. It's the luck of the draw with the draft. And they need more men to fight in Nam."

"Open it, son," his father advised.

John opened the letter and read through it twice before announcing, "Two weeks. I report in two weeks."

They were all silent until the claxon from the tea kettle broke their thoughts. John went to the stove to pour the hot water over the tea bag and brought the cup to his mother. He sat next to her at the kitchen table. All she could do was take his hand. And, he held on.

Thirty-Seven

LOUISA – 1918

Not all beaches have seaglass. The broken glass takes thirty to one hundred years to break down and become a silky, smooth treasure.

Something bothered Louisa. Why was Willie getting worse instead of better? When she was near him, he almost got better before her eyes. The symptoms of shell shock dissipated, and he was calmer and happier. Louisa even thought he was close to getting his vision back. So why? Why had the trembling limbs and anxiety returned?

When she left Fort McHenry that night, it was all she could do not to turn back to Willie. When she stepped off the trolley, it didn't feel right. She turned to get back on, but it had already gone down the street and turned the corner. She watched the tail end disappear and stomped her foot in frustration. It was something in her gut, but she know what it was. Louisa fretted all the way home. She slammed the front door for good measure when she entered the townhouse.

Emma stayed late that night, waiting up for her and emerged at the sound of the door slamming.

"What's wrong, Miss Louisa?" she asked.

Louisa shook her head, "I don't know, Emma. Something's bothering me, and I can't figure it out. I feel I should return to the hospital."

"Not now miss, it's cold and dark. Come have a spot of supper with me and tell me all about it. I'm sad to say that Bertha isn't here. Her husband has the Spanish flu." She told her this as she took Louisa's coat and hat.

"Can we do anything for Bertha and her husband? They're quarantined now. Should we send food?" Louisa questioned.

"That would be nice," Emma said, "and appreciated."

"Can you please make the arrangements?" Louisa asked.

"You seem distracted, Miss, if you don't mind me saying so," Emma told Louisa.

Over plates of scrambled eggs and toast, Louisa confessed her fears about Willie's regression to Emma. It was hard to talk, eat, and try not to cry.

Emma patted her hand.

"I don't know why, but everything will work out. Don't worry, miss," Emma said.

"You know Grandmama never approved of Willie," Louisa said, sotto voce as if Grandmama could hear her.

"But she's not here," Emma said, cocking her head at Louisa. "And the times are changing. There's no reason for you not to go to nursing school. There's no reason for you not to marry Willie. You have this house. You can make a life together here or in Tolchester."

"Thank you, Emma. I just wish Grandmama was still here. I think she would understand how the world is changing. I miss her," she said wistfully, putting her hand over Emma's. Emma squeezed back and patted Louisa's hand.

Louisa looked Emma in the eye, "There's something wrong. I have to go back to the hospital."

Emma looked at Louisa and nodded. "I can see you are determined. I'll call for a cab."

Louisa donned her hat and coat, hovering by the front door until the cab pulled up in front of the townhouse.

"Be careful," Emma advised her, giving Louisa a quick hug.

Louisa fairly flew down the path toward Willie's ward once she left the cab. She stood, outside the door, breathing heavily.

"Louisa?" Nurse Williams voice was right behind her. "Louisa, what are you doing here?"

Louisa spun around, "Oh! Nurse Williams. I just had to come back. Something isn't right."

Nurse Williams nodded grimly. "I feel the same. I came back too." She put a finger to her lips, "We must be quiet."

Nurse Williams took her hand and led her to a back door to the ward. She opened it carefully and peered inside. Louisa squeezed in beside her to peer in too. Nurse Williams put her hand up to her mouth when she observed Nurse Johnston dropping the tray of instruments near a man's head and laughing. Louisa's anger piqued.

"What is she doing?" she gasped.

They watched her again and Louisa tore the door from Nurse Williams's hold. What a wretched woman and excuse for a nurse.

"What are you doing?" Louisa shouted, pushing Nurse Williams aside and rushing into the ward.

Nurse Johnston, looked up, surprised.

Nurse Williams caught Louisa's arm. "No, Louisa. Not like this."

Nurse Williams marched in and snatched the tray of instruments from Nurse Johnston.

"This," she said with a steely voice, barely controlling her anger, "This will be reported immediately."

Nurse Johnston looked at her defiantly.

"Go to the nursing station immediately," Nurse Williams ordered. "Louisa, check on Willie. Stay there until I come to get you."

Louisa did as she was told. She pulled a small stool up to

Willie's sleeping form. How could anyone be as cruel as Nurse Johnston?

"Oh, Willie," she murmured, taking his hand and resting her cheek on it."

Louisa sat, focused on Willie, barely noticing people coming onto the ward and the voices behind the curtain at the nurse's station.

"Oh, Willie. Please come back to me," her whisper pleaded to his still form. She whispered it over and over like a mantra, and telling him she loved him.

Nurse Williams found her a bit later. Louisa didn't hear her approach and jumped at the hand that was placed on her shoulder.

"It's done," she told Louisa, and motioned for her to follow her to the nurse's station. Louisa laid Willie's hand gently back over his chest. She followed Nurse Williams.

When they were out of earshot of the men, Nurse Williams said, "I don't know how much damage she has done. Her abuse has been going on for a few weeks now. Let's hope we can undo the evil she insinuated on the patients. She's a disgrace to all nurses."

Louisa looked at Nurse Williams with huge, bright eyes with tears on the brink. At first she didn't know what to say. "Oh, oh...," and her emotions fluctuated between hope, despair, and anger.

Finally, anger took over and Louisa burst out, "Ooh, I could kill that woman for what she has done!"

Nurse Williams chuckled, lightening the mood, and said firmly, "No murders on my watch. And it will be worth every double that I need to pull to have that evil woman gone."

Louisa nodded and gave Nurse Williams an involuntary hug.

"And now, it's time for you to go home. I will call a cab for you. Go home, and rest, because I will surely need your assistance tomorrow. I'm going to stay here for the rest of the night."

"Do you need me to stay too?" Louisa asked.

"No, I'll be fine," Nurse Williams assured her. "My nursing life has been a series of cat naps. I will need you to be as fresh as a daisy tomorrow to assist me."

Louisa acquiesced to Nurse Williams' wishes. When she opened the door to the townhouse as quietly as she could, she found Emma on the other side. She had changed out of her uniform to her nightgown, wrapper, and nightcap.

"Oh, miss!" Emma exclaimed, "What happened? Come to the kitchen. I'll make us a spot of hot milk and you can tell me all about it."

Louisa followed wearily. Over the warm milk, she told Emma what happened. Emma gasped in horror at Louisa's story.

"It's a good thing you followed your instincts and went back to the hospital," Emma told her.

Louisa nodded sleepily. She yawned.

"You finish your milk and get to bed. I can't have you getting sick too," Emma chided.

Louisa sat at the dressing table, pulling the hairpins from her bun and began to brush her hair in long, even strokes. One hundred strokes seemed far too many at this hour. She opened the small drawer in the dressing table to put away the hairpins when her fingers touched something smooth.

Excitement raced through her, erasing her weariness for a moment. Louisa pulled the sea glass heart from her vanity drawer. She turned the small, cobalt blue bit of glass over and over in her hand, pondering.

"This might be it," Louisa whispered. "This might be the ticket for Willie to remember."

Louisa put the small sea glass heart next to the bed where she would remember it in the morning.

When she awoke the next morning, the sunlight made the little heart glow. It was a sign. Louisa knew it. She went to the hospital with a light step.

She was running late after the shenanigans of the previous night. Nurse Williams was dragging and Louisa fingered the small heart in her uniform pocket. It would have to wait. She held the tray for Nurse Williams as they made their way through the ward, administering medicines, changing bandages, and offering comfort. It took the larger part of the day. When they approached Willie, he lay still on his cot. He wasn't moving. He wasn't reacting. Nurse Williams talked with him.

"Willie, Louisa, and I are here to change your bandage," Nurse Williams told him gently. "Hold still."

Willie lay still. He didn't move. Louisa shot Nurse Williams a worried look. Nurse Williams removed the bandage while Louisa put her hands-on Willie. The wound had lost its red and puffy look. The wound's edges were knitting themselves together with the healing, yellow crystals of serous fluid that would bind the cut. Nurse Williams smiled, and Louisa sighed audibly with relief. urse Williams applied more healing salve and re-wrapped the bandage.

"I'll leave you two together," Nurse Williams told Louisa.

Willie was staring into space. Louisa took Willie's hands in hers. It was a heartbeat or two or three, but Willie seemed to sense that Louisa was there. He turned his head toward Louisa.

"Willie, it's Louisa," she said softly at first and then loudly. Nurse Williams looked on encouragingly before returning to the nurses' station.

"Willie, I want you to remember. I want you to remember our last day together in Tolchester. Do you remember?" she asked him. She waited a moment but continued her story even though he didn't respond.

"You asked me to walk with you the night before I left. Grandmama had a fit. She didn't have an appropriate chaperone and didn't want me to be with you. It was only after I had convinced her that you were a soldier going off to war and that I had to support you that she agreed to be our chaperone. That was the only way I could have met you to walk. I'll have you know," Louisa said pertly.

Willie still lay still, but Louisa had the feeling he was listening.

"I remember every single moment of that day," Louisa told him wistfully. "It was so hot! All I wanted to do was to take a swim in the bay. We walked along the beach. And we couldn't even talk. We didn't know what to say to each other. Sometimes I think we were all talked out, but really, I just couldn't find words to say goodbye. And, you know, Willie, it's never a goodbye between us. We belong together. There's always been something between us, invisible, but with power beyond anything I could imagine that ties us together. We walked to the beach. I couldn't even look at you because I thought I would cry. You were scuffling. Did you know that? You scuffled in the sand and got wet sand all over your shoes and inside your pants," Louisa giggled at this. "And Grandmama was only a few steps behind. But the hot, humid weather got to her. She ended up sitting on the bench with her parasol."

And then, Louisa turned quiet and hopeful. "While walking, you stared at where the water met the sand in small waves. You stopped. I stopped. You reached down quickly and pulled something from the water, getting your sleeve all wet. And you kept it in your hand, closed, like a secret," Louisa stated softly, her thoughts caught up in the memory.

"Do you remember, Willie?" Louisa asked him. "Do you remember what you found in the waves and the sand?"

He still didn't respond. Willie just stared at the ceiling, or at least she thought so. His eyes were unmoving. Louisa, frustrated now, stamped her foot. She took his hand and pried his fingers loose, but not gently.

"Come back to me Willie! I know you're in there," she pleaded with a half-hitch of a sob.

"Please, Willie!" she cried sharply, voice filled with frustration. "Willie!" And then more softly, Louisa said, "Willie, you picked up something very special from the bay. You picked up this."

Louisa reached into her pocket and pulled out the cobalt blue, sea glass heart. It was where the glass folded around the corner of a small, rectangular bottle. She ran her fingers over it and put it in Willie's hand. She closed his hand around it.

"Willie," Louisa insisted, "This is the heart you pulled out of the bay. You told me this is to be your heart that you gave to me until we saw each other again. Willie, I'm here," Louisa insisted. "And as much as I love this blue heart, I love you more. Willie, please, please wake up," Louisa pleaded.

Willie lay still for a few minutes, but eventually, his fingers closed around the heart. Louisa found a tear leaked from her eye and dropped onto Willie's hand. His hand jerked and tightened around the heart. Other than that, Willie didn't respond.

It was too much for Louisa. She kissed Willie on the forehead and left, tears filling her eyes and blinding her, and stumbled away from Willie's bed. She wiped her hands across her streaming eyes and brushed past Nurse Williams.

"I need to go," Louisa choked out, holding her hand to her mouth.

Louisa left the hospital and flagged down a cab. When she got home, she didn't answer the concerned questions from Emma. She ran up to her room and threw herself on the bed, where she sobbed and sobbed. The world felt like it was coming to an end. Grandmama was gone. Now Willie seemed to be far, far away. She didn't think he was coming back.

Louisa didn't know how long she cried, but she cried until she fell asleep. When she awoke, she found that Emma had put a blanket over her. She got out of bed and went downstairs, the blanket still around her shoulders. She probably looked a sight, but she didn't care.

When Louisa stepped into the kitchen, she startled Emma, who was peeling potatoes at the table.

"Miss Louisa!" Emma cried. "Come and sit. Let me get you a cup of tea and a sandwich."

'Louisa let herself be led to a chair at the kitchen table. Emma straightened the blanket around her shoulders and patted Louisa on the back. Louisa put her forehead on the table. Emma set a cup of tea in front of her before returning to the sideboard to busily make a sandwich. She brought it to the table and placed that plate beside her elbow.

"Miss Louisa," Emma said gently, "you need to eat something. Please, Miss."

Louisa raised her head. She scrubbed her eyes and looked at Emma. Her eyes trailed to the tea and sandwich. Louisa pulled the steaming cup of tea closer, watching the curl of steam rise. Louisa looked at the tea and, hesitantly, picked up the cup and raised it to her lips for a sip. She set the cup down.

Emma looked at her expectantly. Louisa took another sip of tea and then another.

"What's wrong, Miss Louisa?" Emma asked.

Louisa's voice came out in a ragged whisper, "Willie. Willie doesn't seem to be coming back to this world. That...that horrible woman did him in," Her voice choked at the end, and tears started to spill again.

With one hand, Louisa tore off bits of crust on the bread. She stopped and squeezed her hands tightly, leaving a trail of crumbs.

"I don't know what to do!" Louisa finally cried. I'm so help-less! This horrible, horrible war! I've lost Grandmama and now Willie. He's lost, Emma! He's lost to me!"

Louisa broke down in sobs again. Emma let her cry. She patted Louisa on the shoulder, making comforting noises.

"It will all work itself out," Emma comforted. "You need to give Mr. Willie a bit more time. I'm sure he'll come round."

Louisa shook her head. "Oh, Emma, these men are so...so addled," Louisa told her, "They can't help it, and they don't know how to handle the horrors they saw. Their brains can't handle the death, the destruction, and the horrors of war! But we thought things were turning around! That's what is so frustrating! He was responding. He seemed to know me! And then, something happened, a horrible, horrible nurse wasn't nice to him and the other men with shell shock. He sank back into the war that is going on inside of his head."

Emma patted her hand. "Miss Louisa," Emma said gently, "The war is not only with the men who fight it. It affects everyone. Look at yourself and how frustrated you've been. And you have been at war fighting yourself, pouring all of your energies into these young men to heal, especially Willie. I know you feel helpless, but we need to do our best. And, it's not in vain. You know, Miss Louisa, I have a little bit of the sight," she said with a twinkle in her eye. "I feel that everything will be all right."

Louisa sighed and looked at Emma with red-rimmed eyes, "I hope so," she said dully.

"Oh, Miss Louisa!" she said sympathetically.

"I know, I know, I am a mess," Louisa said.

"Have a bite to eat, and I'll draw you a hot bath," Emma advised. "And a good night's sleep will do you good. I'll also get you a nice hot water bottle for your bed."

"Thank you," Louisa told Emma.

Emma left the kitchen. Louisa reluctantly picked up the sandwich. She ate a few bites thoughtfully. Poor Willie. And those other soldiers. No one should have to experience such horrors. She pondered why wars even took place when they killed so many, brought such despair, and returned broken men.

Thirty-Eight

WILLIE – 1918

There is an International Sea Glass Museum in Fort Bragg, California.

Willie's hand jerked from a splash on his hand. Was it raining? What was it? There was something in his hand. He ran his fingers around the edges. He ran his finger around the edge over and over. It seemed to be glass to him, but not. It was silky and sanded and had funny divots in it. The shape was unusual too. It wasn't round or square. It felt like a heart.

Willie wished he could see what it was. His frustration manifested itself by kicking the bed. The hard metal springs squeaked raucously as he kicked and kicked and kicked.

He heard running feet.

"Willie!" Nurse Williams called to him.

Willie felt a comforting hand on his shoulder and the calming voice of Nurse Williams. He stopped kicking the bed.

Willie tried to use his voice, saying slowly, carefully, and loudly, "I want to see!"

He pushed at the bandages with the hand that didn't hold the sea glass heart.

"Wait, wait," Nurse Williams told him gently. "Let me get scissors, and I can help you with that. Give me just a moment. I will be right back."

Nurse Williams' footsteps disappeared, but Willie felt he could trust her to return soon. He waited for what seemed like hours, though it was only minutes. His thumb and fingers rubbed the glass over and over again. Finally, he heard her footsteps. Willie breathed a sigh of relief.

Willie felt cool hands on his cheeks and heard metal scissors cutting away the bandages.

"So, you're ready to see now, eh?" Nurse Williams said with satisfaction. "You're ready to see your girl again, I suspect."

Willie couldn't nod while she was holding his head and using scissors, but he tried once again to say slowly, loudly, and clearly, "Lou-Louisa."

"That's right," Nurse Williams said matter-of-factly. "Louisa. She'll be back in the morning."

Willie felt the bandages pull away from his head. Cool air seemed to rush around him. He tried to open his eyes but squinted at the bright lights.

"Can you see?" Nurse Williams asked.

"Bright," Willie said, squinting.

Willie put his hand up to shield his eyes. The world started to come into focus. He saw bright white near him and realized it was Nurse Williams' uniform. He saw the red cross emblem on the apron on her chest. His eyes rose to see the kind eyes of Nurse Williams framed neatly by her graying brown hair that was pulled back in a bun at the back of her neck. A white nurse's cap was pinned to the hair. She was smiling. Her eyes were smiling.

"Hello, Willie," Nurse Williams said. "I'm Nurse Williams. Welcome back to the world."

ELLIE – 1969

Some avid sea glassers snorkel to find their treasures.

Ellie woke up eagerly the next day, ready to go to the Farmers' Market. She hoped that John and his mother would come by. It had only been a day since she had seen him, but it seemed like forever. She had never felt a connection with anyone as she did with John. When he was away, it felt like a piece of her was missing. She wondered how he was faring after Pete's funeral. Last night, she desperately wanted to call his house but didn't want to intrude.

She was happy to connect with Dora again, and after they set up their table and textiles, she spoke with her. Dora had brought wool roving and a drop spindle to demonstrate how to spin the wook into yarn. It was fascinating and almost magical to see how the wool became yarn. Ellie doubted she could repeat what Dora did. Dora insisted she would get the hang of it – with practice There wasn't much of a crowd, but her eyes kept straying to look for John. She didn't hear much of Dora's tutelage.

Finally, she apologized, "I'm sorry, Dora. I'm hoping my

friend will come this morning. I'm distracted as I don't want to miss them."

Dora nodded, understanding. "It's fine, Ellie. We'll get into it this coming Wednesday with less distractions."

Ellie thanked her and left. The crowd was starting to build. Pockets of people moved from booth to booth. Aunt Penny smiled gratefully at her return. The morning turned busy. After ten and in a lull, Ellie realized neither John nor his mother had come by. She was disappointed. When the market ended, she was enthusiastic about packing the van so they could get home as soon as possible.

Ellie shot her aunt a grateful look when she took the long loop through the campground. They finally spied John. He was mowing one of the many grass islands that bedecked the campground. He noticed the Beast and gave a quick, short wave before returning to focus on his work. Ellie, whose heart skipped a beat when they found John, settled back into a normal rhythm once again. She relaxed. It would be a few hours until John was off for the day. After lunch, Aunt Penny noticed Ellie's restlessness and suggested she teach Ellie a new technique.

Penny asked Ellie to cover the picnic table with one of the shower curtains they used when they dyed. Next, she instructed Ellie to get their glasses from the kitchen and get rubber bands from the tie-dye area. Puzzled, Ellie did what she was told. Penny brought out two scarves draped over her arm, her collection of colorful, permanent markers, and a couple of spray bottles. She demonstrated as she stretched the fabric over the glassware and secured it with rubber bands. Next, she drew blousy flowers using the markers on the stretched fabric. Next, she sprayed the flowers with alcohol in the spray bottles, and like magic, the colors spread.

"Oh!" Ellie exclaimed. "That's beautiful!"

Aunt Penny nodded, "I love doing these. I have often thought of selling them. Once it dries, you can outline it with the black marker to give it definition or add more flowers, leaves, or anything you like. You only need to toss the color in the dryer for twenty minutes to set it."

"Wow!" Ellie exclaimed, her eyes shining with enthusiasm.

"And now, it's your turn to try," Aunt Penny told Ellie.

Ellie secured the scarf to the glasses with rubber bands. Next, she sat and looked at the markers, absently rubbing a finger along her chin.

"What about the white spaces?" Ellie asked her aunt.

"What about them?" Aunt Penny returned.

"Can I put color there as well?" Ellie asked.

"Whatever you like, just know that when you spray the alcohol, the ink will run. I would suggest you work on the designs secured over the glasses first. When they are dry, you can work on the designs in the white spaces. It's a warm day, so drying shouldn't take too long." Penny advised.

Ellie got to work using her favorite colors of blues and purples to create the flowers. Some had yellow centers. She was delighted to see how the flowers changed and bloomed before her eyes when she sprayed the alcohol.

"You can also use a paintbrush with the alcohol if you want more control," Aunt Penny suggested.

Ellie fetched a paint brush from the camper and an old cup to put alcohol in. She settled back at the table, put her tongue between her teeth, and worked on the silk scarf creating a design of loose, flowing flowers and leaves that melted into brilliant greens and yellows, holding light within like stained glass.

"Aunt Penny," Ellie asked, "do you have to use silk? Can you work with other fabrics?"

"Natural fabrics are best," Aunt Penny told her. "Each fabric has a different tooth and will change the design subtlety."

"May I try one of the cotton shirts we tie-dye with?" Ellie asked, eager to try more.

"Of course!" Aunt Penny said, "Maybe you want to work on some to sell at the market in the next couple of weeks. I have a few silk scarves, but we can certainly order more. If you're interested, we'll call on Monday. The vendor is in California, and it takes more than a week to arrive."

Ellie nodded, "Yes! Please order more, Aunt Penny. I would love to create these scarves. There are so many possibilities!"

Aunt Penny nodded in agreement and stated sagely, "And it's just the tip of the iceberg for this technique and so many more in textile arts. I'll go and get you a T-shirt. And later, I'll share the catalog with you so that we can choose different types of scarves."

Aunt Penny went to their tie-dye and storage area to find a clean, washed t-shirt for Ellie to find her completing some details on the scarf with a very thin, black marker. Ellie draped it over a chair to dry in the sun. Aunt Penny directed her to clean the area with alcohol and dry it well before setting up the area for the t-shirt. She purposefully stretched the fabric over the glassware and secured it with rubber bands.

"Go away, please," Ellie told her aunt. "This is going to be a surprise."

"All right, all right," Penny acquiesced. "I'll just be over here, facing *away* from you, and reading a book. Eventually, we'll need to figure out something for dinner."

Ellie nodded, but her concentration was on the new piece. She pulled together the colors she needed and fetched her notebook to work out a quick sketch. Satisfied after a few attempts, Ellie began sketching onto the fabric using brilliant oranges and yellows. They looked almost like a combination of op-art and impressionism when she sprayed them with alcohol. She added movement with various squiggly lines resembling ripples across space and time. She was focused on the colors and the piece, catching her bottom lip between her teeth. She could not help smiling. She loved it. Ellie was in her creative element, watching the colors blend and meld. She sat back, observing her work, studying it carefully, and trying to figure out if she needed to do anything else. She thought about adding fine black lines to outline the images and add depth to the ripples of dark blue.

"Aunt Penny, I would loveyour thoughts on this piece," Ellie called over her shoulder.

Penny went to see the t-shirt Ellie designed. The bright, orange butterflies looked like they might fly off the fabric. Ellie created beautiful movement in her design with line, color, and shadow.

Penny cried out, "Oh, Ellie! This is glorious! You need to make more of these to sell."

"Thanks, Aunt Penny," Ellie said, joy filling her voice. "You know, you've opened up an incredible world for me. I am so hooked on the colors and fabrics that I just want to shout and sing when I am creating these!"

Aunt Penny nodded in agreement, "Yup, I feel the same way. The tie-dye is the bread and butter for paying the bills, but I love working the Shibori technique. And more. Maybe, this winter, while we work on your portfolio, you and I can work on a joint exhibition for a gallery. I have some contacts. That would give you an edge for art school as well, to have an exhibition under your belt."

Ellie sucked in a breath, "Oh, Aunt Penny! I would love that!" She gave her aunt an impromptu hug. Eyes shining with excitement, Ellie held up a fistful of markers and requested, "More please, Aunt Penny. I want to work on more scarves. My head is full of designs!"

Forty

JOHN – 1969

Traveling to the islands? Ireland Island in Bermuda has a bounty of sea glass.

John's heart was filled with dread as he read the chilling words, "You are hereby ordered for induction in the Armed Forces of the United States." He read through the letter. His brain was having a difficult time wrapping around the news. His parents were waiting, so he read through it again.

In a voice that didn't seem to be his own, he gravely informed his parents, "Two weeks. I report for duty in two weeks."

Shock and dismay. His mom and dad seemed to turn to stone before his mother cried out about college deferment. At that point, John could only see the sick sense of humor in the situation. He had never been lucky, and this only proved it once again.

The shrill whistle of the tea kettle broke their shock and silence. His father poured the hot water over the tea bag and brought it to the table. But John and his mom sat and he held her hand. They didn't speak. His mother let her tea grow cold. And he couldn't stop holding her hand. It was a lifeline to his heart.

Two weeks! Two weeks! John thought of Ellie. How could he leave her when they had only just begun a relationship? He hunched over and put his forehead on the table. Surprisingly, his father put his hand on his shoulder.

They were all like robotic dolls as they went about the evening routine of dinner and bed. Although his parents sat mutely watching the comedic variety shows on television that evening, John couldn't stand the sound of the laugh tracks. It seemed ludicrous that there could be anyone in this world left laughing.

He went to his room. He knew some men deserted and went to Canada. Others, he had heard, feigned mental illness. In his heart, he knew he couldn't do either. He closed his eyes. Drafted. The reality was harsh. He thought of Pete. But Pete enlisted. Would there be a difference? He wondered if Carl would know.

Carl and Betty. He would need to tell them first thing tomorrow. And Ellie. He would need to tell Ellie and her Aunt Penny.

John didn't sleep well that night. Pete's face loomed large in his dreams that were near nightmares. He kept dreaming he couldn't get home. He was so close, only steps away, and he couldn't reach his doorstep, where he saw his mom, Ellie, and his dad in the doorway. Dawn painted the sky with a peach glow. He stared out his window as the sky brightened. His stomach growled loudly. He hadn't eaten much last night. He sighed and rolled out of bed.

His mom was in the kitchen cooking up eggs and bacon by the time John showered, dressed, and went downstairs. His mom was at the stove, a defeated slump in her posture, but she turned and tried to put on a bright face when she saw John. Behind the smile, her eyes were filled with pain and fear.

"You didn't eat much last night," she commented, her voice strained, "and I thought you should have a good breakfast."

"Thanks, Mom," John told her, more gravely than he intended.

When he got up to go to work, he picked up the letter from

Selective Service to show Carl and Betty. After placing his dishes in the sink, he kissed and hugged his mom. She looked like she was about to cry, so he turned quickly away.

He drove slowly through the tunnel of trees to the campground, enjoying the interplay of light and shadow. He hoped that Carl was in the store with Betty, and he practiced what he would say to them on the way. In the end, he knew he would likely blurt it out. He parked, straightened his shoulders, and went into the store. The screen door banged loudly as he entered the store.

"Good morning, John!" Carl boomed. He stood with his ever-present cup of coffee, elbows on the counter. Betty stood next to him, smiling. John must have had some odd expression because Betty's grin faded, and she cocked her head, looking at John seriously.

"John? What's wrong, hon?" she asked, sensing a change in his demeanor.

John pulled the envelope from his back pocket and handed it to Carl before stating, "I've been called up."

Betty put a hand to her mouth and read the letter over Carl's shoulder.

"Two weeks," Carl commented, "not much time."

John nodded. "Would it do any good to go and enlist, Carl?"

Carl shook his head and returned the letter to John, saying sadly, "Whatever for, son? The deed is done. But what about your college deferment? You would be a junior this year.'"

"Bad luck," John answered ruefully.

"And, it's the way of war." He shook his head before saying, "This war..." and trailed off.

"Here," Carl said, handing John his letter back. "Put this in your car so that it's safe. We've got to work on the usual stuff today – the trash, the bathhouses, and chopping wood. We'll need to talk about your schedule in the next couple of weeks and what you want to do."

"I don't want to sit around," John blurted out impatiently. "I can't."

Carl nodded, understanding. Carl handed his coffee cup to Betty before telling John, "Okay then. Let's saddle up the golf cart and go and get that trash."

At the end of the day, he visited Ellie and Penny. Ellie was concentrating so hard on her piece of art that she didn't hear him approach. He looked at Ellie. Her head bent over her work. Her gorgeous honey-colored hair was tucked behind her ears, her tongue between her teeth, and her sure hands drew details with a black marker confidently on the t-shirt. He looked at her creation.

"Wow," he uttered, unsure if it was Ellie's visage, the t-shirt, or both that he was commenting on.

He startled Ellie, and she jumped before she turned and breathed his name. Her smile was infectious and filled with joy. Penny came around the corner of the camper and greeted him, and asked him to stay for dinner.

"I'm sorry, I need to get home to my folks tonight. But I have something I need to tell both of you."

The two women waited expectantly. John cleared his throat.

"I've been called up," he told them quietly, "I report in two weeks to go to basic training and then to Nam."

He heard Ellie suck in a breath and whisper, "no." And, he saw the confusion and the pain in her eyes that erased the joy that was there moments ago. He didn't have any words of comfort for her.

Aunt Penny broke their silence, "Oh, John. Oh..." She trailed off.

A heartbeat passed and he asked Ellie, "You okay to go for a walk?"

Ellie barely nodded before he took her hand, and Ellie grasped it like a lifeline. He pulled her to her feet and kept her hand in his. With her hand in his, he felt connected. It was as if the world was right when they were together. Melded together. They held hands with fingers tightly interwoven. Ellie still hadn't spoken.

They walked to the beach and sat on the sand. John tried to memorize the feeling of the sun on them and the feel of her hand in his.

"Oh, John," Ellie began but stopped.

"I know," he responded quietly.

They sat, looking at the water, the sky, and the Eastern shoreline—a boat whizzed by. There was the sound of children playing on the equipment near the green. Time passed. John wanted to hold each moment as if it was trapped in crystal.

Breaking their quietude, John stated, "I need to go home. I need to be with my folks. I needed you to know. I need you," he ended in a whisper.

Ellie nodded, understanding. John pulled her up. She looked into his eyes, which had darkened from their usual golden brown to something deeper. His emotions were a medley of love, desire, and fear of his unknown future. He held her for a few minutes and then pulled away. They walked back to Aunt Penny's in silence. This time, he didn't take her hand.

"We'll pick you up at about ten tomorrow morning," John told her.

John held her for a long moment again and didn't want to let her go. Finally, he pulled away from her, cradled her face between his hands, and kissed her, drinking her in with a deepening kiss. Ellie responded by threading her fingers behind his head and pulling him closer to kiss him more deeply. He didn't want to stop but pulled away, knowing he had to get home.

"I'm sorry," he whispered, resting his forehead against hers.

He turned and walked away, leaving Ellie staring after him while he squeezed his emotions into a tight kernel inside of himself. In the coming weeks, he knew he would keep the memory of that kiss alive and that it would get him through bad times.

LOUISA – 1918

*Human civilizations have been using glass since 3500 B.C. and
discarding it into large bodies of water.*

Emma was correct. The food, the bath, and the night's
sleep helped tremendously. Louisa was still worried
about Willie and wanted to get to the hospital as soon as
possible to see how he was doing.

Emma fussed, "What would you like for breakfast, Miss
Louisa? Are scrambled eggs all right? You'll need a good breakfast.
I think you need to wear a scarf today. It's cold out."

Louisa felt smothered. She didn't want to snap at this dear
lady over her concern.

Emma brought a plate to Louisa, overflowing with eggs, toast,
and potatoes. She leaned on the kitchen table. Louisa put her
hand over Emma's.

"It will be all right, Emma," Louisa told her gently. "You are
correct. What did Grandmama say, 'It will all come out in the
wash?'"

Emma laughed at that comment. "You're right, miss. That
dear lady said that a lot."

"You're a dear lady, too," Louisa told her and gave Emma an involuntary hug.

"Oh, you!" Emma cried, flapping a dish towel at Louisa.

Louisa stood and hugged her before leaving the kitchen, leaving Emma bright and teary-eyed.

When Louisa entered the hospital ward, she walked swiftly down the rows of beds until she reached Willie. There was something different about Willie. His eyes were closed, but his skin had a brighter tone. He was still holding the sea glass heart. There was something else. His bandage had been removed! Stubble grew around the wound, which now looked like it was healing.

"Willie?" Louisa said, surprise and hope in her tone.

Willie's head turned toward Louisa's voice.

"Lou...Louisa?" he asked in a quavering voice.

"Yes, Willie! Yes! It's Louisa!" Louisa nearly shouted in her joy.

"Willie," Louisa whispered, hoping against hope.

"Louisa," Willie breathed as he held onto the cobalt blue sea glass heart in one hand and reached for Louisa with the other. Louisa caught both his hands in hers. She didn't know how long they sat, holding hands with the sea glass heart. He looked into her eyes. They drank each other in.

Louisa gasped. "Can you see?" She bent her head to their hands. Tears streamed down her cheeks. She closed her eyes, so grateful Willie had come back. She knew in her heart that he likely had a long road of recovery ahead, but this was a start—a hope burned inside that everything might finally be all right.

"Loo- Louisa?" Willie asked, worry in his voice.

She raised her head and looked at him with shining eyes. She used her other hand to wipe away the tears.

"I'll be fine," she told Willie. "I am so glad that you have come back to me." She smiled a tremulous smile filled with joy. "I have so much to tell and catch you up on, Willie. But I must check in.

I'll return to you as often as possible and sit with you before I go home."

Louisa leaned down and kissed Willie on the cheek. He still held onto her hand. Louisa gently pulled her hand away from Willie's.

Nurse Williams looked at Louisa's face and commented, "So, you've seen him."

"Oh, yes," Louisa said, joy and hope filling her voice. "He can see! He talked to me. Oh, Nurse Williams, he's getting better. Louisa felt like swooning.

Nurse Williams put a hand on Louisa's arm before saying, "Louisa, this is a step, a small, first step. Yes, it's positive, but Willie has a long, long way to go with recovery."

Louisa's euphoric happiness was quelled, and she asked hesitantly, "How long?"

"Recovery will likely be nearly a year," Nurse Williams warned. "We'll get him started here at the hospital, but they'll most likely send him somewhere to recuperate fully. We really don't know. The brain is a funny thing. We don't know enough about how it works. Many people have ideas, but they're really a stab of light in the darkness. For example, the Brits have been sending the men to work on the farms, and they've seen excellent recovery from shell shock. We're just starting to look at this therapy as viable here in the United States."

"Sent away?" Louisa asked faintly, voicing disbelief. "A year?"

"Yes, Louisa," Nurse Williams said solemnly. "A year. You want him to be fully recovered, don't you?" she asked the girl standing before her. Louisa's bright and happy visage had turned pale.

It was as if Louisa woke up, "Of course! Of course, I want him to recuperate completely!" she stated, almost vehemently, yet added, "But, I don't want to see him go away again."

"Of course, you don't," Nurse Williams agreed stoutly. "And, in your heart, you know what's best for him. Willie will be here until the doctors think he is ready to go. We must get him on his feet before he can work on a farm."

Louisa spent a busy day assisting other nurses and tending to soldiers. Her heart and her mind drifted to Willie's bed. At the end of her shift, she returned to Willie's bedside with Nurse Williams. She had him sitting up. He looked frail and a wisp of the man she knew, but he smiled at her. She sat beside him and took his hand. Her heart was too full to speak. She knew Willie would recuperate, and her throat was tight with emotion. She tried to communicate her joy through their interlaced fingers.

"I have so much to tell you, Willie," Louisa said, "and I'm not sure I know where to begin."

Forty-Two

WILLIE – 1918

Port Townsend, Washington, has a glass beach near McCurdy Point.

Willie felt like he had been awakened from a nightmare. The hospital's lights were astoundingly bright. He looked about, drinking in details of the hospital ward with the bustling nurses and the patients in their beds. Willie was in awe of the bustling figures moving through the ward like a well-oiled machine. The nurses in their starched white caps and uniforms looked like swans gliding in and out of the hospital ward. He was never so grateful to see the light and movement. Light streamed in from windows, making the area brighter. He reveled in seeing the subtle changes of color in the monochromatic hospital ward. He wished he could see out the window, to see the colors of the bay and perhaps some green grass or trees.

Nurse Williams came by and greeted him, "Hello, Willie. We're going to work on getting you back on your feet."

His head jerked to look her in the eyes. "Really?" Hope blossomed on his face.

She chuckled. "Really, Willie. But it will take a lot of work on your part. First, we need to get the blood flowing back into your legs. So, we will have you sit and dangle your legs over the bed."

"W-when can I walk?"

"Not so fast, young man. This is a process. Unfortunately, it is slow. I've alerted physiotherapy that you will come to them soon. They'll come to assess you soon." She gave Willie the information as she worked to shift him so that his legs dangled over the edge of the bed, not quite touching the floor.

"There now, won't that be a nice surprise for Louisa when she comes in today? She can sit right beside you on the bed."

"Louisa," Willie said, not stuttering this time.

"Louisa," Nurse Williams corroborated. "You have a fine young woman there, Willie."

He nodded.

"Can I bring you anything?" Nurse Williams asked.

He glanced around the ward, looking at the other soldiers in their beds. Most were lying in bed, but there were a few propped up. One of them held a book.

"A newspaper or a book?" he asked.

"I'll see what I can do," Nurse Williams told him.

A few minutes later, she returned with a newspaper. "Here you are, young man. We're currently scarce on books, sharing them with so many young men. Perhaps Louisa can bring one or two in from home. I suspect she has a few," Nurse Williams suggested.

Willie nodded but was anxious to read the news, and Nurse Williams left him to read. Willie drank in the words and the pictures. There were several articles about the war and about local soldiers that had lost their lives with a listing of numbers of if they lost their lives via killed in action, wounds, or dying of disease.

He had to put the newspaper down for minutes after reading that article. He looked around the ward of the hospital. Despite the moans and injuries, Willie and these men were the lucky ones. They had made it out of France alive.

He remembered the starkness of the burned-out land, the muddy trenches, and the overwhelming smell of death. It disturbed him that he and his comrades became casual about finding bodies. Some men frequently made fun of dead Huns by putting silly things on their heads and in their hands. Sometimes, they put a burning cigarette between a dead man's lips, and they would laugh and laugh and laugh. Willie never found it funny, but he knew it was their way of coping with the atrocities of the war. They were all living moment by moment, thinking at any time a bullet or a shell would erase the possibility of living another day. Willie's legs began to shake on their own. He willed them to stop. The newspaper shook. He looked helplessly at his trembling limbs. He looked wildly around, but no nurses were in sight. He wished Louisa were here.

Louisa. Her presence brought him peace. He thought about her beautiful eyes, smiling mouth, and shining hair. He breathed deeply, keeping an image of Louisa in his mind. His limbs slowed their quivering and eventually stopped. He breathed a sigh of relief.

Willie returned to reading the newspaper. He read stories of Hun atrocities and an article on a bank merger. Willie was astounded by the high prices since the onset of the war. Men's shoes were now $6.98! How on earth could anyone afford those prices? He marveled at all the advertisements for potions and pills to stop liver disease, brighten skin, and relieve catarrh. A few pages in were stories about the Spanish Flu epidemic and how it hit the city and communities with a high number of illnesses and death. The articles described how life came to a standstill in many communities. Willie had not heard about schools and churches closing due to the flu. Willie read of a horrific account where a man died in the room where his wife had just given birth. The visiting nurses found them in a dreadful state. He read another article about how the Spanish Flu wiped out entire villages of native people in Alaska. Willie thought the Spanish Flu was akin to the plague in the 14th century.

And then, Willie spied a small article buried in a column on page four. It was brief, but it told of deaths from the Spanish Flu on the Eastern Shore. Willie's heart went cold. What about his mother? He wondered if she had been affected by this flu. What if she were dead? He shivered at the thought and felt a coldness in his belly. There wasn't anyone that knew he was in Baltimore. He felt hollow from fear.

Forty-Three

ELLIE – 1969

Spectacle Island, near Quincy, Massachusetts, is a former dump site and is popular with glassers.

Ellie pressed her fingers to her lips as if to seal in John's kiss. She wanted the tingling and yearning to last forever. She wanted to get lost in his kisses and body and for him to get lost in hers. Her core was held hostage with pleasant tingling and butterflies. The anticipation of what they couldn't have right now and the desire filled her. And she wanted John with every fiber of her being. She watched him walk down the road, and it took all of her will not to call him back. She wanted to kiss him more and for the two of them to get so lost in the kiss that it would transport them to another time and place, and John wouldn't have to go to war. She stood as still as a statue, staring unseeingly down the road where John had walked. That was how Aunt Penny found her a few minutes later.

"Ellie? Ellie? Are you all right?" Aunt Penny asked her in a worried tone.

Something in Aunt Penny's voice snapped Ellie out of her contemplation. She turned to face her aunt before saying, "I don't think anything will be right ever again. That is, at least, until John returns home safe and sound. This stupid, stupid war!" she ended passionately crying out. She hugged herself tightly and squeezed her eyes shut.

Aunt Penny went and tightly put her arms around Ellie. Her eyes were filled with tears, and she nodded in agreement, her head against Ellie's bright hair, stating, "It's not a nice thing to say, but you're in the boat of millions of women, watching their men go to war for millennia."

Ellie stiffened and twisted around until she faced Aunt Penny. She gave her a sharp look.

"Look, darlin', don't shoot the messenger. You know I'm all for 'make love, not war,' and have been criticized for my hippie stand. But I don't understand why 'hippies' are labeled as bad when peacekeepers are revered throughout the world. Look at Dr. Martin Luther King, Gandhi, and even Mr. Rogers! It's all the same message. Our time is short on this earth. Be positive and be kind."

"But that seems to keep getting beaten down – all the time," Ellie complained wearily.

"I know," Aunt Penny agreed. "But we need to fight that attitude." She changed the subject, "I just happen to have one more scarf. Why don't you make something to give to John's mother tomorrow? When it's done, we can head to the laundromat to heat set it in the dryer."

"Hmm, that's a good idea, but I want to discuss this more. It's so unfair," Ellie said.

"Yes, it's incredibly unfair," Penny agreed. "But, make something beautiful, and some of the sting will go away. I promise."

Ellie was soon focused on creating a lovely scarf for John's mother. She drew a myriad of brightly colored flowers that radiated color beyond their outline of black. Blues, pinks, peaches, and lavenders filled the scarf with splotches of green to represent leaves. When she sprayed the alcohol on the markers, the colors spread and merged into a quilt of color. The design had the movement of modern art pieces, but the colors were gentler. Ellie sat back in satisfaction, looking at her creation. She could imagine John's mother tying the scarf over her hair or around her neck. She hoped she would like it.

Ellie let the scarf dry. The heat had built in the late afternoon, and it took only a few minutes to dry the scarf in the hot sun before taking it to the laundromat. Aunt Penny collected Ellie, the t-shirt she created, and the scarves, and they walked to the laundromat. A few coins and minutes yielded the completed scarves, heat set, and ready to be sold or given away.

It was getting late, and Betty came around to lock up the laundromat for the night.

"Ooh! What do you have there?" she asked when she spied the brightly colored fabric.

"Ellie's new creation," Penny announced proudly. "Aren't they gorgeous!"

Betty touched the scarves almost reverently before saying, "Ellie, I think you're on to something here. These should sell very well. Maybe you should look at a gallery? The farmers' market is fine, but these scarves would be perfect for a high-end gift shop or gallery. There's one in Deerton, I believe."

"Thank you, Betty," Ellie returned, blushing a little. "We're going to send for more scarves on Monday."

"Good idea. These will sell like hotcakes," Betty said. "Now, I need to lock up and get home to cook Carl his dinner." She looked soberly at Ellie, saying, "I was sorry to hear John's news."

Ellie gulped down her emotions. Her eyes filled up. Betty put an arm around her and gave her a small hug. Ellie worked to keep her emotions under control.

"Thank you, Betty. Us too," Penny said, giving Ellie a moment.

The next morning, Ellie paced the camper nervously, waiting for John and his parents to pick her up. The potato salad sat on the counter, and the scarf was tied prettily with a colorful ribbon Aunt Penny found.

"Relax!" Aunt Penny scolded. "You're going to have a marvelous day. Betterton is a lovely spot on the bay."

Ellie sat at the edge of the couch and smoothed her pants.

"Do I look all right?" she asked Aunt Penny for the hundredth time.

"You look lovely," Aunt Penny insisted. "Perfect for a picnic at the beach."

Ellie wore her chambray pedal pushers and the t-shirt she created yesterday. She also took along her swimsuit and towel, 'just in case.' She stood up again after just a minute and checked on the potato salad and her tote bag on the counter.

"They're here," Aunt Penny announced as she heard a car pull up. Ellie gathered her things and went outside. John had hopped out of the car and come up to the door. He greeted Ellie with a kiss on the cheek and looked at her appreciatively. She smiled up at him, albeit a little nervously until Penny went to the car to chat with John's parents. John opened the trunk. He shifted the nylon webbed folding chairs on top and tucked Ellie's bowl of potato salad and her tote bag alongside a cooler. There was a big, round aluminum thermos that rattled with ice cubes when he pushed it aside to make room for Ellie's things. John opened the door for Ellie, and she climbed in.

"Hello, Mr. and Mrs. Black," she greeted as she slid into the seat.

"Good morning, Ellie," Mr. Black returned.

John's mother was still chatting to Aunt Penny.

"I'll stop chattering," Aunt Penny said. "Have a wonderful time!"

"We intend to," Mrs. Black returned with a grin.

They waved at Aunt Penny and drove off, maneuvering through walkers, bicycles, children, and golf carts to get to the main road. Ellie had the scarf in her lap. John took her hand, which helped quell the butterflies in her stomach. She leaned towards the front seat and handed the scarf to Mrs. Black.

"What's this?" Mrs. Black asked as the small package came over the seat and tapped her on the shoulder.

"It's a new thing I'm working on," Ellie explained.

Mrs. Black untied the ribbon and opened the scarf. She audibly sucked in her breath with an 'Oh!' of delight. "Ellie, this is gorgeous!" she exclaimed. "Thank you! I will cherish this."

"You're welcome," Ellie replied. "Thank you for inviting me today."

Mrs. Black craned around and said, "I'm so pleased you like sea glass! We're going to have such fun on our treasure hunt."

Mr. Black made a noise that wasn't quite enthusiastic, but he smiled at his wife indulgently. They drove south towards Betterton. The suburbs of Deerton gave way to open land on either side of the road where corn was peeping a few inches above the ground. Ellie held her breath as they crossed the tall, arching bridge over the C&D canal.

"Look there!" Mrs. Black called out. "Look at that tanker!"

Indeed, a tanker and a tug boat were motoring its way just beyond the bridge to the Bay.

"Have you been down this way, Ellie?" Mr. Black asked.

"Not since I was a little girl. We used to have relatives that lived in the Tolchester area," Ellie answered.

"It was so sad when they knocked down the amusement park and built houses," Mrs. Black said mournfully. "There's good glassing there, too, if you can get on the marina property. We stopped once when we were cruising on a friend's boat."

Ellie's memories of Tolchester were dim. She remembered a rather dilapidated amusement park and some big houses. Her mother told her of steamships that used to come to Tolchester Beach and how it was extremely popular before they opened up the Chesapeake Bay Bridge and made it convenient for people to vacation in Ocean City. The bridge was the downfall of many of the Chesapeake Bay resorts.

"Betterton was a destination beach, like Tolchester," Mrs. Black said. "They had steamboats, beach clubs, and boarding houses. You would never know it today."

They crossed a drawbridge over the Sassafras River. Boats hugged the marinas like cats crowding around bowls of milk. It looked like a picture from a postcard or calendar. It was so picturesque.

"This area is quite historical. Do you know the story of Kitty Knight?" Mr. Black asked Ellie.

She shook her head, and realizing he couldn't see her, she answered, "No."

"In 1813, British troops burned Georgetown to the ground. They made their way up the Sassafras River. Kitty Knight was caring for an invalid neighbor and refused to leave, telling the British they would need to burn her in the house. And, believe it or not, the British general agreed and let her go. She's a legend in these parts, and they say she haunts the old place," he finished his story and pointed to the stately brick home perched on the shore of the river.

"Where's your home, Ellie?" Mr. Black asked.

"Roland Park is where I grew up," Ellie answered.

Mrs. Black gave a soft 'oh' in surprise, obviously knowing and noting it was a premier suburb of Baltimore.

They drove further south, where the land was leveled and flat, with colonial and Federalist homes rising out of the fields every so often between farms. Mr. Black went on about the history along the way. He turned right off the main road, and they drove into Betterton. Beautiful, tall Victorian homes lined the street on the way to the beach. Ellie could see the bay, and Mr. Black drove down a hill and turned into a small parking lot.

They all took turns carrying the cooler and other food to the small, grassy picnic area across the street at the edge of a wide sandy beach.

"Let's go, Ellie! Let's get some glassing in while the charcoal is heating up," Mrs. Black told her.

They left Mr. Black in charge of the grill, and Mrs. Black, John, and Ellie went to the beach where families had gathered. Mrs. Black led them to one end by the rock pilings and systematically walked up the beach, looking at the tideline and the shallows. Occasionally, she would make an excited sound and reach down to pick up a piece of sea glass from the sand or the shallows. She ran back to show Ellie and John a piece of sanded green, white, or brown glass. Ellie found a few pieces. John just held her hand and watched her with a smile. He was at the water's edge.

Suddenly, he pulled away from Ellie and stopped, staring at the water.

"Could it be?" he said softly, staring at the shadows of pebbles in the water. He peered at the shallow water with the sun glinting off the small wavelets. He turned and cocked his head first one way and then another.

A boat zoomed by, creating a wake, and small waves started approaching the shore.

"No!" cried John, and he dove into the shallows to pluck out a dark piece of what Ellie thought was a rock.

John looked at it and cried out, "Yes! Yes!"

"What is it, John?" his mom hurried back to him.

He rinsed off the piece from the shallows, scrubbing it with sand to clean off a millennium of dirt. He held it up to the light, and there was a glint of blue in the bright sunlight.

"Whoa, John!" his mom, "That's an amazing piece! Cobalt blue! I can't believe it! It's huge!"

And it was huge, as large as a fifty-cent piece. It had ridges, but it had also been in a bonfire to the point where the glass had bubbled and reformed.

"Oh, John," Ellie breathed when he handed her the piece of

cobalt blue glass. She held it reverently, holding it in her hand and then raising it to the light. Mrs. Black came up beside her.

"I wonder what it was?" she breathed close to Ellie's ear, bending over her to look at the piece of glass. "Definitely old. A piece of bonfire glass. It looks as though parts of it were melted. And there are ridges underneath that melted part."

Ellie took it in her hand and marveled at the piece as she turned it over and over in her hand. John grinned a silly, triumphant grin. Ellie reached her hand up to touch his face and kiss him.

"Thank you," she whispered, and she kissed him again.

Forty-Four

JOHN – 1969

Abacos Islands in the Northern Bahamas have good spots for glassing.

John whistled triumphantly and draped an arm around his mother's shoulders and the other around Ellie's.

"Wow," his mom kept whispering reverently, looking at the piece of glass in Ellie's hand. "That's an unbelievable find, John."

John was happy Ellie loved the piece of glass he found. It was quite a prize! Pleased with himself, he pulled away from the ladies and ran ahead, doing an impromptu cartwheel and then another as they returned to their picnic area. He received the intended reaction of their delighted laughter at his antics. Then they reached the picnic area, where his mom rushed ahead and gushed about the glass they had found. John watched his dad nod, pacifying his mom with gentle, soothing noises of agreement. Since his father had started grilling the hamburgers and hotdogs, Ellie, John, and his mom set up the rest of the food.

They spent the rest of the day relaxing on the beach. John and Ellie went swimming and then lay on the hot sand. The reality that this would be the last day to enjoy this with Ellie and his family hit him in the gut. He closed his eyes, trying to etch each moment into his soul. When he opened his eyes, he turned to Ellie next to him on the blanket, her skin still glistening from water droplets that beaded up on her smooth, tanned skin. He touched her arm, tracing a water droplet that traveled down her arm to drip off onto the blanket. Ellie shivered. He was acutely aware of every inch of her body.

Ellie sensed something. She turned to look at him. Her movement sent a fresh wave of the coconut smell of her sun tan lotion and the smell of the bay. He breathed in the scent. A hint of Ellie was in that wave, too. He smiled.

"Are you okay?" she whispered, her head close to his shoulder.

She looked up at him with those huge, blue eyes, now filled with concern.

Was everything okay? No. The nightmare of Vietnam lay heavy on him.

"No," he croaked out in an emotive whisper. "I'm not okay."

Ellie squeezed his hand and rested her head on his shoulder. Her honey-colored hair with red, brown, and gold highlights sparkled in the sunshine. He breathed in her scent again. There was something about Ellie that made him feel whole. Even their slightest glance or touch left him feeling complete.

On the way home, he laced his fingers through Ellie's. It wasn't as though the day had a pall over it, but each one in the car was cognizant that this might be the last picnic together for a long time. John felt the eyes of his mother on him. She had twisted around in the front seat to glance at them both, picking up on John's distress. Emotions welled up, and he turned to look out the window instead of meeting her eyes.

Two weeks. He wanted to manipulate time, to have it stretch to give him optimal time with Ellie. He wondered briefly if she would wait for him to return from Vietnam. Could they pick up where they left off, or would they both be irrevocably changed so much that they would be strangers to one another? He couldn't imagine being a stranger to Ellie. Now that they had met, he felt tied to her. He didn't think those bonds would break. Vietnam would stretch their bond and their love to its limits. Would they survive this?

When they dropped Ellie off at the camper, his parents gave them a moment of privacy. John gripped Ellie's arms and kissed her so thoroughly it sent them both reeling. He looked deeply into her eyes before kissing her lightly and returning to his parent's car.

Forty-Five

LOUISA – 1918

Maine's rocky coastline provides a bounty of hidden sea glass treasures.

Louisa wondered how Willie was faring today. When she got home the previous night, she grabbed Emma's arms and danced her around the kitchen, her uniform whipping wildly around her, regaling her with how Willie could see again and that he was also starting to talk. It had brought happy tears to both women. Now, she had to tell him some news and wasn't sure how.

Louisa had to skirt around a bunch of girls playing jump rope on the sidewalk. It was only after she passed them that their chant of "I had a little bird, and its name was Enza. I opened the window, and in flew Enza." The macabre jump-rope rhyme sent a shiver down her back.

Yesterday, she received a letter from Tolchester. It wasn't from Willie's mother but from Cora, one of the women who cleaned at the boarding house. The letter stated that Willie's mother couldn't answer Louisa's letters as the Spanish Flu had struck her and she was quite ill. The letter was dated the previous week.

When she reached the hospital, Louisa resolved to talk to Willie about his mother. Nurse Williams said he would work on physiotherapy for a long time and possibly rehabilitation at a farm for almost a year. She wasn't ready to say goodbye to him again. Not since she had just found him again after losing hope and losing Grandmama.

Louisa was surprised to find Willie sitting up in the bed. He was propped up by pillows and reading the newspaper.

"Oh, Willie, look at you!" she cried.

The eyes that looked up at her were not happy. They were filled with worry and laced with fear.

Instantly, Louisa was sobered. She sat carefully on the bed beside him and rested her hand on his.

"Willie, what's wrong?"

He was quiet for a minute and then two.

"Willie?" she asked again.

"The Eastern Shore," he croaked out, "Tolchester, it's been hit hard with the Spanish flu. I'm worried, Louisa. I'm worried about Mama."

"I am too, Willie." And then she confessed, "I wrote a few letters to your mother to let her know you were here. I hadn't heard from her. Yesterday, I received a letter from Cora."

Willie's face blanched.

"No! No!" Louisa cried, "She's alive, Willie. She had the Spanish flu, and she survived! But Cora said she's still very ill and weak. I was coming today to talk to you about it. What would you like me to do? How can I help?"

"Would you go to her, Louisa? Could you go to Tolchester and care for my mother?" Willie asked in a hopeful voice.

Louisa hadn't thought of that. It made her pause. She could go. Nothing was holding her to Baltimore except Willie's presence in the hospital.

"I can go," she told Willie. "And I can take Emma with me.

Let me talk with Nurse Williams for a bit." She patted his hand. "I'll be right back."

Louisa found Nurse Williams in the office area, updating charts in her neat and elegant hand. She looked up when Louisa entered the room and smiled grandly.

"Louisa, good morning. How are you? Did you see Willie sitting up?" Nurse Williams asked brightly.

"It's wonderful that he's sitting up, Nurse Williams! I'm so happy he is progressing," Louisa returned.

Nurse Williams nodded. "Physiotherapy will be coming today or tomorrow to work with him. I am expecting great things from that young man."She looked again at Louisa, and her forehead creased with worry. "What's troubling you, Louisa?"

Louisa sat heavily on the straight-backed wooden chair near the desk. She spilled out her story of Willie's mother, the letters, Willie reading the paper, and his request.

"Of course, you must go to her! We will miss you here dreadfully. You are a tremendous worker. And Willie will be fine. It might be good because it will spurn him on to get better to get to his mother and be near you. When are you planning on leaving?"

Flummoxed, Louisa stared at Nurse Williams and said hesitatingly, "I, I don't know. This has happened so suddenly. I suppose I must go home, prepare, and get tickets for the steamship. I need to go back and tell Willie, too. And go home and talk to Emma and get word to Bertha. Oh, my!" she ended, realizing the preparations that needed to take place. Her head swam with the details and responsibilities of necessary tasks to complete before she left for Tolchester. Louisa put out a hand to steady herself.

Nurse Williams told Louisa, "Steady on, Louisa. Just take it one step at a time. Take one step, do it well, and then move on to the next step. You will be fine."

"Will you write to me?" Louisa asked, somewhat mournfully.

"Of course!" Nurse Williams assured Louisa.

Louisa stood up and gave Nurse Williams an impromptu hug,

which was returned. She looked into the older woman's eyes and saw true friendship there. She could count on Nurse Williams. Then she returned to Willie and sat beside him on the bed. She took his hand and filled him in on what Nurse Williams said. Willie's worried look cleared when he heard the news.

"I'm going to go home now and break the news to Emma, and we'll start planning the trip. I will come to see you tomorrow before I leave, Willie."

"Thank you, Louisa." He pulled her hand up to his mouth to kiss it.

She wanted Willie to kiss her, but with the Spanish Flu, they advised kissing through a mask or with a 'kissing screen.' She had had only one kiss from him, which had been stolen the night before she left Tolchester. She had not forgotten the feel of his lips on hers and often dreamed of it.

"Willie, I..." Louisa broke off and was bold. She kissed him.

Cheers and catcalls erupted around the ward until a nurse called, "Pipe down, men!"

Louisa turned several shades of crimson at her boldness. Willie just grinned at her. She remembered that grin from last summer. It was the one that she had fallen in love with. Louisa hurried out of the ward.

Emma was surprised to see her and asked if everything was all right when Louisa came home before lunch.

"Let me put on the kettle for a cup of tea, and I can tell you everything," Louisa told Emma.

She made a strong pot of tea and sat at the well-scrubbed kitchen table where Emma was waiting. Also on the table was a small plate of molasses cookies, one of Emma's specialties and Louisa's favorites.

Emma pushed the plate towards Louisa, saying, "I made a batch of these this morning. I thought you could take Mr. Willie a few of them."

"Thank you, Emma," Louisa said, taking a cookie from the

plate and biting into it. The warm cookie, dusted with sugar, melted in her mouth. "Oh, Emma, these are so very good."

"You need to finish that cookie, have a sip of tea, and tell me what's on your mind," Emma ordered. "It looks as though you have something about to burst out of you. What's happened?"

Louisa did as she was told. Over the tea, she told Emma about the letter from Cora and Willie's fears about his mother. She looked pleadingly at Emma, asking her to accompany her to Tolchester.

"We will go and take care of the dear lady," Emma insisted. "I can rustle up some provisions to take along as well." She thought for a minute. "We'll need to get word to Bertha. She can check on the house and care for it when her family is on the mend. You need to go to the bank and also get our tickets. Do you want to go tomorrow?" she asked Louisa.

Louisa nodded. "As soon as possible, I think. It's been a week since that letter was written. I am worried about his mother."

"Then let's get cracking!" Emma insisted.

Louisa pushed herself up from the table, catching Emma's enthusiasm. She called for a cab to take her to the bank and the station. When she had secured funds and the tickets, she dropped by the hospital again, taking Willie some of Emma's cookies.

Willie was lying in bed again, his eyes closed. Louisa hovered nearby. As if sensing her presence, he opened his eyes and smiled when he saw her. He moved over so she could perch herself on the edge of the bed. She filled him in on all that had occurred since she saw him that morning.

"Can you sit up?" she asked. "I have something for you."

Willie nodded and worked to sit up when Louisa fetched pillows to support his body.

"Emma made these for you." Louisa produced a small box tied up with white string. She undid the string and opened the box. The warm, rich scent of molasses cookies and fresh baking wafted out of the box.

"These are the best cookies," Louisa insisted.

Willie took a bite and agreed. Louisa updated Willie on her departure plans.

"I'll try to stop by before we leave tomorrow," Louisa assured Willie. "What I need you to do is to get better, get stronger, and come to Tolchester. But now, I must go and help Emma."

Willie grasped her hand as she stood to go. "I love you, Louisa. I have from the first moment I saw you."

Stunned, Louisa stared at Willie. These were the words she had been waiting and waiting to hear. His words almost seemed surreal, as if everything was a dream. But then she awoke, and her face broke into a huge smile because she realized it wasn't a dream. It was real. "Oh, Willie, I love you too!" she exclaimed.

"And I will get well so we can begin our lives together as we are meant to be," he told her.

Forty-Six

ELLIE – 1969

With its nearly 11,000 miles of coastline, the Chesapeake Bay is a veritable scoop that harbors sea glass on the beaches of its coves and tributaries.

Ellie's emotions roller-coasted. She went from elation when she was with John to despair when he left her. During the time in between, she felt ill at the thought of him heading to Vietnam. She was restless and couldn't concentrate.

John stopped by after his work, and Ellie threw herself into his arms. They stood, their heartbeats settling into a joint rhythm. She breathed in John's sweet, salty, and slightly spicy smell as she buried her face into his neck. Having him hold her gave her a sense of peace.

"Swim?" he murmured in her ear.

She nodded into his shoulder. "Sure," she answered softly and pulled away from him to change. The bay shallows were warm, and John and Ellie floated on the water on their backs, holding hands. An occasional swell from a passing boat lifted their bodies as if they were traveling on a cloud. They didn't speak. Ellie looked at the intense blue of the sky. A bald eagle soared above them. She wanted to memorize each moment with John. This was a moment to keep. It was very dreamlike, and time didn't seem to exist. She floated on the water and floated in a dream.

Ellie didn't know how long they floated. A tern dove for an insect and splashed nearby, causing Ellie to jerk breaking her trance. She panicked briefly when her feet didn't touch the bottom and looked at John, who was laughing. They had drifted out quite far and needed to tread water to stay afloat. Without speaking, they both swam towards the shore until they could stand.

"Will you write to me?" John asked, a note of pleading in his voice.

"Oh, John," Ellie said with a sigh. "Of course. Letters and letters," she promised.

He reached for and held her, the swells lifting them slightly off their feet. She felt so safe and protected when he held her. Ellie closed her eyes, memorizing the feeling. They pulled apart, and Ellie knew John had to go.

Forty-Seven

JOHN – 1969

UV sea glass, or glass that glows under a black light is also known as fluorescent glass.

John had a hard time walking away from Ellie that afternoon. He was so torn between spending time with his parents and spending time with Ellie. Fear of the unknown was eating him up from the inside. Ellie's presence, no Ellie's essence, quelled some of the fear.

He contemplated as he drove home, wondering about Ellie. He thought he fell in love from that first glance of her when the sunlight glinted off her hair and the wind ruffled the gauzy little dress she wore as a cover-up. Now that he knew her better, he loved her laugh, her passion, her independence, and yet, she was an innocent. He wanted to protect her.

He also wanted to do something special with her before he left for boot camp and Vietnam. He found his mom weeding her flower bed when he was home. He dropped to his haunches and pulled some weeds, too.

"Mom, I need your help," he confessed, "I want to have a special date with Ellie before I leave for boot camp. Do you have any ideas? I thought about a picnic by the lighthouse or a nice dinner somewhere. What do you think?"

"John, that's a lovely idea. What about Longwood Gardens? That's romantic, and they have a restaurant there."

"That's a good idea, mom. She would like that, but I don't know," he ended frustrated. "Nothing seems quite 'right.' Going to the gardens or a museum is cool, but I want something *really* special."

"She loves glassing. Maybe go to the Delaware beaches? Old New Castle is lovely, and you can walk along Battery Park. Or, get a couple of kayaks and head south to the small islands in the southern bay. I've always wanted to do that." His mom's eyes got a faraway look. "They say you can find shark teeth and artifacts like clay pipes and stems on the southern part of the Chesapeake Bay," she said dreamily.

"You might have something there, Mom," John replied.

"I have it!" his mom's eyes sparkled, and she snapped her fingers. She pulled John's head close to hers and whispered her ideas.

John nodded, his eyes lighting up, too. "That's perfect."

He and his mom called to make arrangements. Afterward, he called Carl and Penny.

It was difficult for John not to grin when he was with Ellie the next day.

"What is up?" she questioned, "You look like a Cheshire Cat!"

"Nothing," John said innocently, "Just happy to be with you." He pulled her in for a kiss.

He told Ellie he would work just a few more days with Carl and Betty. Carl was looking for someone to take his place. He was apparently asking around town and placed an ad in the local newspaper.

"I still want to keep things as normal as possible until I go," John insisted.

"How can you pretend like that?" Ellie asked, exasperated.

"I'm not pretending inside," John admitted. "I'm scared as hell. Sometimes, I feel like I will start screaming and never stop. Ellie," he said, putting his forehead to hers, "Ellie, you are my sanity."

He kissed her then, and she started to cry. She didn't make any noise, but tears seeped from her eyes and flowed down her face."

"I'm sorry," she whispered. "I'm trying hard to be brave. I keep thinking I'll wake up, and everything will be normal again." Her face crumpled a little before she said, "And it's not."

John put his arms around her and held her, "I know," he whispered back.

He let Ellie cry a little. She wiped away the tears with the back of her hand.

Look at me, Ellie," he commanded.

Ellie turned her face up, and her eyes met his. John was stolid in his answer, "I love you, Ellie. And I'm not saying that lightly. If I don't say it now, I may never have the chance to say it. That's the truth, and that won't change. That's what will get us through this."

Forty-Eight

LOUISA – 1918

Like marbles, old dice, and toys are prized collectibles by glassers.

L ouisa and Emma packed up their things. Emma packed provisions as well to take to Tolchester. They stopped by the hospital on the way to the steamship. It was there that Louisa introduced Emma to Willie for the first time.

"Ma'am, it's a pleasure to meet you. I can't thank you enough for going to care for my mama," Willie told Emma. "And thank you for those cookies!" His serious face changed to his mischievous grin, and Emma was charmed.

"We only have a moment," Louisa told him. "The steamship should get us to Tolchester this afternoon. It's the packet boat for mail?" she asked him questioningly.

Willie nodded. "Yes, from the Old Star Line. It brings passengers, mail, and goods from Baltimore to the Eastern Shore. Then, it heads to Virginia on an overnight voyage. That's something I'd like to do sometime." His attention then his thoughts returned to Tolchester. "When you get to Tolchester, Louisa, see if you can find old Burt. He should be around if the flu didn't get him. He's been around forever and can help you with whatever you need. Cora's a good sort, too."

"That's who wrote to me," Louisa reminded him.

Louisa was distracted by Emma's foot tapping. She glanced at her and raised her eyes to the clock on the wall. Willie followed her glance. His face clouded. Every tick of the clock meant they would be separated. Louisa was torn between wanting to go to his mother and selfishly wanting to stay with him.

"We need to go," Louisa told him. "I'll write to you and let you know how things are going."

She leaned over to kiss Willie on the cheek, but he pulled her face over to kiss her on the mouth.

"I must go," she whispered.

He nodded. "Take care of her, please, Emma."

"I will, Mr. Willie. We'll hopefully see you sooner than later," Emma told him.

They took a cab from the hospital to the port. Louisa took a long, last look at Baltimore and wondered when they would return. The rumble along the cobblestone streets and the sounds of train and boat whistles were well-known and welcome noises to Louisa. She wondered briefly how quiet Tolchester must be without the crowds at the amusement park. Willie had told her it was eerily quiet. She shivered slightly as they pulled up to the terminal. There was their steamship at the dock. The excitement of their new adventure blocked some of her trepidation. She convinced herself she could do this. No, she would do this for Willie. They boarded the boat, and Louisa glanced at the clock tower that topped the terminal as it faded from her sight as the steamship left the port of Baltimore.

Emma tucked herself into the stateroom. It was virtually empty, except for a couple of traveling salesmen heading to Virginia. A rather lazy steward eventually approached Emma and Louisa to bring them hot tea and two pastries that were worse for wear. Louisa took a bite and nearly spat it out into her napkin.

"Stale," she muttered to Emma as dry crumbs made her cough.

Emma urged her to drink more tea. Louisa took a large gulp of tea to soften the rough crumbs and coughed as lady-like as she could into her napkin. She glanced around for the steward to get a glass of water, but he had disappeared.

She looked out the large windows. The clouds were a palette of grays in swirling dramatic sweeps of the firmament. She could almost see the edge of the Eastern shore. She was excited and nervous. What if Willie's mother didn't want them there? What would they do? Where would they go? A sinking feeling settled in her stomach. What if this was a fool's errand? She was doing what her grandmama always scolded her for, rushing headlong into things without thinking them through.

Forty-Nine

Carnival glass lends an iridescent shimmer to the sea glass.

Willie was melancholy. He lay in bed, staring at the ceiling and picking at the bedclothes. He had no interest in the comings and goings on the ward today. Louisa was gone. He missed her. He was glad she would check on his mother, but still, he missed her.

Nurse Williams came by to check on him and asked, "Why the long face, Willie?"

"Louisa's gone," he muttered.

"I know, but she's going to help your mother. I suspect she will write to you right away. Anyways, you will be starting physiotherapy today. That will keep your mind occupied. We're going to get you up and able to walk so you can run to Louisa."

Willie responded, almost wistfully, "That would be nice."

"You need to believe it, Willie. I truly believe that's half the battle. Believe you are well, and you will get well. You are young and strong and have a beautiful young woman who loves you very much."

Willie blushed and confessed, "The feeling is mutual."

"Good," Nurse Williams said stoutly. "That love will get you through a lot of hard times. And believe me, there are always some hard times. I call the wedding ring "the badge of courage" no matter how much in love you are."She paused and added, "I'm not jumping the gun, am I, Willie? You are planning on proposing to Louisa, aren't you?"

"First, I need to walk," Willie said determinedly. "Where are those physiotherapists?"

He tried to sit up. Nurse Williams took his arm and assisted him. This time, she asked him to scoot to the edge and let his feet touch the floor. The soles of his feet reacted to the cold of the floor. He jerked. Nurse Williams smiled.

"That's the spirit, Willie," Nurse Williams cheered. "I'll fetch some socks and slippers and check on the physiotherapists. We'll get you on your feet sooner rather than later. Won't that be a wonderful surprise for Louisa?"

The physiotherapists took Willie to a room where they started with massage therapy and a series of exercises. He was shocked at the pain he experienced as he tried to get old muscles to move again. They warned him it would be quite painful. They weren't kidding. They stood Willie for only a moment. He cried out in pain and collapsed.

The physical therapy wore him out. It took weeks and weeks of small steps, stumbling and falling, and pain. He remembered the children's tale of *The Little Mermaid*. In the story, the little mermaid said it felt like walking on knives when she got her legs. Willie could relate. He gritted his teeth at the pain and pushed one. One foot, three feet, the length of short walks were slow. He gritted his teeth in frustration. Willie was determined. Despite the pain, he was so fatigued that he slept dreamlessly and without nightmares.

In the coming weeks, they strapped weights on his feet and worked to strengthen the muscles. They massaged his legs regularly. Each day, they encouraged him to take more steps. He was determined to walk. Baby step by baby step, Willie was learning to walk again. It was a triumph when he walked to the end of the ward, raising cheers from his comrades and the nurses. He could do this. The next time he saw Louisa, he would walk to her and give her a good, sound kiss.

Fifty

ELLIE – 1969

Frozen Charlottes are small Victorian porcelain dolls prized by sea glass collectors.

Ellie was making Aunt Penny a second cup of coffee when she heard a car pull up and stop outside the camper. She had to pay attention to the boiling water flowing through the drip cone and couldn't look out to see who it was. A moment later, there was a knock at the door. Where was Aunt Penny? Ellie thought she was sitting outside.

"Come in," she called and pulled the dripping cone from the cup before it overflowed.

Ellie heard the squeak of the camper door, and John came inside, grinning at her.

"Hi!" she said, delighted to see him but confused, as he should have been with Carl somewhere on the grounds.

John laughed at her confused look.

"Hi," he answered and explained, "I have the day off. I have the entire day to spend with you."

"Oh!" Ellie began to reply, but John took two steps and

pulled her to him when Aunt Penny came through the door as he was about to kiss her.

"Thanks for the coffee," Aunt Penny said. "And you," she said pointedly to Ellie, "need to get dressed."

"Where are we going?" she asked, looking at John and Aunt Penny.

"It's a surprise," they chorused and grinned at one another.

"Wear your mermaid dress," Aunt Penny advised, "and get a hat and sunglasses."

Confused but delighted there was a surprise, Ellie went to change, following Aunt Penny's directive to wear the mermaid dress and to get her hat and sunglasses. John eyed her appreciatively when she stepped out of the camper where he and Aunt Penny were waiting. Her insides tingled in anticipation.

"Have fun!" Aunt Penny told them as John took her hand. Ellie was surprised as John led her past his car and walked toward the beach.

"Where are we going?" Ellie asked.

"You'll see," John promised, smiling mischievously.

He led Ellie past the beach to the marina. He walked her onto the dock to a gorgeous sailboat waiting at the end.

The captain greeted them with a "Welcome aboard!" and introduced himself as Joe.

He gave them a brief tour of the boat and settled them on cushioned seats in the cockpit. "Let's get underway, shall we?" he asked rhetorically.

Ellie was stunned. She had never been sailing. The boat was beautiful with its dark blue fiberglass hull and crisp, white sails. The captain described his boat as a thirty-five-foot coast cruiser. The galley kitchen and sleeping areas reminded her of Aunt Penny's camper when he gave the tour. Things were compact and had their place. A camper on the water. She almost said it aloud. She tingled with excitement as she looked down the bay. She had goosebumps as the captain motored out.

As they headed south, John pointed out the clay cliffs where he took her glassing, and further south, he pointed to the lighthouse perched on a bluff. The bay opened up, and the captain unfurled the sail. The wind tugged at them.

Suddenly, as if by magic, Ellie felt like she was flying and cried out involuntarily. The sail billowed out, and the sailboat cut through the water like soft butter.

Captain Joe, who had been talking casually to them, turned from the helm and saw the joy on Ellie's face as they sailed down the bay. He gave a nod to John and turned back to the helm.

Ellie thought sailing was like a dream with the sun, the wind, the snap of the wind in the sail, and the feeling of flying. They zigzagged down the bay. John's arm was around her shoulders, and she leaned into him. They didn't need words, just the sun, the wind, and the magical feeling of flying on the water enveloped them. She could get used to this feeling.

After a couple of dream-like hours, the captain gathered up the sails. Ellie was a little sad to slow to motoring speed again. He docked at a marina and turned to them.

He addressed Ellie, "Here you are, young lady, at the next step of your journey today."

Ellie looked puzzled but took John's hand as he pulled her from her seat.

"Thank you, Captain Joe," she told him as they disembarked.

"Where are we?" she asked a grinning John. "Something about this place feels familiar."

"You said you used to come here as a child," John baited.

There was a small cove with a curved sandy beach near the marina. She looked down the beach. A housing development was nestled on the shore. "Tolchester?" Ellie asked. "It's so different! Why, the amusement park and the houses are completely gone!"

Where the amusement park and houses once stood was a housing development. Ellie looked on in awe at the changes to the landscape.

"I thought you might want to do a bit of glassing," John suggested.

"Would I ever! Your mom was going on and on about this place," Ellie gushed.

"Then, let's go! We have about an hour here before the next part of the surprise," he said.

John led her from the dock, and they walked to the small beach. With bent heads, they began to look for the treasure.

"Whoa!" John cried, checking out the tideline where jetsam lay. He had been pushing things around with the edge of his high-top sneaker.

"What did you find?" Ellie called to him. She had been a few feet away, picking up white and green glass. She headed towards John.

He held up a marble, the sunlight gleaming through the cat's eye of clear and teal glass.

"John, you say lady luck doesn't favor you, but it really does with glassing! First, you find that amazing piece of blue, and now this!" Ellie insisted.

"Maybe," he replied, popping the marble in his pocket. He smiled and took her hand, his other fingering the marble in his pocket.

They continued to search, finding a bit more glass until they each had a handful.

John looked up at the sky and the angle of the sun. "We should be getting back to the boat," he suggested. "The next part of the surprise is coming up."

Ellie looked up at him, smiled, and shook her head a little.

"What?" he asked.

"It's just the most amazing day already," she answered in awe.

They returned to the boat where Captain Joe was waiting. They motored north, and the captain turned into a wide-mouthed river. He pointed out Betterton Beach on their right and spoke of the plantations that used to border the river's edge.

Ellie looked eagerly about at the beautiful landscape and homes along the river. Ahead was a bridge, and she wondered how the mast would fit under it. She sank a little lower in her seat as they approached.

John laughed. "That's a draw bridge. Remember, we drove over it with my parents?"

Ellie nodded.

"But, we're not going under it. The captain is going to dock nearby. We're going there," and John pointed to a large building with glass wrapping around the second floor and stairs to decks leading up. People were at small tables, and Ellie realized it was a restaurant. "Hungry?" he asked her.

It had been a long time since breakfast. "Actually, I am famished."

They disembarked, and John led Ellie to an elegant restaurant. The waitress took them to a table by the tinted windows where they could see the boats at the docks and had a view of the Sassafras River from where they had just come from the bay.

"This is lovely, John. Magical," she said, her eyes shining in wonder of the day they had been having together.

"I wanted this to be a special day," John told her as he took her hand. He looked into her eyes.

The waitress interrupted, bringing them menus. They ordered, and John whispered something to the waitress. He took her hand again and looked into her eyes.

"Ellie, you know I love you," he began. "And, I'm not ready for..."

He had to trail off as the waitress brought a split of champagne, popped it, and filled two glasses.

Suddenly, Ellie had a bite of fear, thinking John might want to break up while he went to Vietnam. She was confused. If he wasn't ready to be with her, why the champagne? He started to say he wasn't ready, but for what? She looked at John. His eyes only held love.

He swallowed and continued. "I am not ready to propose to you. But I wanted to make a promise to you." He paused a moment. "A promise that I will always love you, no matter what happens." He picked up a glass of champagned and toasted, "To us."

Ellie picked up her glass and repeated the toast. They clinked glasses and drank. Ellie nearly sneezed over the small bubbles popping, but she loved the wine's bright, crisp, bubbly taste.

John reached into his pocket and then fumbled with something on his lap. Ellie looked at him quizzically, wondering what he was doing. He brought his hand up, and in it was a silver ring. A glint of blue shone out of a small, silver heart. It flashed cobalt blue in the lights of the restaurant, and the sun starting its western dip. Ellie gasped.

"My promise to you," John said, and he put it on her left hand.

"Oh!" Ellie cried softly, and then, "John! It's so lovely! Is it?" she began to ask.

"Sea glass," John answered. "Yup. Remember my mom talked about the artist in Hances Point? She found it on her beach, across from the campground. She sells her sea glass jewelry at the gift shop on the corner in North Bay. Mom knows her. I thought this glass matched the piece we found in Betterton."

Ellie held out her hand and admired the ring. "It does match the piece you found at Betterton. Oh, John, thank you. It's beautiful. It's perfect."

Other people in the restaurant noticed and clapped for them. Ellie was slightly embarrassed. John grinned. The waitress arrived with their food. Ellie tried to eat but kept pausing to gaze at the ring on her hand and smile.

After dinner, they strolled back to the boat, where Captain Joe awaited them. They motored down the Sassafras. Ellie leaned back and snuggled into John. She gazed at the shoreline, noticing some creeks leading off the river. Imposing houses bordered the river. Ellie wondered which ones dated back to the plantation era. Dreamily, she wondered what life was like then. Near the entrance of the bay, they passed a small creek, and Ellie saw a dock through the gathering shadows. Suddenly, she had a shiver.

John tightened his arm around her. "Cold?" he asked her.

Ellie shook her head. "Just a funny feeling," she murmured. She looked down at the ring on her hand. It glinted in a sharp ray of late afternoon sunlight. The blue of the glass flashed. She turned and looked up at John and asked, "I wonder what the chances are of the ring being from the same bottle as the piece of glass you found at Betterton?"

"That would be would be something, wouldn't it?" John commented. "I think they match pretty closely."

"We'll have to look at them together when we get home," Ellie suggested. "Maybe I can find someone to make that piece into a bracelet or pendant."

"Or maybe you can make it yourself," John suggested. "Don't they make jewelry in art school?"

"I think there are some classes," Ellie pondered. "I don't know. I've been so focused on textile arts that I haven't considered anything else. I'll have to ask Aunt Penny."

They passed Betterton on their left and were again out in the open bay. The sun was dipping further into the west, and the sky was painted in ribbons of color. Deep fuchsia and luscious apricot laced the deepening blue of the sky. As the sun set, bruised shadows of lavender appeared, and the sky darkened. Captain Joe turned on the running lights. A star popped out.

"Make a wish," John whispered into her hair.

"You too," She whispered back.

And both closed their eyes briefly, wishing. When Ellie opened up her eyes, more stars had popped out. The boat motored quietly through the water and the eventide was magic. She sighed. It had been a perfect day.

Fifty-One

JOHN -1969

Finding a piece of cobalt blue glass on the Chesapeake's beaches is a rare and prized by collectors.

Their day on the bay was as magical as he had hoped. John wanted to remember this day forever. He knew already it would likely hold him through some upcoming tough times.

His arm tightened around Ellie, resting his cheek against her silky, soft hair. He breathed in the strawberry scent of her shampoo and the smell of the water. He wished he could bottle it and take it to boot camp and Nam.

The sun began its descent in the west, hovering over Kingstown and sending out streamers of colored light. Shadows gathered on the shorelines on either side of the bay. A star popped out in the twilight.

"Make a wish," he whispered to Ellie.

She asked him to make a wish, too. He closed his eyes, wishing to stay alive and return to Ellie. He wanted to be with her forever.

They docked at the campground and thanked Captain Joe for the incredible day before walking back to the camper.

Penny had left a note that she was visiting friends on the other side of the campground. She must have been gone a little while as the fire in the firepit had burned down to coals.

"I need to get home," John told Ellie.

He gathered her and held her tightly, memorizing the feel of her body against his.

"Thank you for this most amazing day," Ellie whispered into his ear.

Their bodies pressed up against one another tightly. John started to kiss Ellie. He didn't want to stop. He wanted to take her into the camper and ravish her and then slowly make love to her. But he couldn't. Not tonight. He hoped that would be in their future. Reluctantly, he pulled away. She gave a little gasp of disappointment. He was glad to hear that, in a way, knowing she wanted him as much as he wanted her.

He took her hands in his and then pulled up her left hand to kiss it above the ring.

"I'll see you soon. Tomorrow," he promised.

Ellie nodded, and John went to his car. He drove toward home. He would need to thank his mom for shopping the other day and noticing that ring. Maybe, just maybe, his luck was turning. He briefly felt for the marble in his pocket and rolled it between his fingers before putting both hands back on the wheel.

The remainder of his few days at home were a blur of activity as he finished working for Carl and spent as much time torn between Ellie and his parents. Their first stop that weekend before he left was the Barber Shop. John chose to have his hair cut before he went to his induction. The barber shop was filled with cigarette smoke and laughter when they walked in. Men were gathered talking, laughing, drinking coffee, and making jokes. He caught the hint of an off-color joke when they entered. The jocularity ended when John told them why he was there. They sat John down immediately. Someone offered Ellie a seat, but she declined. Instead, she stood a few steps away from

John, out of the barber's way, a little shy. She watched as the barber shaved his long, wavy hair and it dropped to the ground in long, limp locks. He noticed Ellie bending over. She picked up one long lock of hair. The light caught it, and hints of red glimmered in his brown hair in the lights of the barbershop before she tucked it away in a small purse she carried. He had to blink back his emotion, and he couldn't look at Ellie, but his heart was full, and her gesture touched him. When they were finished, there he was, with short hair or what they called a 'high and tight,' which looked as bristly as a hedgehog. His short hair was sobering to both of them. Ellie marveled and commented at how mature he looked, almost like his father, but not quite. John knew he had his mother's eyes and her easy smile. The barber refused to take payment from him. Instead, he shook his hand and told him to stay alive and to pay him when he got home. John nodded. The other men shook his hand, wishing him good luck as they left.

They went from the Barber Shop back to his house. John told Ellie his mom's goal was to make all his favorite foods before he left. Today, his mom made them a lunch of grilled frankfurters and homemade macaroni and cheese. His dad snapped many photos. He promised he would get copies to Ellie and send copies to John. They played bocce and jarts on the lawn. Their conversations were light. It was like a normal family gathering on a sunny summer afternoon. But there was a tension beneath it. No one wanted to admit that he would leave Monday morning for basic training and head off to war in a few weeks.

That evening, they drove back to the campground for a farewell dinner with Carl and Betty. Aunt Penny joined them. Carl told them the history of their home. It was originally a duplex for two families to spend the summer on the bay in the 1930s. The stone foundation and fireplace came from the quarry just a few miles away. After what Betty called the 'nickel tour,' Carl laughingly called the houses in the area 'weekend and a case of beer cottages' without a lick of insulation and not a square corner.

"Luckily, Carl is handy," Betty said, looking proudly at her husband.

"It's not much, but it's home," Carl said, looking slightly embarrassed by Betty's praise.

Carl went on to tell the history of the place and how the original well was only fifteen feet deep and hand-dug. He told them about the old wooden boats left on the property. Carl donated those to the Waterman's Museum in North Bay.

John watched Ellie. She became animated, asking if there was sea glass on their beach.

Sadly, Betty shook her head, "No, I don't think the current is right here. Sea glass is on the other side. I have an artist friend living in Hances Point who steps out the door at her small cove and finds lovely glass. She's told me she's found amethyst too, but I don't believe her."

"Is that the artist that made this ring?" Ellie asked.

Betty leaned in, looked at the ring carefully, and nodded, "Why yes, it is! She sells her jewelry and artwork at that gift shop in North Bay. The one on the corner."

"We'll have to go shopping!" Ellie commented.

The men rolled their eyes. Carl changed the subject.

"We have arrowheads," Carl interrupted. "This used to be a Native American settlement. Some days, when the mist rises on the water, I can almost imagine seeing them."

"Maybe that's why this place feels so special and so peaceful, Carl," Aunt Penny said. "Maybe it's hallowed ground."

"Maybe," agreed Carl, lost in his musings.

"Maybe," Betty told the group, "it's time to get dinner."

Betty had been watching the grill that Carl lit when they arrived. The coals were glowing red, and she went into the house and emerged with steaks on a platter. Before she went back into the kitchen, Ellie and Penny asked if they could assist. Betty accepted their help.

"Ellie, you can set the table, and Penny, you can begin to get the food to the table. I need to keep an eye on these crabcakes that I'm going to broil."

Once again, John thought over the light banter at dinner, everyone was trying to pretend that life was normal. Part of him could understand and accept this, but part of him wanted to scream, rant, and rave and not go to boot camp and go off to war. After Betty served dessert, she pulled out a bottle of something from her buffet.

"I keep this for special occasions," Betty told them. "I'm of Polish descent, and this is the drink my grandparents used to toast with on important occasions. It's Wisniowka, a Polish cherry liqueur." She pronounced it "Whiz-neuf-ka" and poured it into small, liqueur glasses.

When everyone had their glasses filled, Betty held hers up to toast, "To John, may you come safely home."

"Here! Here!" they chorused and downed the liqueur. Betty refilled the glasses.

Carl toasted, "May you be ready for every foe!"

They drank again, and Betty filled the glasses. Aunt Penny toasted. Ellie tried, but her eyes filled with tears, and she was too choked up to continue.

"Excuse me," she apologized and left the deck to go to the water's edge.

"Thank you, everyone," John told the group and went after Ellie.

John noticed Ellie hugging herself as tightly as she could. It was a perfect summer's evening when the fireflies were blinking in and out as the stars began to pop out in the sky. The water rippled swathes of deep blues as a boat went by. Lights near the water and from boats cast golden ribbons on the blue. How could it be perfect when he was leaving?

John approached Ellie and took her in his arms. It was then she broke down into great, wracking sobs. John held her.

"I'm sorry," she gasped. "I'm so sorry, John. I've been trying to be brave. I don't want you to go!"

"I don't want to go either," he told her, his mouth near her ear. "But I don't have a choice. C'mon, let's walk."

They walked along the familiar lane to the boat house and the marina. Campfires glowed and wafted sweet woodsmoke their way. Someone nearby was playing the radio, Elvis's "Love Me Tender" floating into the night. That's when John took her in his arms and started to dance slowly on the sand, crooning the lyrics in her ear. Her crying had ceased, but the bittersweetness of this moment caught Ellie. Her eyes filled, but she didn't cry. She wanted to memorize every millisecond of his voice in her ear, the feel of his body against hers, the warmth of the summer night, and the gentle waves on the shore that added rhythm to the song.

When the song ended, John took her face in his hands. He didn't kiss her. Instead, he looked at her, memorizing her face in the darkening night. Ellie ran her hands over his face and touched and stroked as she memorized the lines of his face. He kissed her then, and she kissed back, expressing what they could not say through their kiss.

He walked her back to Aunt Penny's then. Kissed her again and said goodbye. He could feel her eyes on him, watching him walk away. She would be a tall, slim, ghostly shadow, getting swallowed up in the shadows of the trees that populated the campsites like old friends.

Fifty-Two

LOUISA – 1918

Sea glass is polished into its jewel-like form from wind, sand, and waves.

The Tolchester shoreline grew closer. It wasn't a bright, sunny summer's day like her last visit. Everything appeared gray today. The cool mist in the air made everything look ghostly. Doubt fogged her mind.

"Oh, Emma, are we doing the right thing?" Louisa asked her worriedly.

"Of course, dear!" Emma replied.

Louisa still wasn't sure. She watched as the steamship docked. When she had been to Tolchester with Grandmama, there had been a crush of people exiting the boat. Now, it was just Emma and Louisa. They disembarked and found their bags neatly stacked on the wharf to the side of the gangplank. Louisa asked Emma to wait with the bags, and she told her she would be back in a few minutes while she went in search of a cart.

Halfway down the pier, she spied an older gentleman making his way to the steamship.

"Excuse me, sir, can you tell me where I might find a handcart or someone to help me and my companion?" Louisa asked.

"Eh?" the old man answered, "What was that?"

Louisa repeated the question.

"I can be of some assistance," he told Louisa.

Relieved, she led the man back to where Emma was standing.

"Just a moment," the old man said. "First, I must get the mail from the boat, and then I can assist you ladies."

He was back moments later with a small satchel filled with letters."Now there, ladies, how can I assist you?"

"We're heading to the boarding house," Emma told him.

"The boarding house? Why they're not open right now. The proprietress has been ill. I'm sorry. Perhaps you want to return to the steamship?" he asked.

But, at that moment, the steamship blew its horn and pulled away from the dock.

"You misunderstand us," Louisa explained over the noise. "We're here to care for Mrs. Evans. I promised her son, Willie, that I would."

"How do you know Willie?" the man asked sharply. "He's in France serving in the war."

"He was wounded. He's at the hospital at Fort McHenry," Louisa continued. "And," she added shyly, "Willie is my sweetheart."

"Oh! So that's how it is." The old man tipped his hat back and scratched at the side of his head.

"That's how it is," Louisa stated succinctly, smiled, and asked, "Are you Burt?"

"Why yes, yes I am," Burt stated.

"Willie told me about you. I'm Louisa, and this is Emma." Louisa made introductions. "Do you know how Mrs. Evans is doing? Cora wrote to me last week."

"Is that so? Last I heard, she was pretty weak," Burt informed

Louisa and Emma. "I hope that you can help her out. She may not want you around, though."

"I know. She's a very proud woman," Louisa stated.

"You got that right, young lady," Burt chuckled.

They made their way off the pier, each carrying a bag. Burt had two.

"If I had known you were coming, I would have brought the wagon," he complained.

"If necessary, I can make more than one trip," Louisa said.

They started up the path to the boarding house. It seemed so odd to Louisa that the amusement park was so eerily silent. The previous summer was filled with so many happy voices and the noise from rides and barkers. Willie had often told her how different things were in the winter – almost desolate. They were. She shivered.

They arrived at the boarding house, silent and dark as the amusement park. At first, they knocked. There was no answer or answering call. Louisa was worried. When they pushed at the door, it opened.

"Mrs. Evans?" Louisa called out, pausing for an answer. "Mrs. Evans?"

Louisa remembered that Willie and his mother lived in quarters adjacent to the kitchen. She led the way.

"Mrs. Evans?" Louisa called out again when they walked through the kitchen.

A voice cried out faintly, "Who's there?"

"It's Burt, ma'am, and two ladies," Burt called out.

"I'm not open. You know that, Burt," she scolded, her voice slightly stronger with consternation.

Louisa walked through a small parlor and knocked on the door that was ajar. She could see flickering candlelight through a crack in the door. She knocked again and entered.

"Mrs. Evans?" Louisa asked again. "It's Louisa. I'm not sure if you remember me. Willie asked me to come to check on you."

"Willie?" Mrs. Evan's voice was an astonished whisper. "You've seen Willie?"

"Yes, ma'am. He's in Baltimore at Fort McHenry. He's recovering from some wounds. He's doing very well. I can tell you more about it. We came to help out. This is Emma, and you know Burt," she introduced, waving a hand.

Mrs. Evans was pale and lying under many blankets on the bed. The room was chilly as there wasn't a fire going.

"Let's get you set to rights," Emma said, and she bustled about. "Burt, can you help me get some fires going? Louisa put a kettle on for tea. I thought I would make some good soup, and I brought bread. That should suffice for dinner tonight. We'll sort through our things, and I'll pull out the ingredients for soup. I'll have it made in a jiffy."

Louisa and Burt hurried to their chores. Emma examined Mrs. Evans before she went to the kitchen to put the soup on. Burt's fire caught up quickly, and it wasn't long before the room started to warm. Louisa brought Mrs. Evans tea and held the cup and saucer for her to take sips.

"However, did you come?" she asked, the hot tea and warm room bringing color back into her cheeks.

"When Willie was in the hospital, I wrote you a couple of times. But I didn't get an answer. And I was worried. I read about the flu here on the Eastern Shore. It's terrible in Baltimore, but I understand it's been bad here too. Cora wrote to me last week, asking for some help. Willie and I decided it would be best that I come. So, here I am," Louisa told her.

"What does your grandmama think of that?" Mrs. Evans asked, a slight tone of sarcasm at the edge of her voice.

"Grandmama died a few months ago when the flu first hit Baltimore," Louisa informed her, her voice hitching. The empty feeling settled inside of Louisa's stomach again. When she had been here last, Grandmama had been alive and well and her bright and feisty self. Louisa missed her.

"Oh, I am sorry," Mrs. Evans relented. "And what about Willie?"

"He had a wound on his head that is healing well. Unfortunately, he has shell shock and lost sight for quite a while."

Mrs. Evans gasped, and Louisa said, "But, his sight has returned. His limbs still tremble at loud noises. They are starting physiotherapy today. He may go to a farm to rehabilitate. It depends on how he does. But he is a lucky one. You see, I've been volunteering at the hospital for several months now. That's how we found each other again."

Mrs. Evans drank in the information. She looked like she was about to say something, but Emma entered the room with a bowl of soup and a piece of buttered bread.

"Here now," she said. "Louisa can help you eat if you need assistance."

"I can manage, thank you," Mrs. Evans said primly.

"All right," Emma agreed, a twinkle in her eye.

"Burt's going to have a bowl as well in the kitchen. Louisa, you come out when you're ready. Mrs. Evans, I'm hoping we can stay here?" Emma asked.

"Nothing's ready for guests," Mrs. Evans said.

"Oh, we can manage, I'm sure," Emma said.

She left Louisa and Mrs. Evans alone. Louisa told her about Willie being in the hospital and how she realized it was him when they changed his bandage. She told her of his miraculous recovery and the setback due to the evil Nurse Johnston.

"Nurse Williams assured me he would take good care of Willie. I trust her. She was an excellent teacher to me. I'm hoping to return to attend nursing school in the near future," Louisa said.

"You've grown up quite a bit since last summer," Mrs. Evans commented.

"I've had to," Louisa said, "especially after Grandmama died.

If Bertha and Emma weren't around, I would be completely alone. I don't have any family left."

Mrs. Evans had finished her soup and was nibbling at the bread.

"More soup?" Louisa asked.

Mrs. Evans shook her head. "I'm so weak," she complained.

"You'll get better. It's a slow process. Now that we're here, we can ensure you have good food and help you with things. I think you'll be on the mend," Louisa assured her.

"Is that so?" Mrs. Evans replied.

Louisa looked her straight in the eye, "Yes, it is. I will get a little soup and make up a couple of beds for Emma and me. I'll send Emma in to check on you in a few minutes."

Louisa took the bowl and spoon to the kitchen, where Emma and Burt were chatting amiably over their bowls of soup and pieces of bread. Louisa helped herself to Emma's rich vegetable and beef soup. She took it to the table and sat down with Emma and Burt, feeling she was interrupting. Emma was a little flushed, and Louisa had never seen her that way before.

"How's she doing?" Burt asked.

"Better, I think, with some nourishing food and the news about her son," Louisa responded.

"Two good things," Emma said. "Two good healing things."

"You got that right," Burt said. "Thank you for the dinner," he nodded to Emma, "and let me know if you ladies need anything. I'll drop by tomorrow to check on you."

"Thank you, Burt," Emma and Louisa chorused.

Louisa turned to Emma, "If you can tend to Mrs. Evans, I'll wash up from dinner and work on making some beds for us."

Emma agreed. Louisa quickly washed the dishes from their dinner. She went in search of linens to make up beds. She vaguely remembered linen closets on each floor. Even though it was chilly, she opened up the windows a crack to let in fresh air. The one fire gave her some trouble, but eventually, she got it lit and going well.

She made up the beds. The linens smelled faintly of lavender, just like at home. When Emma came upstairs, Louisa put on her nightgown and wrote a brief letter to Willie telling him she had arrived and that his mother was weak but all right. She would ask Burt how to post the letter tomorrow.

WILLIE – 1918

Ussuri Bay is also known as "Glass Bay" in Russia, where you can find a bounty of sea glass.

Willie was worried. "I should be at home," Willie told Nurse Williams when she dropped by to see him. "You know my mother's been ill. She needs someone there for her. She needs me."

"Even with Louisa there, she needs you?" Nurse Williams said soberly. "Do you think it's that bad there?" she asked.

"It's an old boarding house," Willie explained. "Something's always falling apart. I do most of the upkeep in the winter. The summers are much too busy. And when I can, I want to add modern conveniences like a telephone and maybe even electricity."

"My goodness! Don't you have lofty goals!" Nurse Williams exclaimed.

"It's a beautiful spot on the Chesapeake Bay. The swells from Baltimore will want all the bells and whistles," he said. "And I don't know how Louisa is making out. She's never fed chickens. I wonder if she knows how to chop wood or build fires in a stove or a fireplace."

"You're not giving her enough credit, Willie. Louisa is a resourceful young lady. She may find some things challenging, but I suspect she's making out just fine. And that Emma, she has a steady head. And from what you've told me of your mother, she expects nothing less than things to be done correctly," Nurse Williams exhorted.

"You've got that right!" Willie said.

He paused, "Now that I'm walking again, I need to do something. Can you help me?"

"Now that you are on your feet, you might be able to do it yourself," she said saucily. Nurse Williams put her hands on her hips. "Can you get dressed on your own today? I would like to see you try. I brought you some street clothes."

Willie worked to get the clothes on. Getting up from the cot was still a slight challenge, and Nurse Williams steadied him. The trembling had all but ceased except for times of stress.

Willie's brow furrowed as he concentrated on dressing. He concentrated so hard to do the thing properly that his fingers trembled, and he couldn't fasten the buttons.

"Damn it," he muttered under his breath, "Damn it, damn it, damn it."

"Be easy on yourself," Nurse Williams chided. "You're doing really well. Let me help you with those pesky buttons. I think it's time you started vocational training between physiotherapy sessions. We can keep you busy, don't worry, Willie."

"And we'll be transferring you out of this ward to a ward where the men will be recuperating like you, Willie. They are also learning skills to use in the world and working on healing their bodies."

"I'm ready. And when this dang-blasted war ends and life returns to normal, you'll have to come to Tolchester for a holiday, Nurse Williams. I will treat you to an extra-long ride on the carousel. You will love it. Louisa does. That was her favorite ride," Willie said.

"You know why, don't you?" Nurse Williams asked Willie.

"What?" Willie asked. "She came around the carousel hundreds of times. She didn't go to the other rides like that."

"And just who ran the carousel?" Nurse Williams asked pointedly.

Realization dawned on Willie. He turned beet red, "Oh," he said and paused, "Oh!" as the realization hit him. In his heart, he knew Louisa came to the carousel to see him. In his memories, he envisioned her riding the varied steeds on the merry-go-round with joy in her eyes and a smile just for him. He smiled inadvertently at the memory.

"See, you know," teased Nurse Williams. "And, the 'swells,' as you put it, are taking care of the soldiers here. They're setting up dinners and dancing at Fort McHenry to entertain the soldiers. You can join them, you know."

"I don't want any of those mamas to get any ideas," Willie replied. "Louisa is the only girl for me."

Nurse Williams nodded, stating, "I understand, but you could practice dancing now that you're walking again."

"I'm not that steady yet! If I try to dance, I will likely fall down!" Willie cried.

"Practice," Nurse Williams told Willie. "Dancing will help, you'll see."

He looked around the ward; Nurse Williams had proposed a lot of changes. He had watched comrades come and go from this ward. He was doing better than a lot of them. He had moments of guilt that he could walk and talk. At least, pretty well. There were soldiers on the ward who might not survive, or if they did, without limbs or pieces of their body. He had seen one soldier whose face was blown half off, fitted with a mask to make his face look like a face again. It was spooky but better than seeing the ravages of war. Willie took a deep breath and thought of Louisa. Thinking of her made him happy and helped calm his limbs.

Nurse Williams, who had checked on a couple of other soldiers, had returned. She looked at him quizzically. "Are you all right, Willie?"

He took another deep breath, "Yes, ma'am. I am ready. Let's check out this vocational stuff. I'm interested in learning about electricity and how I can make that old boat of a guest house more modern."

She chuckled and walked with him down the ward, keeping a sharp eye on how steady he was on his feet.

"And, about that thing, you can help me with," Willie said, leaning closer to Nurse Williams to whisper his idea.

Fifty-Four

ELLIE – 1969

Manganese Oxide is added to the process of making glass purple.

Ellie reeled from the fact that she might not see John again until he returned from Vietnam. The horrific thought of 'if' was an insidious whisper she tried to quell. She felt hollow inside. The last couple of weeks had flown by, and her time with John was magical and bittersweet.

Ellie looked at the ring on her finger in the early morning light. The cobalt blue looked as dark as a midnight sky in low light but gleamed a deep rich blue in bright light. She found herself twiddling the bottom of the ring with her thumb to catch hints of the deep, rich blue.

She also pulled out the large shard John found and gave to her. She held it next to the ring. It was easy to imagine they were from the same bottle. She wondered what bottle it came from and how old? The large oval shard had been through fire and storms. Ellie ran her fingers over the odd texture of the piece.

John mentioned making jewelry. Could she do that too? She wondered if the lady who created her ring gave lessons or if she would need to wait until art school. Maybe she and Aunt Penny could spend a day in North Bay and learn more about the jewelry artisan at the gift shop. Or, ask Betty. She had a connection with the artist, too.

The shard was large. Ellie held it to her chest, imagining a pendant. Next, she balanced it on her wrist, imagining a bracelet. She liked the bracelet idea. That way, she could wear the bracelet and see it when she looked at her hands. It would remind her of John and their day at Betterton.

Her thoughts kept returning to John, wondering if she was in love with being in love or in love with John. John made her feel safe, special, and cherished. It wasn't a 'fancy fling,' as her mother would say. Her feelings for John were in her core.

Restless, Ellie left the trailer and walked to the beach. It early. Penny was still asleep. The campground was asleep. The sun rose over the Eastern shore, and the day was beginning. It was a beginning for her, as well as it was her first day without John. She didn't want to think about it. Saying goodbye last night was agony. In the end, she and John were both at a loss for words, other than the whispered "I love you" with their last kiss.

She walked to the beach finding the water was as still as glass and reflective of the sky and landscape bordering the bay. A fish jumped out in the water, causing circular ripples to distort the surface of the mirror-like water. An osprey screeched in its sharp, repetitive cheeps somewhere in the distance.

Ellie plunked herself in the sand, feeling the coolness through her shorts. She pulled her knees up to her chin and hugged them. She stared at the water, not thinking, just being. Her heart already ached, missing John.

Ellie looked again at the ring on her finger. It flashed dark blue in the sunshine. She smiled as not only was the ring a thrill, but she knew that the cobalt blue glass was a rare and special find on the Chesapeake Bay. She was getting to be as passionate as John's mother about sea glass. Ellie was glad they had that in common. She would need to share her theory about the ring and the shard the next time she saw her.

Fifty-Five

JOHN 1969

Calvert County, Maryland, is known for shark teeth, fossils, and sea glass.

John tossed and turned that night, his sleep filled with vivid and unusual dreams. He woke, exhausted.

His mother insisted they go to church that morning. John wasn't sure why. She was convinced that God would protect him and keep him safe. The minister's sermon was all about faith and trusting in God. The minister droned on about how God rules our lives and makes our paths.

John wasn't so sure. In his life right now, he wasn't sure if God or the Government ruled his life. His thoughts were bitter, and his faith in God was on a tightrope. Dutifully, he thanked the minister and shook his hand as they left the church.

His parents wanted to take him to lunch, and they drove back to Kingstown, where they went to the Shoals Restaurant. It had been a private hunting and fishing club in the late 1800s. Their food was superb, and it was where they celebrated special events as he grew up. The plaque boasted that it was a place for optimists, where men could while away the hours to create a 'happy habit.' John always wondered what stories the walls would reveal if they could talk.

"Order anything you want, son. There's no limit. Do you want lobster?" his father asked him.

John shook his head. "No, no lobster, thanks." He looked over the menu and decided on the club's famous chicken pot pie. His mother ordered scallops, and his dad a snow-topped or crab-topped steak.

"Have you decided on what kind of training you want to go to out of basic?" his father asked as they ate their dinner.

"I've had several thoughts. I don't think I want to be a sniper or a radioman. Carl steered me away from those. I was thinking of a draftsman and surveyor. It would give me a good background for my engineering degree when I come home," John answered.

His father nodded in agreement with his son. John looked around the room. The club looked like what John imagined an anti-bellum mansion looked like. There was a claret red carpet and white plaster walls with decorative plaster fixtures and moldings on the ceiling, around doorways, and fireplaces. The stark white of the walls and deep red of the carpet contrasted with the dark, polished fireplaces. It was filling up with the after-church crowd.

After lunch, his mother asked, "Is there anywhere you want to go?"

John shook his head, stating, "No, I think I just want to be at home. I need to pack."

At home, John finished packing and put his duffel bag by the front door. They tried to have a normal Sunday, and it would have been if the duffel bag didn't seem to scream that John was going away in the morning. They played cards on the back porch with the ceiling fan blowing a gentle breeze. His mom made his favorite meatloaf and mashed potato dinner. It was heavy for such a warm day, but John didn't care. It was delicious. He couldn't get it out of his head that it was his last meal at home.

After dinner, he asked his dad, "Okay, if I borrow the car? I need to see Ellie. I need to…" he broke off, emotion getting the better of him.

"Of course, son," his dad told him, tossing him the car keys.

John drove to the campground in the twilight. He had to drive carefully as the deer were traipsing in and out of the forest. He suspected they went down to the bay to drink but saw their spooky blue eyes as his headlights when he went around the curve. He wondered why there were so many deer this year. And belatedly realized it might be because many of the hunters were hunting human targets in Vietnam.

The campground was fairly quiet as the bulk of the people had left to go home and leave their vacation weekend behind. Penny and Ellie had a small fire going. Ellie leaped from her chair when John pulled up and jumped into his arms when he exited the vehicle.

"I'm so glad you came by. I didn't think I would see you." Her words tumbled out. "Do you want to sit by the fire?"

"No." He shook his head. "Are you okay with going to the beach?" he asked.

"Of course!" Ellie told him. "Let's grab a blanket to sit on."

She went inside to find an old quilt, and they carried it to the beach. The summer insects started their evening summertime chorus. John always loved the sound. It was soothing. They sat, not talking, legs stretched out in front of them, hands touching.

"I want to remember every second with you," John murmured.

Ellie nodded, not trusting her emotions or her voice.

"Ellie," John said quietly. "I just want to hold you for a little bit."

They lay on the blanket, spooning in together, their bodies fitting perfectly together. And John wanted Ellie. His desire flared, but he also wanted to hold her, to protect her, to be close. He ran his hand up and down her arm and then up and down her leg. She turned towards him, kissing him deeply and taking one of his hands and putting it on her breast.

"Please," she whispered when she pulled back a moment from their kiss. "Please," she whispered again raggedly.

They stopped kissing. John put his forehead against hers. "Are you sure, Ellie?" he whispered back with the question.

Ellie was biting her lip. John desired her even more. Darkness had fallen completely. The stars were popping out one by one into a glittering blanket above them. He felt her nod in the darkness. She nodded, and he heard her barely whisper, "Yes."

They explored one another, and he found a passion he didn't know existed. His love for her burgeoned as he enveloped her, drinking in her hair, her touch, her body. Time and place didn't exist. Ellie was his entire world and his entire universe. Her soft moans of passion thrilled him and drove him to pleasure her more. He wanted to keep the feelings with him forever. With Ellie, he almost always felt at peace with the Universe. Ellie was his home.

"I love you," he whispered as he drifted off into one of the best sleeps he had ever known.

They woke up hours later when it was deep night. The stars had shifted, and so had the moon. They giggled as they floundered back to the camper in the little available light. Aunt Penny left a light on the inside but not the outer light due to the bugs. The campfire had burned down. The remaining coals glowed weakly, barely giving off a hint of heat.

The moment had come for them to part. Neither knew for how long. The fears he had kept bottled up inside threatened to spill out. He held Ellie as tightly as he could and wrenched out, "I don't know when I'll see you again. I don't want to leave. I don't want to leave you."

Ellie returned his hug. But, she straightened and seemed as

though she had matured in an instant. She told John in a serious tone, "Just come home, John. I'll be here for you. I'll be waiting for you. Come home safe and sound. I love you, John."

"I know. I love you too," he said before he gave her one long, last kiss goodbye.

Fifty-Six

LOUISA -1918

Bonfire glass is sometimes called campfire glass.

Willie's mother was slowly recuperating and gaining strength. Louisa's respect for her grew daily as she realized the sheer amount of work to upkeep the boarding house, and her life fell into a rhythm at Tolchester.

Louisa volunteered to care for the chickens. She loved scattering seeds for them around the yard and having their soft, feathery bodies gather around her. Occasionally, she would sit and put one in her lap, stroking their soft feathers. Emma advised her not to name them, but Louisa couldn't help it. Rusty was a Rhode Island Red who came to her easily. Rusty would sit in her lap and make contented noises as she petted her. Louisa loved her.

She also loved gathering the warm eggs. At first, she was scared to reach under a hen for an egg but found her courage. Louisa considered it a treasure hunt and spoke softly to the hens when culling the nests for eggs. She proudly took in her stash, and Emma would turn the eggs into delicious breakfasts and use them in cakes and custards to tempt Mrs. Evans to eat.

After her chores of feeding the chickens and gathering the

eggs, Louisa would take a few minutes and sit on the steps that she and Willie used to sit on, just out of sight of the boarding house. Here, she could sit for a few minutes and look at the water and sky. Willie was over there, west of Tolchester, in Baltimore.

She spent a lot of time on those steps thinking about Willie. She imagined that one day, they could be here together, in Tolchester. If that dream happened, she imagined what their lives would be like. Mrs. Evans ruled this place with an iron fist, but Louisa had great respect and awe for all Willie's mother accomplished, running the boarding house nearly single-handedly for years.

She could think of everything and think of nothing as she stared at the sky and the water. The interplay of light on the watercolor and sky was an everchanging dance. The vista before her brought her peace. She sighed after sitting for a few minutes. The weather was changing, cold was beginning to seep through her skirts, and the breeze had a sharp edge to it.

Louisa's cheeks were bright red when she returned to the house with her quarry of eggs.

"Ahh, thank you, my dear," Emma said as she brought in the eggs. "Just put them in this bowl. I am finishing this bacon, and we can cook some of those eggs in the bacon grease in just a few minutes. Could you take this cup of tea to Mrs. Evans, please?"

Louisa filled the teacup from the pot and turned to take the cup and saucer to Mrs. Evans. When she turned, she nearly dropped the cup when she saw Mrs. Evans in the doorway.

"Oh!" Louisa cried, "Let me help you!" She put the cup on the counter and raced to support Mrs. Evans as she walked to the kitchen table.

"And what do you think you're doing?" Emma asked Mrs. Evans briskly.

"I have to get out of that dang bed some time," Mrs. Evans complained. "And today is a good day to do it. I won't get better until I start moving around a little."

Louisa brought the tea to the table. She had added a dollop of honey to the tea to help Mrs. Evan's cough. Indeed, the exertion of her walking from the bedroom to the table caused her to cough again. Louisa patted her back and urged Mrs. Evans to drink the tea.

"Thank you, Louisa. How are the chickens doing?" Mrs. Evans asked.

Louisa's face shone with happiness as she told Mrs. Evans that she had gathered nearly a dozen eggs this morning.

"And one of them had a double yolk!" Emma crowed. "What good luck we'll have today!"

She brought steaming plates of eggs, bacon, and buttered toast to the table. She gave Mrs. Evans the double-yolked egg, telling her to eat every bit to help her build up her strength.

"What do you hear from Willie?" Emma asked Louisa.

She put her fork down and smiled before answering. "He writes that he's getting stronger each day. The physiotherapy is helping him gain strength, and he's walking again. His head wound is healed. He thinks they'll move him out of the hospital soon. He doesn't know if he can stay at Fort McHenry for more physiotherapy, or if they will send him to a farm to recuperate. They also have some training on the campus too. He's not sure."

"I wish they would send him here," his mother stated. "This is as good as working on a farm. We have a lot to keep him busy. I don't know who to hire with all the young men gone off to war. Burt can only do so much."

"Burt has been a wonderful help," Louisa said. "He's been coming nearly every day."

"Really?" Mrs. Evans stated. "I didn't realize it was so often. He used to only come around once or twice a week."

"I think it's Emma's good food and conversation he's coming for," Louisa teased, looking pointedly at Emma.

Emma blushed, and Louisa giggled.

Mrs. Evans raised an eyebrow and added, "Burt is a good man.

It was a shame his wife died a few years ago. He's mighty handy. I couldn't have managed without him while Willie has been gone."

She sipped her tea and said, "I think I would like to get dressed today."

"You are feeling better then! That's wonderful news!" Emma turned to Louisa and said, "Louisa, be a good girl and wash up. I'll help Mrs. Evans get dressed."

Louisa set about pouring the bacon grease into a crock dedicated to it. She knew Emma would use the bacon grease in cooking and flavoring many dishes. Louisa filled and turned on the kettle to heat the water to wash the dishes. She didn't mind washing the dishes. There was a window over the sink that looked out into the kitchen garden. Louisa noticed a cabbage or two they could harvest and some Brussel sprouts.

There was a knock at the back door, and it opened a crack, revealing Burt's twinkling eye.

"How do, Miss Louisa," he greeted, tipping his hat to her before taking it off and stepping inside.

"Good morning, Burt," Louisa greeted. "How are you today?"

"Oh, as best as I can be. Rheumatics are kicking up a bit in this chilly weather," he answered.

"Tea?" Louisa offered.

"Don't mind if I do," Burt said. "I brought the mail and a newspaper from Baltimore."

"Lovely! Please sit down. I'll get you the tea and join you. Emma and Mrs. Evans should be out in a moment."

"That so?" Burt replied, eyeing the door to the private quarters. "Mrs. Evans is doing well today?"

"Exceptionally," Louisa answered. "She walked to the kitchen for her breakfast."

"That's just fine," Burt remarked, taking a steaming cup of tea from Louisa. But he put it down quickly and stood up as Emma, supporting Mrs. Evans on one arm, guided her into the kitchen.

Louisa hopped up, pulled out a chair for Mrs. Evans to sit, and then got tea for the ladies.

Mrs. Evans spied the small pile of mail and the newspaper at Burt's hand. "What's the news?" she asked.

"They're hoping this danged war will end soon," Burt stated.

They were all quiet for a minute.

"And then, hopefully, Willie can come home," Louisa commented.

They went on to discuss the cold snap. Burt and Mrs. Evans said it would warm up again and not to worry. It wasn't like last winter when it was the coldest winter on record. Burt talked about the oyster harvest and mentioned he could get some oysters for them.

"Oh, please, Burt!" Louisa cried. "Emma makes the best oyster stew in the world! And her oyster casserole at holidays…" she trailed off and then turned to Emma, "Emma, could you make the oyster casserole for Thanksgiving? Please?"

Emma chuckled. "I can surely do that, Miss Louisa."

Mrs. Evans said, "I see you have some mail there, Burt. Who's it for?"

There was nothing from Willie today, and Mrs. Evans and Louisa were disappointed. But Louisa received a letter from Nurse Williams. She stated in her letter that Willie was doing just fine and that she was taking good care of him in Louisa's absence. She mentioned he was walking pretty well and that the tremors were lessening. She said she missed Louisa's presence at the hospital and her good work. She also went on to tell Louisa that she was involved with "Votes for Women" and had been to some rallies with several other nurses for women's rights.

Louisa read Nurse Williams's letter aloud. The rest of the group listened eagerly.

Mrs. Evans stated, "Louisa, you go and write to that Nurse Williams and tell her she is welcome here at any time, free of charge, for taking care of my Willie."

Louisa grinned. "I will do that, Mrs. Evans, after my morning chores."

"Oh, and I almost forgot," Burt interrupted, "Word's about that a tramp is going around these parts. You ladies, keep an eye out."

"A tramp?" Emma exclaimed.

"These have been hard times with the war," Burt stated. "I don't know if it's a soldier that's returned home or just someone wandering around. You may want to lock your doors at night."

"I have never felt the need to lock my doors!" Mrs. Evans exclaimed. "Good heavens! What is this world coming to?"

"It's changing quickly," Louisa said. "Unbelievably so. Electricity is in Baltimore. I don't know when it will reach here. Telephones, too."

"It will take a while for the electricity to come here," Burt predicted, "but people are getting telephones right and left."

"It's a marvel," Emma commented.

"Thank you for the tea, ladies," Burt said. "I'll get you some of those oysters for stew, Emma. And I'll be back to get some more wood chopped for you. Miss Louisa, can you manage to bring in the wood?"

"I can. Can you stay for another cup of tea while I write a quick note to Nurse Williams?" she asked. "And then you can post it for us?"

"I can do that," Burt replied, settling again into the chair.

Emma bustled about to make more tea.

The day passed by pleasantly. Burt brought them a pail of oysters, and he worked with Emma shucking them so that she could make the stew. Emma made them a rich stew with biscuits for dinner. Satiated and sleepy, Burt went home, and Emma toddled off to bed after Louisa assured her that she would clean up. She was restless.

She gathered up the vegetable scraps to take outside to the compost pile. Dusk was deepening, and night would be coming fast. Louisa made her way to the garden and dumped the scraps before taking a minute to look at the stars popping out in the sky. Childishly, she started to make the wish, 'Star light, Star bright,' when she heard a chicken squawk.

What was it? The chickens were restless. She wondered if a fox was about. A chicken squawked loudly again.

"What is it, girls?" Louisa called to the chickens. "It's all right. No nasty fox will get you!"

She turned toward the hen house and saw a tall shadow and shrieked. A dirty man dressed in ragged clothes clutched her favorite chicken, Rusty.

"You let her go!" she shouted at the man.

He leered at her. His face wore a scar that went down one side of his cheek.

"And what are you going to do about it, girlie? This here chicken will make me a nice meal. You have plenty of others," he said in a gravelly voice.

Louisa didn't know what to do. She had the pan from the vegetable scraps, but it wasn't much of a weapon.

"Let the chicken go, please!" she begged him.

"Maybe I should take you instead." He lunged at her, grabbing her arm as he released Rusty, who squawked and flew to the ground.

Louisa screamed, but he held her arm tightly, knocking the pan to the ground. She tried to swing with her other arm, but he caught it and just laughed with an evil laugh.

"One more sound out of you, and I'll knock your lights out," he threatened.

Louisa became silent, but inside, she was screaming. She had learned about bad men and what they would do to a woman from some of the nurses at the hospital. Grandmama had kept her naïve, and she didn't have a clue about some of the badness in the world. Working at the hospital had opened her eyes. She heard about rape and domestic abuse with descriptions of injuries that made her skin crawl and sick to her stomach. This man meant her harm. Her stomach twisted in knots, and bile filled her throat. She thought she might lose her dinner. Her legs turned to stone. Her entire body went rigid.

"And I'll knock yours out with this buckshot," a voice came from the shadows.

It was Mrs. Evans, and she had a rifle leveled at the man. "Let her go and git!" she commanded.

He hesitated. Mrs. Evans cocked the gun. She stared at the man levelly. She wasn't spoofing. She would shoot if she needed to.

Louisa was too frightened to breathe. Would she do it? Would Mrs. Evans really shoot him while he held her? Would she get shot, too? Louisa looked at Mrs. Evans. Raw, wild fear was in her eyes.

"I'll give you to the count of three," Mrs. Evans said, "And I'm a dang good shot. Ask anyone around these parts."

He let Louisa go and ran, disappearing around the corner of the house. Louisa sagged to the ground, rubbing her arm and wrist where he had wrenched it. She breathed in shallow, ragged breaths.

"Are you all right?" Mrs. Evans asked Louisa.

She pulled herself up and took another shaky breath. "I'll be all right."

"I can see the reason why people need those telephone things now," Mrs. Evans stated. "I wish I could call the sheriff."

"We can tell him in the morning," Louisa said.

"Well, I'm taking Burt's advice and locking up tonight. That tramp could be hiding anywhere in the Amusement Park. I didn't like the looks of him," Mrs. Evans said.

They went inside. They locked the boarding house up tight between them, checking locks on doors and windows.

"Let me wait on you tonight, Louisa. I'll make you a cup of

hot milk. Did you know my mother used to put pepper in it?" Mrs. Evans said.

"Pepper?" Louisa asked, wrinkling her nose.

"Pepper," Mrs. Evans said. "You can try it if you want to. Or not. And, by the way, perhaps you should start calling me Mother Evans now."

Louisa sat at the kitchen table. Her hands still shook a little. Her arm and wrist were sore, and she suspected she would have bruises in the morning.

Mother Evans brought the milk and a plate with buttered bread to the kitchen table. Louisa felt her heart rate returning to normal as she sipped the warm milk. She tried the pepper in the milk and found the savory flavor delicious and told Mother Evans so.

"Are you sure you're all right?" Mother Evans asked.

Louisa put a hand to her heart. "I think so. I'll be a little bruised tomorrow, but I'll be fine. Thank you again for rescuing me."

"No one is going to hurt someone in my family!" Mother Evans stated.

Louisa stared at her.

She stared back, meeting Louisa's eyes, "You heard me. I am very grateful you and Willie found one another. I was wrong last summer. And I owe you and Emma a huge thank you for saving me."

Louisa didn't know what to say. Tears filled her eyes, and she pushed herself up from her chair and hugged Mother Evans. Mother Evans was not a demonstrative person, but she hugged Louisa and patted her back.

"Now, now," she said, and Louisa noticed her eyes filling up, too, when she pulled back from the hug.

The warm milk and the shock of the attack made Louisa very tired. She yawned and yawned.

"You go on up to bed. I'll clean up," Mother Evans told her.

"Thank you," Louisa replied.

As tired as she was, she was floating on a cloud of happiness from what Mother Evans told her about her and Willie. Now, they had no obstacles, except for him to get well. She would write to him tomorrow to see when he might be able to come home. Perhaps he could get leave for the Thanksgiving holiday. Perhaps Nurse Williams could accompany him. Ideas swirled in her head as she succumbed to sleep with a serene smile on her lips.

Fifty-Seven

Sometimes, bonfire glass is created when trash is burned at coastal landfills and not from campfires.

Willie was healing nicely. He now enjoyed physiotherapy and having his body become strong and whole again. He felt so fortunate that he hadn't been maimed in any way, even though the mental issues were insidious. The nightmares and trembling hadn't ceased, but they had calmed tremendously. The attacks that came were seemingly random. He was fine one minute, and then the next, he was back at the front with all of its horrors. It was as if something overtook him, and Willie's real self, switched back to his soldier self, and he could smell the acrid smell of gunpowder and the stink of death that never went away. The psychologist that he was working with was trying to help him figure out the triggers of the episodes. Willie was thinking part of it was when he smelled some of the stink of the wounds, and sometimes sounds. Certain hospital foods reminded him of the vittles they had eaten at the front. Sometimes, the whiff of someone's cigarette was the same brand of someone who had died fighting. Willie could only guess.

Fort McHenry had become a community with the hospital on the grounds. Baltimore had turned itself out to help soldiers and sponsored entertainment and educational opportunities. Willie was going to occupational therapy to learn electrical work. He thought it would come in handy for the future with the boarding house and the amusement park. Metalwork also interested him, but he had a feeling that electricity would take off in this world, and he wanted to learn as much about it as he could.

He attended the concerts, the movies, and the dances sponsored at the hospital, but he couldn't think about another girl except Louisa. What he didn't like about the social activities was the bevy of eager mamas simpering over the soldiers and seeking husbands for their daughters. Most of the girls were all right. Some were embarrassed by their mothers' obvious machinations of husband-seeking. Others were bold and clear they wanted to get married. Some were mourning their sweethearts that had been lost in the war. He had met one of the desperate ones the other night. She clearly had had too much punch of which someone had spiked. She flirted with him shamelessly and kept putting her hand on his arm. He was polite as he could be, not wanting to show her his disgust over the situation. Eventually, he could dance with her and stop 'conveniently' in front of another soldier he knew was unattached. He made brief introductions, gratefully placed her hand in his, and bowed out. He left the dance then and stood by the sea wall, staring south to where he knew Louisa was, with his mom. Louisa. All he could think about was Louisa, her long brown hair, and beautiful blue eyes. How he missed her.

Love was a funny thing. Willie and Louisa were apart, but their love was still like a small flame that was perpetually burning inside him. He had read that somewhere, in one of the books that made its way through the hospital ward. It talked about 'love's eternal flame.' Willie could understand it now.

Willie kept pushing Nurse Williams on a date that he could go home. He begged her to use the hardship excuse that his mother couldn't manage without him. He didn't feel he needed to go to a farm to recuperate for a year. He had plenty of fresh air and a lot of work to keep him busy in Tolchester. He couldn't imagine how many things he would need to repair since he'd been gone.

Nurse Williams came and found him one evening after dinner. "Hello, Willie. How are you doing?"

"Good evening, Nurse Williams. I am doing just fine," he answered. "Do you have news for me?"

"Actually, I do," Nurse Williams explained. "Your mother and your lovely girl, Louisa, have invited me to Tolchester for Thanksgiving! I can't begin to tell you the last time that I have been away. I was thinking of taking them up on their offer."

"Oh, you should go, Nurse Williams!" Willie cried. "I wish I could go too. I am so close to home, and yet so far."

"Well," Nurse Williams's eyes twinkled with mischief, "I was thinking that if we could arrange it, perhaps we can get you discharged, and you could surprise your family for the holiday."

Willie's eyes grew round. He grasped her hands and held on to them, "Nurse Williams, that would make my dreams come true. Please, please tell the doctors that I am well enough to go. Please."

"I'll see what I can do. I can't promise anything," she said warningly, "but I will try my best. You need to try your best too. I think we can convince the team of physicians that you need to be at home to help your mother and that you live in a healthful place. I will tell them I am accompanying you to make sure you adjust to home life." She winked at him.

They whispered conspiratorially like two children with many secrets.

Fifty-Eight

ELLIE – 1969

Some sea glassers are concerned about sea glass becoming depleted, so they 'plant' sea glass by dumping bottles at the beach or just off-shore.

L ife without John began. Ellie wasn't sure what to do with herself. Depression slammed her, and she had no will to get up, shower, or do daily tasks. She lay in bed crying and waiting for what she didn't know, turning the piece of blue sea glass over and over in her hand. The depression surprised her. John had only been part of her life for a short time, but it was enough. She loved him, yes. She loved him deeply, but beyond that was a bond that she had never felt with another person. It was more than friendship, too. If asked, she wouldn't be able to put it into words. It felt like a piece of her was missing now that he was gone. It was as though a piece of her soul was missing from her body.

Aunt Penny was patient with her at first. She let her wallow for a couple of days. By the third day, her patience ebbed. She sat, crossed-legged, on the floor next to the bed.

"Ellie, you need to be part of the problem or part of the solution," Aunt Penny told her sternly.

"How?" Ellie asked miserably, turning her tear-stained face towards Aunt Penny.

"Wallowing in misery does no one any good," Penny snapped. "I know you miss John. Nothing in our immediate power will bring him back. But, we can voice our protest about the war. Interested?"

Ellie nodded.

Ellie hadn't written to John yet. She didn't want to sound whiny and didn't know what to say. Aunt Penny suggested she tell John about her days and what she's been doing.

"It will give him a sense of home," Aunt Penny suggested.

So, Ellie began to write.

Dear John,

I've been missing you so much and just, plain miserable for the last few days. I haven't done anything except lay around and cry. Aunt Penny snapped me out of it. So, here's the beginning of my letters and letters to you.

Aunt Penny suggested we add our voices to those protesting the war. I heard on the news that people were angry with the soldiers coming back. I don't understand people sometimes. Aunt Penny will keep me busy between her business, helping me create a portfolio for art school, and protesting the war. Did I tell you she wants us to have a joint show at a gallery? She thought having a gallery show on my resume would be good when I apply for art school. I want to work on more scarves and perhaps a kimono with the same technique I used to create your mom's scarf and my butterfly t-shirt. It probably sounds weird, but seeing how the colors merge, blend, and stretch with that technique is exciting. Next week, I promised Dora I would go to her house for the natural dye lessons and lessons on spinning. There's so much to learn.

Carl said a new guy is starting later this week to do your job. I haven't met him yet. He's going to live in an old camper on the grounds. Aunt Penny met him. She told me privately she thinks he's a grifter. I don't know.

What is boot camp like? Is it terribly hard? You must be exhausted. I can't stop thinking about you. I love you, and I miss you.

Your,

Ellie

Ellie sealed the letter and walked to the campground office to mail it. The humidity level was skyrocketing, and Ellie felt like an old, wrung-out rag when she reached the office. She was happy to step into the coolness of the story.

Betty greeted her with her usual cheerful countenance. "How are you, Ellie? How are you holding up?"

"I've been immersed in my own sadness, Betty. I miss John so much!" Ellie told her, biting her lip so as not to cry.

Betty nodded sympathetically. "I remember when Carl went off to war. I thought I would curl up and die, but I didn't."

"How did you manage it?" Ellie asked

"One day at a time," Betty answered, "and I kept busy and sent as much positive energy as I could to Carl."

Ellie nodded and handed her letter to be mailed. "The first of many," she told Betty.

"We're going to send him a card and letters too. Carl said that mail is a lifeline in the Army."

"Then, I will write as many letters as I can," Ellie promised.

Fifty-Nine

JOHN – 1969

Sea glass bottle stoppers are usually very old and prized by collectors.

John's world changed on a dime the moment he stepped off the bus for basic training. The bus was filled with other young men. They were all terrified, the same as John. And they needed to survive basic training. They pulled into the base to deboard with a sergeant yelling at them at the top of his lungs.

As they waited in line to depart the bus, one guy muttered loudly for many of the men to hear, "Baby, we're not in Kansas anymore."

Another joked nervously, "And don't get caught with the ruby-red slippers."

And a third said, "But, that might get you home."

"...or in jail," another added.

John waited his turn, quietly listening to the quips ahead. He couldn't understand what the sergeant was yelling ahead. Whatever it was, it was derogatory. And that was his beginning. They lined them up off the bus, all the time yelling, yelling, yelling.

Expectations were high. John felt like a robot. Up early and drill, drill, drill until they practically passed out at the end of the day. The training officers were constantly screaming at them, telling them, "We'll get the civilian blood out of you! You're Army now!' The drill sergeants and other officers drilled everything out of him until he became a fighting machine. They were no longer themselves but the property of the US military. They were trained that their primary mission was to become a grunt and a grunt that could kill.

John soon learned that his M16 was his best friend. He kept it with him constantly, wrapping the strap around him so that he was hugging an odd, cold teddy bear. They practiced on M14s, M16s, and a 45 revolver too. He learned that it was a matter of life or death if he didn't keep his weapon clean. His one sergeant yelled, "If your weapon isn't clean, it's not reliable. If your weapon isn't reliable, you wake up dead. Game over!" It was a constant reminder they were preparing for war.

They ran them for miles and miles and miles. John was starving. He never ate so much in his life when he had mealtimes. Breakfast, he learned, was the most important meal of the day for him. It was where he could nearly gorge on eggs, coffee, orange juice, bacon, pancakes, toast, and fruit to get him through the harsh training. For many days, he felt like an animal, corralled through food, training, food, and brief rest. He read Ellie's first letter when it arrived. He smiled at the memory of her bent over an art piece with her tongue between her teeth as she worked. He loved watching her work at her art. She became so focused she turned off the world. It was as if she was welded to the art she was working on, with her spirit traveling through her hands, adding a bit of her essence to each piece. He only saw paints and materials and was in awe of her beautiful creations.

> *Dear Ellie,*
> *It's a different world at boot camp. We drill, and drill, and drill. The training instructors yell so much it echoes in my*

ears even when we have free time. I've turned into one of the army's robots. They're drilling us so much that we don't have time to think about going to Vietnam. We're all scared. But they drill us to the point of exhaustion, and we can't think a thought of our own.

I miss you. I miss holding you and kissing you. I miss our lazy summer days at the beach. Please give your Aunt Penny, Carl, and Betty my best.

I love you.

John

John paused after writing the letter. He imagined Ellie reading it, perhaps out by the firepit, or maybe she took it to the beach to read, stretching out her long, tanned legs in the sand. Next, he penned a quick letter to his parents. He told his mom he missed her meatloaf and that he even missed his chores at home. That would make her smile. John took his letters to mail. A bunch of guys were playing football. Others were sitting and smoking. A few were polishing their boots. Walking back to his bunk, he wondered how many of them would survive this. Would he?

The next round of training was out in the field. Drill. Drill. Drill. John learned to hate mud. He learned to hate C-rations. Some, he learned, were leftovers from World War II. But he didn't care. It was food. Inside the C-rats were three cigarettes. At first, John gave them away to men he knew who smoked. Boredom and curiosity led him to smoke.

And, in eight weeks, it was over. The military machine chewed him up as a naïve young man and spit him out as a slightly jaded, hard-muscled soldier.

Dear Ellie,

It's over. Boot camp, I mean. I feel like I've been in a meat grinder, but now I am a solder. I'm heading to a school for surveying and civil engineering. It will give me some hands-on experience after my couple of classes in college. Hands-on expe-rience can't hurt. But I don't know what to expect. This is the next step before we're shipped to Nam.

How are you doing? Are things still going well at the Farmers Market? You said in your one letter that you had fallen in love with Dora's sheep. Are you turning into a hippie farmer? What are you making now?

I love you.

John

John scored high on the ASVAB test and was sent to his school of choice for training to be a combat engineer. He was disheartened to find that the engineering teams were often the ones to lead in the jungle, paving the way for the troops and, therefore, in high danger. He spent time practicing mine-sweeping and blowing things up with C4 explosives. He learned they would be in construction and demolition. He learned how to drive a bulldozer and a dump truck. Vietnam was coming soon, and he knew it. A small trickle of fear seemed permanently lodged in his brain. The unknown was out there. Vietnam was out there. Eventually, they corralled them onto a plane and were flown to Vietnam.

The plane banked hard as they neared Vietnam, and the beauty of the tropical country struck John. The water was turquoise and drastically different from his Maryland Chesapeake Bay water. The mountains shot out of the earth like pointed cones covered in green vegetation. They reminded John of the conical volcanoes he made as a kid and filled with baking soda and vinegar to erupt.

When they deboarded the plane, the heat hit them like they were walking into a wall. He was familiar with the heat and humidity of Maryland, but this was heat and humidity that took your breath away.

They were rushed off the plane with their belongings, and

they watched as coffins and body bags were loaded onto the plane quickly. John felt sick. He had a rock in the pit of his stomach. His comrades at arms were shocked too, and many stood, mouths open, staring, until a sergeant pushed them onto their buses and took them to barracks.

Dear Ellie,

I made it. I'm in Nam. I know it's hot in Maryland right now, but you can't even begin to imagine the heat in this coun-try. It whacks you when you deboard the plane. I want to move to Alaska or the North Pole when this is over. I dream of being cold.

I don't know when I'll be able to send letters again. We're headed out to the field.

I love you.

John

He penned the letter quickly and took it to post. He was so very tired, and it was beastly hot. From what the guys said, they were heading to the jungle to build a road. He crawled into the bunk assigned to him, briefly thinking of his bed at home. And he thought of Ellie, of holding her when they fell asleep on the sand that last night. God, how he missed her. He fell asleep, dreaming about Ellie's eyes, hair, and lips until they were roused rudely and shoved onto copters to be taken out in the field.

It was a nightmare, only it was real. The men smoked cigarette after cigarette out of nervousness and to wake them up. The copter was crowded, and they didn't talk much. Some of the guys fell back to sleep. John looked out over the expanse of jungle. It was a medley of deep greens and shadows. He couldn't get over the mountains. They were so different from the rolling hills in Maryland and the mountains he was familiar with from family trips to West Virginia and Pennsylvania. He remembered the gentle blue-green expanse of mountains that rolled like ripples on the water. These mountains were jagged and very, very green. He didn't see any outcroppings of rocks like the ones he saw along the highways in Pennsylvania. These mountains were dramatic and surreal at the same time. He thought of Ellie and how she liked to blend colors. She would love to see the brilliant greens of Vietnam and the sun rising through the mist. He would need to try to write about what he was seeing in his next letter to her.

John's troop of engineers landed near the edge of a road. It was a road, he learned. They were to continue. The helicopter pilot shooed them off with their belongings. Crouching, they ran to the outer edge of the helicopter's blades, rushing toward the sea of tents. The copter took off quickly.

They were introduced to a Lieutenant who showed them their sleeping quarters – tents near the edge of the jungle where they dumped their stuff and proceeded to the Mess tent. It was crowded and noisy. Some of the people were friendly and introduced themselves. Some completely ignored them.

John had made friends with Lenny, his seatmate on the plane. Lenny told John not to be surprised if people ignored you when they landed. His brother, who'd served in Vietnam earlier, said when you first arrive in Vietnam, many people ignore you, just in case you get killed right away. Lenny told everyone this to their table at dinner that night. The guys at his table were stunned into silence with this announcement. Then, they all looked around the mess tent. They were being ignored. It was like they didn't exist, an invisible island in a sea of conversation and the sound of cutlery. They turned back to their food soberly.

After dinner, his group tried to shake off Lenny's conversation. Some went to play cards, smoke, or smoke dope. The heavy, sweet, but acrid smell of marijuana was prevalent as heavy clouds around the camp. John went back to the barracks. He tried to write a letter to Ellie. His words to her seemed stilted. He tore up the letter and tried again, but it was of no use. He couldn't tell her about the cold-shoulder reception at the camp.

Screeching woke him up from his dreams of Ellie. He didn't know where the sound came from. He reached for his M16, terrified the Viet Cong were going to attack at any moment.

Stan, from the bunk next door, stage whispered, "What the hell is that?"

"I don't know," he returned in a whisper.

Someone down the row growled, "It's monkeys. It's the damn monkeys. Go back to sleep."

Despite the knowledge that it was the monkeys screaming, John kept his M16 by his side at the ready. He slept fitfully; his sweet dreams of Ellie were long gone. Now, ghosts and monkeys roiled in front of his eyes in nightmares that filled any moments he slept.

Morning came much too early. They were roused and, after breakfast, sent out in a convoy to begin the roadwork. Jungle bordered the road like rickrack on a dress. The jungle looked dark and deep; no matter how hard he tried, John couldn't see anything through the vegetation. He kept looking for movement, for something, but it yielded only dark silence this morning. He had a bad feeling about the dark and foreboding jungle. It wasn't the friendly forests of Maryland with spaces between the trees and sunlight streaming through the branches. He remembered Pete had told him a Japanese word for the light between the trees – Komorebi. The scouts used to chant it softly when they were out on a hike. There was something beautiful about the word and seeing that filtered sunlight through the leaves. Almost holy. Pete. He had been here, somewhere in Vietnam. He wished he could talk with him about this forest. He wondered if Pete would have had a word for this jungle. It was so alien to John. He thought there was something sinister about the darkness and the vegetation pressing down on them, with the road the only ribbon of light.

They stopped at the end and poured out of the vehicles, awaiting the next orders, sweating heavily in the building heat of the day. John swiped at the seat, pouring down his forehead. The sergeant posted guards even though everything seemed quiet. There was a tension in the air. He was puzzled by this. He couldn't see anything in the jungle shadows but noticed how the guards' eyes darted back and forth, occasionally stopping to look piercingly into the darkness. The guards' tension bred fear among the new guys. John and the other newbies had been told that the Vietcong were vigilant in setting mines and that one of their daily tasks was to sweep for mines. Intelligence said the Vietcong would use almost anything to make a landmine. They had to be careful if a bicycle or a beer or soda can were lying about. The Vietcong used mousetraps, watch batteries, and flashlight batteries to arm the mines. Some of the men used mine sweepers, others spread out down the road in a slow and tedious search, looking for any sign of digging or detonating wires. If all was clear, they could move ahead with their work.

John was one of the soldiers at the edge of the road, looking for any signs of mines. It was hot, slow work as they had to check every inch. Peering down at the road, he noticed that his shoelace was loose. He reached down to tie his boot tighter. As he bent over, he felt a zing fly past his ear and another near his feet. Sniper fire. It was real. He hit the ground as he heard counterfire from the guards. He reached for his M16 and began to shoot into the darkness. He shot, randomly firing into the vegetation, fear overtaking everything else, and the one shred of sanity he had was to keep himself alive. And that was day one.

Sixty

LOUISA – 1918

17th and 18th-century pipe stems are treasured artifacts that can be found on Chesapeake Bay shores.

Louisa found a rhythm to her days. She loved Tolchester. She loved the peace and quiet and the freedom she had to wander the beach. Mother Evans scolded her for tracking in the sand and finding her beach treasures of glass and pretty stones all over the boarding house.

Louisa was stunned by the brilliant color of the sunsets of autumn. She thought the sunsets she saw with Willie were beautiful, but now, the sky seemed to be on fire when the sunset. She wished she could paint and knew in her heart she didn't have the skill to capture the beauty of what she saw. And, it was so fleeting. Every breath brought a new nuance of color, painting the sky. She couldn't tear herself away even though Mother Evans called to her.

"Just a moment," Louisa called back. She held her breath as clouds moved, creating a dramatic shadow in the sky painting.

"Here you are! You're going to catch your death by getting cold. It's chilly out here!" Mother Evans chided Louisa.

She sat, somewhat heavily, beside Louisa on the steps.

"I'm fine," she insisted.

Mother Evans dropped a woolen shawl over her shoulders, and Louisa was suddenly grateful for its warmth. She hadn't realized how chilled she had become.

"You like it here, don't you?" Mother Evans asked after a minute. She, too, watched the drama of the sun setting.

"I love it here," Louisa breathed. "I think I like it better now than in the summertime."

Mother Evans nodded in agreement. "If you can survive the honky-tonk and the flibberty-gibbet tourists for a couple of months, we're rewarded with this." She waved a hand at the sky and continued, "Now, mind you, the winter is another story. It can get mighty cold with the wind from the bay."

"But you love it, don't you?" Louisa asked.

"I wouldn't trade this spot with Buckingham Palace," Mother Evans said determinedly.

"I feel the same," Louisa confided. "Now, if we can only get Willie home. That would make everything perfect," she said with a sigh.

"I'm in agreement with you, Louisa. I worry about him and what the war did to him. Your stories of the men in the hospital and how Willie can't control his legs, why I..." she broke off.

"Willie's getting better. Honest! Nurse Williams told me he was much better. They're sending him to classes. Willie's learning about electricity. You know he has a lot of plans for the boarding house, don't you?"

Mother Evans answered slowly, "Yes, he's told me some of his ideas. I thought they were flights of fancy. I know some of them are pretty good, though. Won't Willie be surprised when he comes home to find that we have a telephone?"

Louisa chuckled about this. After the tramp incident, Mother Evans had a telephone installed. They were all a little frightened of the new technology but were becoming used to it. The phone didn't ring much, and when they used it, it was scary-magical how the crackling voices came through the line. Louisa wondered if they might talk to Willie sometime. How she would love to hear his voice again.

"Come on, girl. It's getting dark, and I didn't bring a lantern," Mother Evans said, breaking Louisa out of her reverie.

Louisa tore her eyes away from the vista. The colors of the sky deepened into shadows and twilight. Shadows stretched out into the water, turning swathes of its blue-gray surface into purple-blackness that rippled, grew, and receded like storm clouds. The beauty of the stark winter landscape almost made up for the fact that Grandmama was gone and Willie wasn't with her. Louisa scrambled up the steps after Mother Evans and into the warmth of the kitchen, where Emma was pulling something savory from the oven.

Sixty-One

WILLIE- 1918

Some sea glass looks like it was frosted with sugar, while other glass, known as "silkies," are soft and smooth.

The doctors wanted Willie to walk. There were days when he thought it would never happen. How did babies go about it so cheerfully? Walking was painful, and he was unsteady. If his limbs began to tremble, he feared he would fall. His doctors drummed into him that he needed to overcome the fears and nightmares of the war to be fully healed. He wondered if that would ever happen. The nightmares were woven into every cell in his brain. They had diminished to an extent, but they still haunted him.

As he became more mobile, he was astounded by the small city at Fort McHenry. There were nearly one hundred buildings in this hospital. It always seemed to be bustling. Willie heard through the grapevine of men in the barracks that this was one of the largest army medical surgical centers. They brought hundreds of men here for surgery and also plastic surgery, where they tried to repair some of the ghastly wounds so that the men looked normal again.

As he practiced walking through the wards, he saw the vestiges of the horrors he witnessed. He watched the doctors perform many miracles to recreate a prototype of bone and sinew. But, seeing the horrific wounds caused his limbs to tremble and nightmares to haunt his nights.

Even with the nightmares, he was sure he was getting better. He was frustrated by the doctors keeping him at the hospital. He missed Louisa, and he missed his mother. Apparently, from their letters, they were getting on famously. He was a little surprised and a little jealous.

His mother wrote, *"That girl of yours, Willie. She loves the chickens! She likes to feed them and gather the eggs. She's named every chicken and thinks of them as pets. One of the Rhode Island Reds is her favorite. She named it Rusty. That chicken sits on her lap like a cat. I don't know what she will do when winter comes and one of the flock becomes dinner."*

Willie could imagine Louisa with the chickens. She had told him she always wanted a pet but her grandmama said no. Maybe when he got home, he would get her a puppy. When he got home...whenever that would be. He pestered Nurse Williams with the topic of going home. He didn't want to go to some farm. He had plenty of physiotherapy opportunities in Tolchester. He wondered who had put the park to sleep for the winter. Burt couldn't do it by himself.

And preparing for winter, that was another story. He wondered how his mom and Louisa would survive this winter. What about wood? How would they ever get enough wood to last them through the winter?

Willie put his mother's letter away. He needed to find Nurse Williams and beg her once again to find a way for him to go home.

Sixty-Two

ELLIE – 1969

Safety glass sea glass is an unusual find where you can see the wire mesh patterns within the glass that form unique patterns.

The sunny summer days of farmers' markets and festivals had a pall over them. Without John, she had difficulty feeling joy.

Dora pulled her aside one day. "Ellie, you need to snap out of this. Women have been sending their men off to war for millennia. You need to be strong," she advised Ellie.

"Strong? What's that?" Ellie asked.

And that was when her grief turned to anger. The daily body count on the news rose and fell like the tide on the bay, but it didn't get any better. It was senseless death, and her John was in the thick of it. She didn't know where he was. The rare letters she received she shared with his mom, who would come to visit her at the Farmers' Market. Sometimes, they went out for pie and coffee at the local diner. They bonded in John's absence. And they hung onto each other for hope that John would come home alive.

The tide of campers waned as the weather grew cooler. Ellie and Penny were so busy on weekends with the markets and protests, that she barely noticed the quietude of the campground on the weekends because she was so weary from the days. Ellie and Penny joined thousands as they protested the Vietnam War. Ellie woke up hoarse from shouting, "Peace now! Peace Now!" Her feet hurt from what seemed miles of walking and marching in protest.

She noticed the change in the campground during the week, knowing children were in school and campers were scarce. Ellie traded her shorts, t-shirt, and flip-flops for jeans, boots, and a cardigan. She sat on the beach, thinking about John, wondering how he was doing as she stared at the line where the water met the sky. He complained of the heat and the humidity in Vietnam. She wondered if she could send him an autumn leaf or two to share the changes of the seasons. Time continued to pass, and her heart ached.

In November, when the weather had turned crisp, Penny and Ellie drove to Washington, D.C. It wasn't their first protest there, but this time, Ellie was worried. She had a gut feeling that this protest would be different. They parked on a side street this morning, just off of DuPont Circle. The protest was to take place outside of the Embassy of South Vietnam. Ellie and Penny had not formally joined any groups protesting the war. They independently showed up at protests and helped where they could. Today's march focused on the South Vietnamese Embassy to hand them an 'eviction notice.' It was a planned peaceful protest.

As Ellie and Penny got into the thick of it, they heard rumors that the permits for a demonstration were not approved. The already enormous crowd grew and moved forward, marching up Massachusetts Avenue. Penny and Ellie had linked arms, shouting and carrying their sign touting "No More War!" It was a familiar invocation at every protest.

Ellie wasn't sure what happened next. The crush of humanity made walking difficult. The marchers moved and squashed into one another, and there wasn't room to move or step. The shouting became louder. She thought she saw armed police on the perimeter. The crowd surged forward, step by step, until smoke and chaos filled the air. Teargas.

Ellie tried to pull her t-shirt over her nose, but the tear gas enveloped her. Her chest was tight, she couldn't breathe, and she let go of Penny's arm to cough and cough, each breath becoming more painful as the chemicals seared her eyes, her nose, and her lungs. Ellie stumbled. Someone caught her elbow. She moved, unseeing, through the crowd, crying out Penny's name.

Somehow, she found the sidewalk. She didn't know where she was and sank on some steps to cough more. Hands, stranger's hands, pulled her inside a building. Terrified and unable to see properly, she tried to protest and pull away, but the hands pulled her forward. Through her streaming, burning eyes, she saw shadows and darkness.

Inside, it was cool but not cold. It was quiet and away from the chaotic crowd outside. She wiped at her eyes with the backs of her hand. The chemical was on her hands, and her eyes continued to burn.

Someone spoke to her soothingly, but she didn't understand them. The shouting still rang in her ears. She wanted the burning in her eyes to stop. A cool, wet cloth was put in her hands, and she wiped away at her face. Relief came as some of the chemicals were wiped away.

When she could open her eyes and look around, Ellie saw that she was in a church. The smiling, kind eyes of a priest were in front of her. She only knew he was a priest because of his collar. Her terror subsided a fraction. He wore a signet ring and held a pan filled with damp towels. His navy blue cardigan was buttoned up. He reminded her somewhat of Mr. Rogers of the PBS children's television program. This man and Mr. Rogers had the same kindness emanating from them. She calmed.

"Welcome to St. Thomas's church. I am Father David. You're

in the sanctuary for sanctuary." He smiled at his play on words. "And you are?"

"Ellie, Ellie Ryan," she told him. As her wits returned, she said, "I was with my aunt – Penny Blackwood. Is she here?"

"I'll check," he said. He handed her another cool, wet cloth and told her to continue to wipe the chemical off her skin.

Ellie did and closed her eyes. She was sitting on the floor against a pew. Where could Aunt Penny be? She hoped she was all right. The acrid smell of the tear gas was coming from her clothes. She wanted to rip the shirt off her head. She noticed another priest was coming with t-shirts and scissors. People were cutting off their clothes and putting them into a trash bag. They pulled new shirts over their heads. She could see from their faces that it was a relief from the tear gas. She waited her turn, albeit anxiously.

Eventually, Father David returned. He had not found Penny, and Ellie grew worried.

"I must go," she told him. "I have a place to meet my aunt."

"Ellie, it might not be safe outside," he paused and frowned, "We've been hearing reports of violence with this supposed peaceful protest."

"But I must see if she's there," Ellie insisted.

"Promise me that you'll return if you can't find your aunt?" the priest asked.

Ellie hesitated and thought better of it. If she couldn't find Aunt Penny, this was a safe place. One step at a time. Isn't that what her grandmother used to say? It was definitely a time to listen to those wise words.

She looked at the priest. "Father David, I promise I will be back if I can't find my aunt. I will need more assistance then. Thank you. Thank you and your colleagues for..." There was too much to thank them for, "for the sanctuary."

He nodded in understanding and placed a hand on her shoulder, squeezing gently. Ellie made her way to exit the church.

Ellie stepped outside into the afternoon sunshine. She gaped at what she saw before her. The tear gas had dispersed, and the streets were littered with signs and shirts that had been ripped away from people. They looked like roadkill made of cloth. Ellie needed to get her bearings. She stood on the steps of the church, trying to remember how they had arrived at that spot. She had to find the Beast and Aunt Penny. Worry niggled her, and she tried to quell the panic that wanted to rise inside of her. What had happened to everyone? She tried not to think about what to do if she couldn't find Aunt Penny. Call the police? Call her parents? Those were not pleasant thoughts. She needed to find Aunt Penny and the Beast.

Ellie began to walk. She asked for directions and eventually found DuPont Circle. From there, she proceeded to find the side street where the Beast was parked. Ellie was never so happy to see that old van in her life. Sitting inside was Penny, head back, eyes closed.

"Aunt Penny!" She must have screamed her name as Penny's eyes flew open and Penny flew out of the van and gathered Ellie in a hug.

"Oh my God! Oh my God! I'm so glad you're all right!" Penny said over and over again.

They both collapsed into their seats in the van and started talking at once. And they both stopped talking at once. And then they giggled and laughed in relief. Laughing made them both cough.

Penny drove them home.

After they showered, they lounged on the small couch in the camper. Ellie drew her knees up to her and hugged them.

"I'm missing the campfire tonight," Penny told Ellie. "There's something about watching the flames that is soothing."

Penny turned off the television. The talking heads bothered both of them this evening. They went to bed, exhausted, only to have the phone jangle them out of deep sleep.

Penny answered the phone first with a quavering " Hello?" She listened and clutched the phone.

By this time, Ellie was awake, "What is it?" she whispered, "What happened?"

Penny handed the phone to Ellie, telling the caller to hold on a minute.

"Hello?" Ellie asked into the heavy receiver, a cold fear settled inside of her. Her hands shook.

"Ellie, it's Margaret Black," the voice came through the line. Ellie could tell that she had been crying.

"Ellie, are you there?" Mrs. Black asked.

Ellie swallowed hard, knowing she had to be brave for whatever news Mrs. Black had called to share in the middle of the night.

"Ellie, I couldn't wait until morning to call. I don't have much news. The only thing I know is," and she stopped to sob, "Ellie, John has been shot."

Ellie heard the news as if it had been whispered down a tunnel.

"But, Ellie! He's coming home! Home!" Margaret Black's voice broke. "I'm sorry to wake you, but I needed you to know. He's coming home."

"Thank you. Thank you, Mrs. Black!" Ellie told her.

"I'll talk to you soon, dear, as soon as I get more information, alright?" Mrs. Black's voice came through the telephone.

"All right," Ellie said as she hung up the phone.

"He's coming home!" she said in an elated whisper. "Home." It had been nearly six long months since he had been gone, but he was coming home, and he was alive. But, he was wounded. What did that mean? Ellie's relief and worry merged into a swirl of emotions. The unknown loomed before her, and her imagination ran wild. Wounded? How wounded?

Sixty-Three

JOHN – 1969

Collectors often try to solve the puzzle of letters they sometimes find on sea glass. Bottle guides are a useful tool for this.

John felt ancient as the tropical rain pelted him on his helmet and plastic poncho that did little to keep the dampness out. He had never been as wet in his life as in Vietnam. This had been the longest months of his life, crouching in the jungle, always on edge, and with little to no sleep. Ellie's cheery letters of life in Maryland were a wonderful and terrible reminder of the life he had left back home.

It was autumn. He had been gone six months. He should be in classes, complaining about homework, raking leaves with his dad, and watching football. What he wouldn't give for a crisp apple or the chill of the evening air in October. It was still beastly hot in Vietnam. The rain wasn't cooling; it only made it more humid, if that was even possible. Some days, he felt like he was breathing liquid, the air was so dense with humidity.

He felt old. He had seen more men killed or maimed in the last few months than he cared to see. He wasn't squeamish, but the gaping wounds of blood, organs, and tissue were like a macabre modern painting of garish colors. His innocence was gone. He felt grim and hardened. And now it was his turn to ignore the new recruits shipped into his camp. He had made acquaintances with the new guys only to learn they returned in a body bag the next day. Death was everywhere. It sickened him. But now, he was in the 'kill or be killed' mode of survival. He used his weapon almost without thinking. Surviving was his prime directive. Surviving and getting home to his parents and Ellie.

He smoked weed now, like the rest of them. It brought him a small sense of calmness instead of the constant, heightened edginess they lived daily. He even tried a tab of LSD, only to have his 'trip' bring him garish nightmares that returned every so often, and he would wake screaming hoarsely. He vowed he would never take it again.

Now, the noises of the jungle were calmer with the beating rain, but everyone was on edge. They all knew the Viet Cong attacked when it rained because you couldn't hear them in the forest. They were stealth itself, moving through the trees like ghosts. And they were out to kill you. It was survival of the fittest. And he didn't want to become a prisoner of war. That was a fate worse than death. He had heard the stories. He had heard stories of the unspeakable horrors of the torture they put the prisoners through.

John didn't blame the Viet Cong. He still saw no point in this war, and here they were, invading another country, tearing and bombing it to shreds, killing the men, the women, and the children. He had heard horror stories, most of which he knew were true. Fear was his constant companion. He was tired of seeing, hearing, and smelling death. He and his buddy Lenny had survived thus far. They had a mutual mantra of three hundred sixty-five days and a wake-up. And any attack erased the thought of how many days. When the Viet Cong attacked, it was kill or be killed.

They had dumped them in the jungle to work on a helicopter

pad. He hadn't seen the camp for days. They were dirty, smelly, hungry, and now wet. They couldn't work with the constant rain, so boredom had become his companion as he kept watch.

Lenny crawled up next to him, bringing him more cigarettes. They smoked together as the rain continued to pour down on them. It was a beautiful country, but at that moment, he hated it. He closed his eyes for just a moment and thought about Ellie. He needed to survive to get back to Ellie. He just wanted to go home. He daydreamed. And that was his downfall.

A crack of a sound. Slight, but different from the rain, brought John out of his daydream. And they were upon them. A rain of bullets now. He shot blindly into the forest. Kill or be killed. Chaos reigned in the camp. Everyone was shooting and shouting. Explosion after explosion. There was an explosion next to him, a bright flash, and a sound of agony. Lenny. He couldn't look. He needed to shoot. He did, round after round after round. And then he felt something hit his thigh, and a searing pain penetrated his leg as his body arched. His head banged into the tree, and all went black.

Sixty-Four

LOUISA -1918

Small clay pipes are rare and coveted finds along the Chesapeake Bay.

Louisa looked forward to Nurse Williams coming for the Thanksgiving holiday. The boarding house in Tolchester had become her second home, and she raced around like a dervish, getting everything perfect for the visit.

Mother Evans and Emma smiled indulgently at Louisa. They knew Louisa was anxious not only to see her friend, but to hear from Nurse Williams about Willie's condition. Willie's letters had been vague on his recovery lately. His letters were filled with his interest in electricity and the goings on at the hospital. He described the moving pictures and balls held for the servicemen. But he didn't write how he felt, only that he missed them.

Louisa raced to the pier, swaddled in a heavy coat and scarf against the wind that constantly blew on the bay. The steamship pulled up to the dock and Louisa fairly danced on the dock in anticipation. Nurse Williams disembarked with a large carpet bag. Burt had also come along and had the cart waiting with one of the donkeys to take them to the boarding house.

"Nurse Williams! Nurse Williams!" Louisa cried. "Welcome! It's so very good to see you!"

Louisa flung her arms around Nurse Williams in an impromptu hug.

Nurse Williams held Louisa a bit away from her after her hug.

"My, you're looking well, Louisa," Nurse Williams commented, "but I am no longer your supervisor. You should start calling me Eliza as my friends do."

Louisa blushed but said, "All right, Eliza," and grinned. And then Louisa began asking her questions about how she was, how everyone was at the hospital, and most importantly, how Willie was doing.

"I need you to tell me everything!" Louisa insisted. "But let's get you back to the boarding house where we can have a cup of tea and a proper chat. Burt is waiting with the cart. We need to go to the end of the pier. Brr, that wind is cold!"

Nurse Willams – Eliza laughed at Louisa.

"All right! All right, Louisa! I will tell you everything. But, about Willie," she paused.

"What? What?" Louisa questioned, panic clear in her voice.

"Well," Eliza said slyly, "I think he should tell you how he is himself," she ended triumphantly.

And coming down the gangplank was a soldier. His gait was slightly wobbly. Louisa squinted, staring at the figure. Louisa paled. Could it be Willie?

Her breath stopped. Her heart seemed to stop and then restart, dancing in her chest. She couldn't help it. She picked up her skirts and ran down the pier, her breath steamy white in the cold air. Willie couldn't run to her. Instead, he stopped and held out his arms. She ran into them, laughing and crying all at once. He laughed and gathered her into his arms.

"Surprised?" he asked.

"What do you think, sir?" Louisa laughed at him, pulling

away for a moment. "Oh my! Just wait until your mother sees you!"

Sixty-Five

WILLIE – 1918

The top part of a 'kick-up' is known as a mamelon. Glass bottle producers used to 'kick-up' the center part of the bottom of a bottle when glass blowing.

Willie was beyond pleased at his surprise arrival at his home. The look he saw in Louisa's eyes when she realized it was him was something he would hold in his heart forever. After giving Louisa a resounding kiss to the applause of Eliza, they made their way to the end of the pier to an astonished Burt.

Willie couldn't get enough of the view of Tolchester on their short ride back to the house. In all the places he had been in the last few months, there was nothing more beautiful than home. The tall, white-washed boarding house shone in the afternoon sun with the windows like beacons as they mirrored the late afternoon sunshine. The sun on the water glittered like gold-spattered crystals as the water riffled in the passing breeze.

Louisa and Eliza went straight to the kitchen to introduce Eliza. Willie held back a moment before making an entrance.

Mother Evans was at the stove when Burt and Willie came through the door.

"Hello, mother," Willie greeted with his rakish grin.

Mother Evans turned at Willie's voice. She paled and reached out for support. Louisa ran to her, but Willie reached her first, catching her up in a hug and giving her a resounding kiss on the cheek.

Willie had seldom seen his mother cry. But she sagged in his arms, crying tears of happiness and relief. Willie was shocked to see his mother. She looked well enough, but she had lost a tremendous amount of weight from her illness, and it seemed to him that she had aged considerably. He gathered her into a hug, feeling how small and fragile she felt in his arms. He was so very glad they had permitted him to come home. He knew he was needed here.

Emma prepared a feast that evening. Willie had forgotten how delicious food could taste. The hospital food hadn't been bad, but Emma's cooking was par excellence.

"You're spoiling me, Miss Emma," he told her when they had finished their meal. He stretched back and had to loosen his belt. That was something he hadn't done in years.

"And I will continue to do so, Mr. Willie," she returned stoutly.

"I don't know, Miss Emma, perhaps I should ask you to marry me. I wouldn't want to lose a good cook like you to someone else," he teased, winking at Burt. He saw how things were between Emma and Burt almost immediately after his arrival. He was glad to see the older man happy again. His wife's death had taken quite a toll.

"Oh, go on with you." Emma blushed. "Let me go and get dessert."

"No, wait," Willie told her. He turned to Louisa. "Since you turned me down, I must ask Louisa instead."

Louisa had been chatting non-stop with Eliza. She turned to Willie, questioning, "Ask me what?"

"Will you marry me, Louisa Dunn?" Willie asked, his tone serious, his eyes filled with love.

Willie had pushed his chair back from the table and had gone down on one knee. He pulled a small box from his uniform pocket. He opened it to reveal a beautiful gold gypsy ring with a small diamond shining from the center of the gold.

"Oh, Willie!" Louisa cried, throwing her arms around him and almost knocking him down. "Yes! Yes! I will marry you!"

He slipped the ring from the box and put it on her finger. She gave him a kiss in front of everyone.

Sixty-Six

Kick-ups are usually found on wine and champagne bottles.

John. John was home. She could barely believe it. It didn't look like 'her' John when he stepped from the cab. She wondered how he would be. John held her awkwardly, balancing crutches and trying to hold her while she cried into his shoulder. She felt him bury his face in her hair. She heard him sigh. It was as if a part of him melted into her, but there was a stiffness. She pulled back only to see a wary glance in his eyes. A wary glance and a pleading look. She didn't know what that meant. Where was her, John? Was he still in Vietnam in his mind? He pulled away from Ellie and went to hug his parents.

They took their joyful reunion inside the house. Thanks-giving had passed over a week ago, but Mrs. Black had prepared a replica feast with turkey and all the trimmings for her son. The conversation was slightly stilted. Aunt Penny kept up some lively chatter. John kept reaching out to touch her hand or leg, almost to see if she was real. Ellie could tell that he was trying hard. They had cleared the table and sat for a few minutes, letting their food settle before getting dessert. Ellie looked at Carl, and he caught her worried glance.

"Ellie, help me with getting dessert for these fine people. I have a special treat, a Concord grape pie. It was my mother's recipe and boy, is it yummy," Carl boomed.

"Ellie, don't forget the apple pie and the pumpkin pie, too," Mrs. Black called after her.

"Pie for everyone coming soon," Ellie called, hoping her anxiety wasn't apparent in her voice.

In the kitchen, Carl pulled the apple pie from the warm oven and the grape and pumpkin pie chilling on the back porch. Deftly, he cut the pies and put pieces on plates.

He looked Ellie square in the eye. "You'll have to give him some time, Ellie. Be patient with him. Lord, Betty waited a long, long time for me to come back to myself when I returned home. You see, the war is still part of him. This homeworld is what he wants, but if John is like me, it feels very surreal. He probably thinks he will wake up at any moment needing his M16." Carl's eyes had a faraway look, "There are still days I imagine hearing the crack of a bullet or the whistle of a bomb. You'll need to give him time. Lots and lots of time."

"Okay," Ellie said, her eyes filling with tears.

Carl came around the kitchen table and gave her a bear hug. Ellie hiccoughed, trying not to cry.

"Don't worry," Carl said, "he'll come back."

He let Ellie go, picked up several plates, and called out in a jovial, booming voice, "Pie for everyone! Who wants pie?"

Ellie took a deep breath and, pasted a smile on her face and picked up more plates with slices of pie and took them to the dining room.

Pie, conversation, and coffee lasted a while. Ellie excused herself to clean up the kitchen for Mrs. Black. Betty and Carl came to help. She patted Ellie's shoulder.

She caught Carl's eye, and he caught her worried glance. "It will be all right in the end," she advised. "But, you have some tough times ahead, girl. And you can always come to talk to me, or cry, or scream."

Ellie nodded. Betty kept the rest of the conversation light, asking about the craft shows Ellie and Aunt Penny had scheduled before the upcoming holiday.

Returning to the dining room, Ellie saw John barely able to stay awake.

"We should be going," Aunt Penny suggested.

They had come in Carl and Betty's sedan. Carl, Betty, and Penny went ahead after saying thank you and goodbye. Ellie hugged Mr. and Mrs. Black and went outside where John stood. He stood, eyes closed, breathing in the cold air like a lifeline.

"I dreamed of cold air in Nam," he said when he heard her approach.

"Brr," Ellie said.

"Nah, it's amazing," he returned, but his words were caught in a huge yawn.

Ellie stepped close to him, and he put his arms around her. She felt the distance from inside of him but still turned her face up for a kiss. His kiss was on the edge of perfunctory. She pulled away and went to the car, her feelings jumbled between love, hurt, and despair.

JOHN – 1969

Some people see sea glass as a representation of hope and renewal.

John's time in the hospital was spent in a haze of pain and drugged pain. The bullet that hit his leg tore through the tendons and muscles and shattered his femur. He was one of the lucky ones. It was his ticket home. And he wouldn't need to wait 365 days and a wake up. And he wouldn't arrive in a body bag. In many ways, he was elated, but he also felt guilty.

The hospital in Vietnam was crowded with every injury imaginable. John was helpless, his leg bound in a heavy cast, and he passed his days barely conscious. When they finally stopped medicating him heavily, he began to wonder what had happened to him. What had happened to his buddy Lenny? What had happened to the rest of his company?

No one gave him answers. Before he was hit, he remembered the explosion. Vaguely, he remembered Lenny's anguished cry. He thought he remembered seeing Lenny's foot beside him. He didn't remember if it was attached to Lenny.

They fixed him up and put him in his uniform, then sent him home, crutches and all. The flight home seemed more surreal than the jungle that had been his home for the last several months. Gunshots and cries of pain haunted him in and out of wakefulness.

But there he was, deplaning and being driven home. Someone must have given his family notice because there was a huge "Welcome Home, John!" sign on the lawn. He cringed. He just wanted to crawl into bed and wake up before he went to Vietnam.

But his wish wasn't granted. With the jungle and the cries and bullets in the back of his head, he thanked the cab driver. Ellie was there, shiny and golden, and in his arms in the next instant. He held her awkwardly and listened to her sobs. She kept whispering his name over and over. Next, he went to the anxious arms of his mother. His father approached him, too, and put his arms around the two of them, their tears of joy coursing down their cheeks. John couldn't cry. He stood as still as a statue, not really knowing how to react. He was happy to see his family, but part of him was still with his comrades in Vietnam. As much as he hated the war, he felt guilty. His comrades were still fighting and he should be supporting them. This stinking, useless leg brought him his greatest wish of coming home, even though the jungle felt more like home. He shook his head a little to clear it. He saw Carl out of the corner of his eye. Carl nodded to him. He understood. John nodded back with a small sense of relief. At least someone knew how he was feeling.

His mom's Thanksgiving -like dinner was delicious. But it was hard to eat. The war still played incessantly in his head, like the shred of a song. He felt he had to keep pulling himself back to the reality of the friends and family at the table. He didn't want to sink into the memory of the war or explain the horrors that he had seen.

He could tell that Ellie sensed something different about him. She looked slightly hurt, but he couldn't take that away. He was changed. Vietnam had changed his normal, and at the moment, he didn't know if his normal would ever be the same again. He was a jumble of longing and hardness, joy and resentment, alongside an edge of anger that he feared would never go away.

After he said goodbye to Ellie, he went inside to tell his parents he was exhausted and going to bed. Upstairs, he sank into the bed in his room. Vietnam. His mind flashed memory after memory of the horrors and devastation he had seen. It had been a nightmare, but no one prepared him for the pandemonium of emotions of coming home. He wasn't sure how to juggle his Vietnam self with the person that was dropped of on his home doorstep earlier that evening. Who was he now? What was he supposed to do? He took a couple of the pain pills the hospital had prescribed and dropped gratefully into a dreamless sleep.

Sixty-Eight

LOUISA – 1918

*The frosting on sea glass comes from the soda and lime components
added to the glass that have dissolved in seawater.*

Louisa couldn't imagine being happier. She and Willie were going to be married! She didn't want a big church wedding but asked Mother Evans if they could be married at the boarding house in the parlor. She only wanted Emma, Bertha, and Burt as guests. Louisa wanted Eliza to be her maid of honor. And she wanted the wedding sooner than later. She and Willie felt they had been parted too long.

The day was planned for Christmas Eve, just a few weeks away. Louisa took the steamboat with Eliza to Baltimore. She wanted to look in the attic for her mother's wedding dress. Bertha was waiting for her at the house, looking a little pale from her bout with the flu. Louisa fell into her arms with a huge hug.

"Oh, Bertha! It's so good to see you!" Louisa told her.

"Oh, Miss Louisa. You look wonderful, a true blushing bride. That air in Tolchester must agree with you," Bertha told her. "You go on into the kitchen. We'll have a cup of tea and chat before we go up to that cold, drafty attic. I'll take your bag up to your room."

Louisa stood in the foyer for a minute, watching Bertha go up the stairs. She missed this house but loved living in Tolchester. She and Willie would need to decide what they wanted to do with this property. She wondered if they could live in both places.

Louisa and Bertha made their way to the attic, properly fortified with tea and shortbread cookies. Dusty trunks lined the walls. Louisa sneezed. "Where do we begin?" She hadn't remembered all the things stored in the attic.

"Your parents' trunks are over there," Bertha pointed a finger to trunks near a half-moon window.

They set about opening trunks, pulling out old-fashioned clothes. Finally, Louisa spied the gleam of ivory silk.

"I think I found it, Bertha!" Louisa cried.

Carefully, she pulled out a heavy, silk satin wedding gown. The leg of mutton sleeves were huge at the top, but Louisa loved how the folds glimmered a golden amber in the light.

"I love this, except for the sleeves," Louisa told Bertha.

Bertha made a sound, "No need to worry about that. I can fix those sleeves and modify the bodice," she told Louisa.

"Really?" Louisa asked, her voice hopeful.

"Absolutely!" Bertha insisted. "You are going to be a beautiful bride!"

Sixty-Nine

Deep teal sea glass comes from cobalt and chromium added to the glass in the making.

Willie was slightly nervous, standing in the parlor of his house, waiting for Louisa. They had decorated with holly and pine boughs. Louisa had brought back two dozen fairy light candles from Baltimore. They gave a magical glow to the room. They were a small, happy group waiting for his bride.

Cora was at the seat of the piano that was tucked into the corner for guests to play. She was waiting for a signal to begin playing the music. The minister was tall and somewhat imposing. Willie ran his finger around the inside of his collar.

"Not having second thoughts, are you son?" Burt asked, a teasing edge to his tone.

"No, sir! Not at all," Willie grinned. He had one additional surprise for Louisa.

The music started, and all eyes turned toward the door. There was Eliza in a deep, blue velvet gown. It was trimmed in snowy white lace. She glided gracefully through the small gathering and stood to Willie's left. She winked at Willie.

And then, there she was, Louisa. She was breathtaking. She wore a silk satin gown that caught the light of the candles. The ivory silk complemented the single strand of pearls at her throat. Someone had looped and braided her long, chestnut hair into an elaborate style. Her delicate, lacy veil streamed down her back. Willie could barely breathe seeing her. She gave him a shy smile. He grinned back at her, the tension leaving him. She was going to be his forever. Louisa caught his joy, and her smile went from shy to dazzling.

They said their vows. Willie whispered to Louisa, 'There's one more thing."

He held his hand up to stop the clapping and cheers from the gathering. He pulled out the piece of cobalt blue sea glass from his pocket. He had had a hole drilled and placed on a delicate chain.

"My heart to your heart," Willie said, holding up the cobalt blue heart from sea glass. Flashes of deep blue light twinkled as he dangled it from the chain in his hand.

"Yes," Louisa agreed. "Our heart. We're together again, and we won't ever be separated."

Willie smiled up at Louisa. "I love you, Mrs. Evans."

And he kissed her as their family and friends cheered and clapped.

Seventy

ELLIE – 1969

Teal sea glass likely dates back to glass from the mid-19th century to the early 20th century.

Ellie tried her best to be patient with John. She and Penny were busy with December craft and art shows. Ellie's scarves were selling like crazy at the North Bay gift shop and a Deerton gallery. She stayed up late creating the scarves at a small folding table inside the camper.

It's not that she didn't have time for John, but he didn't seem to want to see her. When they got together, their conversation was stilted. She wistfully remembered the summer days when they talked for hours. Ellie felt hurt, and she was worried. According to his mom, he was busy with physical therapy, and all he seemed to do was exercise. She suspected the exercise helped him cope.

Ellie didn't know what to do. She knew they needed to talk.

He came by one afternoon unexpectedly.

"No crutches!" Ellie said, amazed when he came to the door.

"No crutches," he said firmly and asked, "Do you want to go for a walk?"

"Sure," she reluctantly agreed.

It was chilly and felt like snow. They walked down to the beach. His gait was slow, and he had a slight limp. They took their time to get to the chilly shoreline where they stood looking out at the water.

"I missed this," John said quietly.

"Missed 'this' not 'you.'" Ellie wondered if he still wanted her in his life. Her heart lurched, and she fiddled with the ring on her finger. She had to ask.

"John," she started to say, her voice quavering. She had to stop. She couldn't get the words out. A snowflake fell, and then another. It looked like a gray mist on the bay.

"Snow," John said with wonder.

Ellie felt like she was invisible. Anger simmered inside of her, but it was the hurt that lashed out, "John, what happened to you?" she cried in anguish.

John first froze and then spat out the word, "War!"

"It's a shitty, useless war! You have no idea, Ellie! Everyone, just about, was considered the enemy. We shot at soldiers but also killed women, children, and old people!"

Ellie was aghast. What else was he holding back if he was holding in this horror?

"Did you kill any women, children, or older people?" Ellie asked.

John cried out in a strangled voice, "I don't know, Ellie! I don't know!"

His fisted hands shook along with his voice, "It was the jungle. You couldn't see. I don't know who was in the jungle. I just had to shoot. It was kill or be killed. You have no idea."

Ellie went over to put her arms around John.

"No, I don't know," she said quietly, "but I'm here for you."

The snow started falling in huge flakes around them. John buried his head in Ellie's hair. And he started to cry in great wracking, painful sobs. She held him tightly, and he held onto her like a lifeline.

Seventy-One

JOHN – 1969

Cobalt blue glass is also known as 'smalt' when it's ground as a pigment.

It was such a relief for John to hold Ellie and to have her hold him. His anguish and pain came out in tears. Damn war. But the tears and anguish released something. He had been fighting to return to normal every minute he was home. It wasn't easy. It was a war on its own. But he was ready to get back to life. Ellie.

He kissed her hair. And then he lifted her hand to his lips. Something blue glinted in the sunshine. It was the sea glass he had plucked from the bay what seemed years ago at Betterton. Ellie had written to him that she had taken a jewelry class and made the shard into a bracelet. The lines on the bracelet were simple. It caught the light of the sun and shone bright blue. Treasure. His mother had always told him sea glass was a treasure. Here it was, his blue treasure with his treasure of a girl. He brushed away his tears. He looked into her eyes and kissed her slowly. He was home.

Epilogue

TIDES OF BLUE AND CURRENTS OF BLUE CONNECTIONS

- Anna Grace and Josiah are grandparents to Louisa (1918 portion of Currents of Blue.)
- Anna Grace Cadwallader (born 1840 and died 1918 – age 78) and Josiah Bryant – Baltimore – (1840 – 1910 – aged 70 - Tides of Blue)
- Daughter – b 1870 – Amelia Anne Bryant m Benjamin Dunn (died in an accident 1911)
- Louisa Grace Dunn b 1899 m William Thomas Evans (Willie) 1919
- (Currents of Blue)
- Daughter - Anna Louise Evans m Richard Blackwood
- Parents of:
- Penelope (Penny) Grace Blackwood and Amelia Anne Blackwood
- Amelia Anne Blackwood m Thomas Ryan
- Daughter Eleanor Grace Ryan (Ellie) b 1950

About the Author

Sharon, born 1959, grew up in central Pennsylvania surrounded by the beautiful mountains. Writing has been a lifelong passion for Sharon. For Sharon, writing is like breathing. She says she has more stories in her head to write down than lifetimes to live. Sharon is a nationally award winning Librarian and the author of several educational publications. She is also an avid gardener and jewelry artist.

www.ingramcontent.com/pod-product-compliance
Lightning Source LLC
Chambersburg PA
CBHW021227310726

48971CB00006B/1712